SWEET SUNSHINE

A PEMBROOKE NOVEL

JESSICA PRINCE

PROLOGUE

CHLOE

I'VE NEVER HAD the best of luck when it came to men. No matter how hard I tried, I always seemed to pick poorly. If there was a loser, a poser, a thief, or a cheater in my vicinity, I had a gift for sniffing them out.

That was the only reason I could think of as to why I was so embarrassingly hung up on Deputy Derrick Anderson. He wasn't a loser, a poser, a thief, or a cheater — as far as I knew — but he was completely and undeniably unattainable.

Maybe that was why I was so pulled to him.

"You know," my best friend Harlow started, "if you'd just talk to him you'd see he's a normal guy, and you wouldn't have to be so socially awkward every time he's in the same room."

I looked over into my friend's smiling eyes and glared.

"I'm not socially awkward," I insisted. "And I'll have you know I *have* talked to Derrick. Plenty of times."

"Oh, yeah?" she laughed.

"Yeah," I replied somewhat angrily before turning my attention back to the people milling around Harlow and Noah's backyard. It was Fourth of July weekend, and I swear to God, it seemed the entire town of Pembrooke was stuffed into their yard for a fun, family barbecue. But I only had eyes for one person.

Unfortunately, he didn't even notice I existed.

"Well, if it's any consolation, I totally think you two would look adorable together."

That got Harlow another glare, because, really? The truth was Derrick Anderson was so far out of my league, he'd need a map to find me. That was, if he even had any interest in looking, which I doubted he did.

"You have to say that, you're my best friend," I grumbled.

"I mean it!" she insisted. "You're cute! I'd totally do you."

"And I'd totally watch," her husband Noah chimed in as he walked by us with a platter of hamburgers ready for the grill. "Seriously, let's make this happen. Name a time and place." It was so nauseatingly sweet the way he stopped to plant a hard kiss on his wife's lips before continuing on his journey.

I brought my beer to my lips and took a refreshing gulp. I didn't know if it was the summer heat outside, or the fact that Derrick had taken off his t-shirt during a sweaty game of football with Harlow's little brother Ethan and some of the other barbecue-goers, tucking it into the back of the pants, but suddenly my mouth was parched.

Jesus, he was so perfect, all hard muscles and chiseled lines, my fingers itched to draw him. Problem was, I couldn't draw for shit. Looked like there wouldn't be any Leo DiCaprio via *Titanic* reenactments going on any time soon. Bummer, 'cause that was totally one of my fantasies.

"Oh my God!" Harlow laughed loudly. "Look at you! You're totally smitten!"

I reached over and slapped her arm. "Shut up!"

"Okay, okay," she grumbled, poking out her bottom lip in a pout as she rubbed her arm. "I'm just teasing. But seriously, Chlo, you're gorgeous. Derrick would be insane not to want you."

I let my eyes travel over my friend's perfect frame. Even with a massive pregnant belly, there was no denying how stunning she was. All long, lean legs, flawless olive skin, and perfect, shiny dark hair. Harlow could have been a model, no doubt.

But me? Well I was short with round hips, a bubble butt, a big chest that was the bane of my existence, pale skin that fried with the smallest amount of sun, and unruly, reddish blonde hair. On top of all of that, I had a teeny tiny little potbelly I couldn't get rid of no matter how hard I tried. And owning a bakery did nothing to help that.

I loved my pastries, so sue me.

"Harlow..." I started, but she cut me off, hearing the doubt in my voice.

"Don't you *Harlow* me!" she chastised. "You're gorgeous

— you are!" she snapped when I rolled my eyes. "Any man, and I mean *any* man, would be lucky to have you. You hear me?"

I felt a smile curve my lips despite my misgivings. Harlow was just so damned passionate. "I love you," I told her, leaning in to wrap my arms around her. She returned the embrace, squeezing tightly.

I heard an excited "Yes!" shouted from across the yard and turned my head to see Noah, his eyes on me and Harlow, with his arms raising up in the air in triumph.

"Not happening!" Harlow shouted back.

"Damn it!"

I laughed and took another pull from my beer as Harlow stood and made her way to her husband, her big, pregnant belly making her waddle adorably.

I finished off my drink and turned back to the football game going on a few yards away. God, Derrick really was the best looking man I'd ever laid eyes on. Then he threw his head back in laughter at something Ethan said and those looks just got even better. As I stood and walked to the cooler for another beer, my movements must have caught his eye. When he turned and offered me a sweet smile, my insides melted and my heart picked up a frantic pace.

But more than that, I began thinking *what if*.

What if Harlow was right?

What if he was interested in me?

What if I did have a shot?

What if, what if, what if.

In that moment, I started to hope. It was enough to get my feet moving in Derrick's direction just as the football game came to a pause.

"Hey there, sunshine," he grinned as I made my way to him. Just like every time I heard that name from his lips, I shivered with pleasure. I wasn't lying when I told Harlow that Derrick and I had talked. We had. Our conversations just never held anything of substance. But that could be easily changed, right? All I had to do was push past my insecurities and awkwardness, and make that happen.

"Hey Derrick," I offered nervously. "Having fun?"

He lifted one sculpted arm and brushed a bead of sweat from his forehead. The strong muscles in his bicep bulged beautifully and I was hit with a wave of yearning to reach out and run my fingers over his tan, glistening skin. "Yeah, it's been great."

Looking down at the cold bottle in my hands, I picked at the label with my thumbnail as I garnered up the courage to say what I truly wanted to say.

I sucked in a deep breath and dug deep for courage. "So, I was thinking... I don't know if you're busy... it's cool if you don't have time, but..." *Jeez, Chloe, get your shit together and just ask him out already!* I berated internally.

Before I even had a chance to finish that thought, Derrick spoke. "Yeah, sure. Sounds good."

My gaze shot up at his distracted tone to find that his eyes weren't even on me. Looking over my shoulder to see what held Derrick's attention, I saw Tammy Bradford, the town doorknob, smiling at Derrick seductively. When I

5

looked back at him, the corner of his mouth was quirked up in a knowing grin as he kept his focus pinned on Tammy.

A sharp pain stabbed through my chest as my stomach dropped. And standing there in front of my insane crush, I felt my hope die a slow, agonizing death.

Derrick patted my arm and moved to step past me. "'Scuze me, Cathy, I'll be back in a few."

Cathy? What the hell?

He didn't call me *sunshine* out of endearment. He did it because he couldn't remember my actual name!

"Uh... y-yeah. See ya," I stuttered as I fought to keep from bursting into tears. I couldn't remember a time in my life where I'd ever felt more humiliated than just then. And I'd had a boyfriend clean out my checking account in college, for Christ's sake!

This was so much worse.

My bottom lip began to tremble as I made my way through the large backyard and along the side of the house. My vision swam with unshed tears that I refused to let fall. Embarrassment and heartbreak fueled each of my steps as I made it to my car, thankfully, undetected.

I was such a fool to think someone like Derrick would ever be interested in someone like me.

As I put my car into gear and pulled away from the happy sounds of the party, my tears finally brimmed over and fell. All I could think was that I'd never make that mistake again.

1

CHLOE

 ne Month Later

MY FEET WERE KILLING ME. But that was par for the course when you started your day at four in the morning. Such was the life of a bakery owner. I rose long before the sun and spent hours baking away before ever opening the doors. It was exhausting, but I wouldn't have had it any other way. I'd worked hard to build everything around me, and I was extremely proud of my little bakery, Sinful Sweets. I'd poured my heart and soul into the place, and it showed the moment you walked through the door.

The atmosphere was warm and inviting. I'd handpicked everything from paint color to décor all by myself and loved how it turned out. That didn't mean I wasn't dead on my feet come four o'clock.

And I still had three more hours until closing. The best gift I'd ever given myself was the massive, industrial espresso machine. Sure, I claimed it was for the bakery, and I made a mint off the coffee drinks the customers ordered. But mainly, it was my source of fuel for my long days.

I'd just finished filling my gazillionth cup of the day when the bell over the door chimed. I spun around, bright smile on my face, and started my typical greeting, only to have it die on my lips. Like all the other times I'd seen Derrick since July fourth, I felt the same prickly ache creep up my spine just like it always did. Luckily, his back was turned to the counter and I was able to secure the pleasant mask I'd been forced to wear in his presence for the past month in place.

"Eliza, what'd I say?" His voice held a hint of exasperation as he continued to hold the door open for his daughter as she walked through. Her face was scrunched up in a way that only nine-year-old girls were able to pull off, communicating her fury as she crossed her arms over her chest. I'd met Eliza a handful of times when Derrick would bring her into the bakery, but I couldn't really say I knew the girl. I'd seen her around town with her father in passing glances more than anything.

"You're not being fair!" Eliza declared, stomping her foot for dramatic effect. "Mom already said I could go!"

"Well it's not your mom's weekend," Derrick continued as he stalked toward the counter, his own face reflecting the agitation coming through each of his words. "It's my weekend, and your mom had no right to tell you that you could go to Cindy's sleepover on my weekend."

Eliza's head fell back as she shouted, melodramatically, "You're ruining my life!"

"Yes, that's exactly why I'm doing this, Eliza," Derrick replied dryly. "Because I want to ruin your life. It's got nothing to do with the fact that I only get to see you two weekends out of the month."

"Cindy Sanford's the most *popular* girl in school, and she invited *me* to her sleepover two weeks ago! I have to go!"

My eyes bounced between father and daughter.

"I told you you're not going, and that's all there is to it. You wanna be mad at someone, be mad at your mother for making promises she couldn't keep."

"Gah! I hate you!" Eliza cried at the ceiling before trudging over and throwing herself into one of the chairs along the glass windows that made up the entire front wall of Sinful Sweets.

"Tell me something I don't know," Derrick murmured under his breath as he turned to fully face the counter. He shot me a smile in greeting, but I could see the pain his daughter's words had inflicted in the backs of his eyes. "Hey there, sunshine. Sorry about that. She gets a little dramatic every once in a while."

"No problem," I replied softly, looking down to break the hold his eyes had on me. Now that I knew the truth, every time he called me by that particular nickname, it was like a punch to the gut. Ignoring the pain in my stomach, I asked, "Uh, so what can I get you?"

His eyes danced across the menu boards hanging along the top of the wall behind the counter. I'd decided to go old school and bought chalkboards. The first one contained our daily specials that I wrote out by hand each morning, taking the time and care to make sure the handwriting was pretty as well as legible. The other three boards were the standard menu that only changed with the season.

"I don't know." He smiled at me, and seeing as I was still harboring an unrequited crush, the beauty of that smile actually physically hurt. "What do you suggest for winning over a nine-year-old whose life is over because she can't go to a sleep over?"

"Um..." I licked my suddenly dry lips, looking anywhere but his face. "Maybe a chocolate croissant," I told his chin. "Or I have some strawberry cupcakes cooling in the back I was just about to ice if you don't mind waiting."

"Strawberry is Eliza's favorite. You might have just saved me from an entire weekend of a pre-teen's silent treatment. You're a life saver, sunshine."

I wasn't sure why I did it, or what even possessed me, but my head snapped up and I met his hazel gaze head on. "My name's Chloe."

His head jerked back in surprise, his brow furrowing in confusion as he asked, "What?"

"My name, it's Chloe."

"I know what your name is," he informed me, the

befuddlement growing on his face. "What I'm not sure of is why you're telling me something I already knew."

"Oh, well," I was back to staring at anything other than his face as I told his shoulder. "I just figured you didn't know since you always call me 'sunshine.'"

"Chloe—"

I continued, "And you know… since you called me Cathy at Noah and Harlow's Fourth of July barbeque, and all. I just figured you didn't know, so I told you."

"Chlo—" he started again, but the incessant need to escape proved to be too strong to ignore.

"I'll just go frost those cupcakes really quick so Eliza doesn't have to wait. Be back in just a sec."

I shoved through the door to the kitchen and collapsed back into the wall next to it, releasing the breath I hadn't realized I was holding until my lungs began to ache. I felt like such an idiot. Not that it was all that surprising. I typically lost all brain function when Derrick was around, anyway.

I made quick work of the cupcakes, taking extra care with Eliza's for some reason I refused to acknowledge. Putting the beautifully decorated cupcake on a tiny china plate, I pushed through the door that separated the kitchen and dining area, grabbed a chocolate croissant from the pastry case for Derrick, and made my way to the table where both of them sat in complete silence. Eliza was staring out the window, pretending to be oblivious to her father's presence, while Derrick regarded his daughter with that same pain in his eyes I'd seen just minutes earlier.

"Here you go," I told them as I sat their pastries down on the table.

"Thanks, Miss Chloe." Eliza smiled. "Strawberry's my favorite."

And once again, I let my mouth get the best of me.

"I know." I smiled back. "Your daddy told me."

Eliza's eyes darted to her father in surprise. I wasn't sure if it was surprise that he'd do something so nice after how she'd just acted, or surprise that he'd remember his own daughter's favorite cake, but either way, it broke my heart.

I made sure my voice and expression were both gentle as I spoke to her. "You know, you're really lucky. You have a dad that really cares about you and wants to spend time with you. That's a really special thing, sweetheart. And I know you love him just as much, and would never want to cause him pain, but when you tell your parent that you hate them, it hurts. I know, because I did the same thing when I was your age. I didn't mean it when I told my mom I hated her, and I'm sure you didn't mean it when you said it to your dad, right?"

She stared up at me with wide eyes, the same hazel as her father's, and shook her head. "No ma'am."

"I didn't think so," I whispered on a grin as I reached down and tucked a strand of hair behind her ear. "A girl as sweet as you would never want to hurt someone on purpose. Your heart's too kind for that."

I let myself glimpse in Derrick's direction just long enough to see him looking back at me, something I couldn't quite recognize in his eyes, but I wouldn't allow my gaze to linger.

"You guys enjoy the treats, they're on the house."

"Chloe," Derrick started, but I cut him off once again.

"I've got something in the oven back there, but if you need anything else, Ellie behind the counter will be more than happy to help you guys out."

I spun on my heels and disappeared into the sanctuary of my industrial kitchen. Wondering for probably the millionth time why I couldn't just be *normal* around Derrick Anderson.

Derrick

I sat out on the deck that ran along the back of my house as the sun began its descent, looking out on the Tetons. The way Chloe had looked at me earlier when she told me her name kept replaying in my head. I wasn't sure why the conversation was bothering me so much, but, for some reason, it sat like a brick in my stomach, leaving me feeling unsettled.

"Daddy?" Eliza called, her head full of long, dark brown hair just like mine, sticking out the back door.

"Yeah, baby girl?"

Taking a hesitant step onto the back deck, she wrung her hands in front of her. "I, um... I just... wanted to say sorry," she murmured in soft embarrassment, her eyes downcast. "You know, for what I said today. I don't hate you."

"I know, angel," I told her softly, my heart stuttering in my chest at her apology. An apology I wouldn't have gotten had it not been for a certain little baker. A sense of appreciation washed over me when I thought about what Chloe had done. The sweet, gentle, yet unmistakable way she set my little girl straight. That had definitely been something I wasn't used to seeing. The only woman in my life who'd ever really interacted with Eliza was her mom, Layla. And the cold, manipulative way she acted was a juxtaposition to Chloe's caring demeanor. I had to admit, it threw me off a bit.

What Chloe couldn't have realized was that she'd managed to save me from an entire miserable weekend of silent treatment, only broken up by the occasional tantrum. *Shit*, I though. *Maybe I should send her a fruit basket or something.*

Women liked fruit baskets, didn't they? It was a perfect way to hopefully kill two birds with one stone. I could say thanks for helping out with Eliza, and maybe ease whatever was causing her somewhat prickly demeanor, and get myself back on her good side.

It was a win-win.

If there was one thing I was good at, it was getting on women's good sides. I figured I'd have Chloe acting her typically bright-as-the-sun self in no time.

2

CHLOE

"*A* FRUIT BASKET?"
I looked from the chocolate-dipped fruit pieces, all cut to reflect different flowers shoved into a vase, to Harlow and shrugged.

Her face was scrunched in confusion as she looked at the arrangement sitting on the counter between us. "Why'd Derrick send you a fruit basket?"

"No idea," I answered honestly, seeing as the card that had been delivered with it just ten minutes ago only had two simple words written on it. "Thank you." That was it. Thank you. Thank you for what? I'd barely talked to him in the last month, let alone done anything to warrant his thanks. For crying out loud, the last time I'd seen the man was four days ago. And we'd hardly done more than nod at each other... if you didn't count that brief, yet humiliating conversation about my name.

She snatched the card from my hand and stared down

at the two words as I picked up my eleventy-billionth cup of coffee of the day and gulped.

"That's so weird," she huffed, tossing the card back down and picking up her own decaf coffee. "Derrick never struck me as the fruit basket kind of guy. You should call him and find out what the hell you apparently did."

A sharp twinge radiated through my chest as I shook my head adamantly. "Derrick and I aren't really like that, Low-Low. I don't even have the guy's number."

Her pretty face pinched together in a scowl as she focused on me. "What the hell happened between you two, anyway? Last I saw, you were gearing yourself up to ask him out on a date, the next thing I knew, I couldn't find you anywhere and you weren't answering my calls. I've left you alone about it so far, but now chocolate-covered strawberries are in the picture. I want answers."

"There's nothing to say," I shrugged casually even though, on the inside, I felt the sting of rejection all over again. "I just changed my mind."

Harlow actually had the nerve to give me the "bullshit" cough. What were we, eighth graders? I shot her a look that portrayed exactly what I was thinking of her adolescent behavior. "It's true."

"Chlo, you've been mooning over the dude for... how long has he lived here?" she tapped her chin in thought, then snapped her fingers. "Right! You've been mooning over the guy for over a year and a half. That's not something you just *change your mind* about. What really happened?"

I huffed out an exasperated sigh. "I *tried* asking him out, okay? But he was too busy staring at Tammy Bradford's tits to pay attention to me," I finished with a bitter sneer.

I clenched my teeth at her sympathetic expression. "Oh sweetie…"

"Then the asshole called me *Cathy*."

The sympathy disappeared instantly. "Wait — what?"

"Yep." I popped the "*p*" to add emphasis. "Tammy batted her fake eyelashes and gave him that *I'm-a-sure-thing* look, and that was it. He excused himself, called me by the wrong name, and more than likely ended up banging her in one of your bathrooms."

"Ew!" her face pinched in disgust. "What a prick! I can't believe he called you '*Cathy*.' I should punch him right in the nuts next time I see him."

Even though the visual of Harlow, lying in wait for Derrick to walk by so she could slug him right in the balls made me smile, I knew it was pointless. "Don't do that," I told her, knowing that if I didn't, she wouldn't hesitate to go through with it. "He's Noah's best friend, I'm not sure that friendship would survive if you were to rupture his testicles. Things would just get awkward."

She harrumphed and crossed her arms over her chest, resting them on her protruding belly. "Don't care," she all but pouted, "still wanna punch him."

I took another sip of my coffee. "You could always try and make it look like an accident," I suggested, causing her to brighten.

"There's an idea," she smiled wickedly, and I began to

17

worry for Noah's safety whenever he crossed her. Although, he was a big boy; he could take care of himself.

"So, what are you gonna do with the fruit basket, then?" Harlow eyed the basket up and down, actually licking her lips in the process.

I ripped off the cellophane and pushed it in her direction. "Have at it," I offered, even though those chocolate dipped strawberries were calling my name. The only thing better than fruit was fruit dipped in *chocolate*.

"You aren't going to eat any?" She eyed me suspiciously. "Since when do you turn down chocolate?"

Then I made the mistake of saying the one thing that would set her off. "I'm on a diet," I announced casually, snatching up a dishcloth and scrubbing down the countertop as an excuse to keep from looking her in her eyes-

"You're *what*?"

A few of the customers enjoying their midday pastries shot curious looks in Harlow's direction. "Shh!" I hissed. "Will you keep your voice down? Hell, any louder and only bats will be able to hear you!"

"Why the hell are you going on a diet?" she demanded to know.

I scoffed and gave her my best, *are-you-kidding-me-with-that-question* look. "I can spare a few pounds, Low-Low. Believe me."

"You're insane."

"Says the woman with a model's body," I mocked.

"It's because I'm tall!" she insisted. "You're petite, Chloe. And you've got curves most women would kill for! I know

I would. You don't need to lose any weight. You're built like a woman."

"No, I'm built like a potbelly pig." I pinched the roll on my stomach as evidence. For a woman nearing the end of her pregnancy, Harlow was a lot quicker than I'd expected. The next thing I knew, she was standing on the top rung of her barstool, leaning across the counter, and smacking the shit out of my hand. "Ow! What the hell!"

"Stop talking about yourself like that or the next one'll be worse," she warned, sitting back down and resting a hand on her stomach as she scowled at me. I rolled my eyes and lifted my coffee cup back to my lips. "Don't you give me that resting-bitch-face either," she scolded, pointing her finger at me in a way only a mother could pull off. She'd gotten good at it in the months she'd been back in Pembrooke, what with Ethan turning into an adolescent bag of raging hormones and all. The kid had definitely given her some practice.

I was just about to reply when the bell over the door chimed, alerting me to a new customer — or two, I noticed once I looked over. "Hey, Ms. Harlow!" Eliza practically shouted as she came skipping over to the counter, her father in tow just feet behind her.

"Well, hey there, honey. This is a pleasant surprise." Harlow grinned widely, leaning down to give her a hug.

"Mommy said she had a headache so she asked Daddy to get me from school. Now I get to spend an extra night with him!"

"That's great!" Harlow smiled tightly, careful to not let

Eliza see the look she shot Derrick over the little girl's head. He simply raised his hands in defeat.

Since she and Noah reconciled, and Noah and Derrick were such good friends, I knew that Harlow had gotten to know Eliza pretty well. She also filled me in on all the drama that took place between Derrick and his ex-wife. Apparently Layla wasn't the hands-on type of mother, more interested in shopping or finding the next wealthy, eligible bachelor to hook her star to instead of spending time with her own daughter. I'd never met the woman, but I didn't need to in order to know I'd despise her on sight.

What mother willingly tossed their child aside like that?

"Hi, Miss Chloe," she smiled shyly.

I leaned my forearms on the counter, smiling widely at the beautiful little girl who looked so much like her father. "Hi, sweetheart. Did you have a good day at school?"

Her face seemed to light up under my and Harlow's attention, which just made the sour feeling in my gut in regards to her mother that much worse. "Yes, ma'am!" she beamed. "I got a hundred on my spelling test, so Daddy said I could have a strawberry cupcake as a reward."

"That's amazing!" I cried, her little girl enthusiasm rubbing off on me.

"Yep, I even spelled all the hard words right! Mechanical, chemical, behavioral, and combination."

My head jerked back. "Those are fourth grade words?!"

It wasn't until I heard the sound of Derrick's deep laughter that I even remembered he was standing there. I'd been so engrossed in this adorable little girl that everything else around me seemed to fall way. "Tell me about it," he murmured with a prideful grin. Just the sight of that beautiful smile was enough to make my stomach dip. I had to look away.

"I see you got the basket." His velvety smooth voice rolled over me and I had to suppress a shiver.

My mouth hung open with an embarrassing, "Uh…"

"Come on, Eliza. Let's take a look at the pastry cases? Maybe you can talk your dad into letting you have *two* treats." My traitorous, *ex*-friend Harlow hopped off the stool and took the girl's hand, shooting me a shit-eating grin and Derrick a glare over her shoulder.

I scowled at her as she walked away.

"Man," Derrick chuckled under his breath, "gotta hand it to Noah. The man must be a saint."

My head tipped to the side. "Why's that?"

"Well," he waved in the direction of Harlow and his daughter. "Pregnancy hormones. One minute Harlow's sweet as sugar, the next she's looking at me like she's plotting to kill me in my sleep."

I bit the inside of my cheek to keep from laughing, knowing damn good and well it wasn't pregnancy hormones behind the daggers she'd just shot.

"Mmm," I hummed noncommittally, going back to wiping the countertop in even circles, anything to keep my hands busy and my eyes off the perfection standing before me.

"So, did you like it?"

My head shot up. "Like what?" I asked.

His grin grew to an almost devastating level — at least it was devastating to me. "The fruit basket."

"Oh!" Damn it! It had happened again. Why the hell couldn't my brain work whenever he was around? It was seriously beginning to piss me off. "Yes, thank you. It's very nice. But... I'm not sure what I did to deserve it." I shrugged.

His biceps bunched, the corded muscles drawing my attention as he bent his elbows and propped them on the counter. *Stupid gorgeous arms*, I thought, trying not to picture myself sinking my teeth into them.

Damn it! And there it is.

"I just wanted you to know how much I appreciated what you said to Eliza. You know, about saying hurtful things. It saved me an entire weekend of pre-teen girl drama."

"Oh..." I started, somewhat stunned that a few simple words to his daughter packed enough of a punch to warrant a chocolate dipped fruit basket. "Well... you're welcome, I guess. Glad it worked out."

His eyes narrowed, his head cocked to the side, and I got the distinct impression he was watching my face very closely. I was suddenly self-conscious that I'd somehow gotten food on my face at some point during the day.

"What?" I asked as I discreetly brushed at my nose.

"You okay?" he asked and my stomach flipped again.

"Sure," I shrugged.

He looked like he wanted to argue but before he had a chance to get anything out, Eliza and Harlow came sauntering back. "Dad! Ms. Harlow said I should get a strawberry cupcake *and* a puff—pruf—po—"

Harlow took pity on her and offered the correct pronunciation, "Profiterole."

Eliza clapped and shouted, "Yeah! That one!" and Harlow cast a smirk in Derrick's direction.

"Fine," he relented with a sigh, and I went about boxing up Eliza's sweets. As Derrick paid and I handed them over, I offered her one last smile and leaned in. "Congratulations on your spelling test. Just goes to show you've got beauty *and* brains."

She positively glowed and my heart expanded in my chest.

She skipped to the door, and I took the opportunity to turn around and lower my head, giving my back to Derrick and using my hair to block my face, in the hopes of cutting off anything else he could potentially say. I thought my luck had failed when his velvety voice said my name, but then Eliza chirped from the door, "Come on, Dad! I can't wait to eat these. I'm *starving*," she finished with a dramatic flair.

Just to be on the safe side, I didn't turn around until I heard the bell over the door.

"Pretty sure hiding behind a curtain of your hair won't work forever," Harlow chided.

Picking up my forgotten coffee, I dumped it and went for a refill, muttering, "Shut up," in my friend's direction.

Because I was *so* mature like that.

3

DERRICK

*F*UCK.

I stifled the groan that wanted to work its way from my chest as I pulled my cell from my pocket before I collapsed into the worn, cracked faux leather chair at my desk. The piece of shit was uncomfortable as hell, but with the department dealing with budget cuts, we had to take what we could get. At least I *had* a chair.

"What do you want, Layla?" I said by way of greeting.

I could hear her indignant huff through the line, not that I gave two shits what upset her. I stopped having to give a damn once the ink on the divorce papers was dry, a process that I never wanted to go through again. Getting married once was the biggest mistake of my life. Staying married for eight miserable years was the second worst. At least I got Eliza out of it. That made all the bullshit I had to stomach for damned near a decade worth it. She was the only thing I had in my life that mattered for anything.

If the last several years of hell had taught me anything it was that I was never, *ever* taking those goddamned vows again. Marriage just meant a woman got to sink her claws into you and tear your ass apart. No, thank you. Once bitten, twice shy. It might be for some, like Noah, the sorry son of a bitch, but I was bowing out.

"Wow, nice way to greet your wife, asshole."

"*Ex*-wife," I reminded, clenching my teeth at the fact I had to remind her of that over a year after the deed was done. "And the fact you've got some old, rich dick paying your way should be reminder enough of that."

"God," she cried through the phone. "Why the hell did I ever marry you?"

"Ask myself that same question every goddamned day," I grunted. "Now, you call for a reason, or did you just want to help me start my day with your own personal brand of bitch?"

"You're a pig," she seethed, and I'll admit, I got a little bit of pleasure out of ruffling her feathers, after all, she'd only called to screw with me, might as well get some shots in for myself, right?

"You've got two seconds to tell me what you want or I'm hanging up. One—"

"I need you to take Eliza for the rest of the week and through the weekend," she talked over my counting. "Harold surprised me with tickets to Barbados. We're flying out tomorrow."

I clenched my eyes closed over the red haze that was building behind my vision. How I was ever stupid enough to stick my dick in this woman once was beyond me, let alone enough times to knock her up. But the fact that she was the definition of world's worst mother had that stupidity leaving a sour taste in my mouth. She didn't *deserve* to call herself a mother, especially not to a kid as sweet-natured as Eliza. I was convinced the woman had snake venom running through her veins.

"Are you fucking kidding me?" I gritted out. "It's not enough you couldn't bother to pick her up from school yesterday, *or* come get her last night, but now you don't even want her to come home? Jesus fuckin' Christ, Layla! Doesn't this Harold douchebag realize you've got a kid? You can't just go flying off to the goddamned Bahamas or some shit whenever the hell you want! You have responsibilities!"

"It's Barbados!" she snapped. "And I don't have to sit here and listen to you talk to me like that! We're not married anymore, *remember*? If I'd have known watching your own *daughter* was such an inconvenience to you, I would have asked my sister to do it!"

"Don't you dare," I warned in a low voice, not caring that I'd drawn the attention of the entire department. It wasn't the first yelling match they'd witnessed when it came to Layla, and it probably wouldn't be the last. "The only woman on this planet more toxic than you is that sister of yours. You are *not* asking Lilith to watch my kid while you go gallivanting off with your sugar daddy, you hear me?"

"Why do you insist on making my life so difficult,

Derrick? Jesus Christ! It's like you never wanted me to be happy! First, you made me suffer through that marriage, now you're killing whatever chance I have at happiness with Harold!"

She was so full of shit. And the sad thing was, she actually believed the stuff spewing from her mouth. She'd done her best to bleed me dry, and had it not been for the fact I was smart enough to keep our bank accounts separate when she *conveniently* ended up pregnant and insisted I marry her, God only knows the damage she would have done.

"You want happiness so badly? You want to build a life with your old-as-fuck, wrinkly-balled boyfriend? Have at it. I won't stop you. All you have to do is give me full custody of Eliza and we'll be out of your hair, that's what you want anyway, right?"

It was a fight we'd had incessantly since I told her I didn't want to be married to her anymore. She held Eliza over my head, using her as a pawn through the entire proceedings. I tried to get custody of my daughter, I fucking fought for it, but there was nothing to prove she was an unfit mother. That's what killed me the most, knowing she had no interest in raising her own flesh and blood, but wouldn't give her to me because she was a game piece she could continue to play even when we were officially over.

Her sharp, biting laughter echoed in my ear. "And miss out on making you as miserable as you make me?" The manipulative bitch. "I don't think so, Derrick. You could always try and take me to court, but seeing as your income as a *deputy* is laughable, and Harold would insist on paying for me to have the best lawyers in Wyoming, you don't have a leg to stand on. Now are you going to keep Eliza or not?"

"You know I am," I ground out.

"Good," she chirped and that damned smile I could hear in her voice grated on my already frayed nerves. "See, that wasn't so hard was it."

I pulled the phone away from my ear and disconnected before I could say something that would put everything I was working for in jeopardy. I'd been keeping a log of every time I kept Eliza on Layla's days, of how many times her school had called me when her mother just *hadn't shown up* to get her, of the bronchitis she got last winter that was left unattended so long it turned into full-blown pneumonia that put my baby girl in the hospital for three of the worst days I'd ever had to live through.

I kept a record of everything. If it was the last thing I did, I was going to get my child out of that house and into a home where she was surrounded by nothing but love. But I had to be patient in order to do that, and when it came to my Eliza's welfare, patience was a virtue I struggled with on a daily basis.

That was why, at only nine years old, I'd given her a cellphone so she'd always be able to reach me. Did it make me feel like shit, having to explain to a little kid that she couldn't let her mom know she had it because she'd take it away? Of course it did, I never wanted to have to put Eliza in that position. But desperate times called for desperate measures. And I wouldn't leave her without a way to get to me.

"You okay, man?" Perkins, one of the other deputies in the Sheriff's department, asked.

"Yeah," I grunted, standing from the battered chair and re-pocketing my phone. "I need coffee. I'll be back in a few."

I turned without a backward glance, my mind set on one thing, and that was getting the best cup of coffee in Pembrooke to try and calm my tattered nerves. I should have known better than to answer the phone to Layla without caffeine in my system. Wouldn't be a mistake I made twice.

Pushing through the doors of the station, I dragged my ass, and my bad mood, down the board walked sidewalks toward Sinful Sweets, silently praying no one stopped me to chat. I was just pissed off enough to rip even the most unsuspecting person's head off. And it didn't help that in order to get my favorite coffee, I had to deal with the *other* woman in my life hell bent on doing my head in.

I could only hope Chloe wasn't working the counter when I got there. I still hadn't figured out what the hell was up with her, why she'd gone from sunshine to snow queen in the flip of a hat. And in my current mood, I didn't care to find out.

Chloe

I SHOULD HAVE KNOWN things were about to go south — or even more south than they were already going — when Derrick pushed through the door of the bakery with a thundercloud hanging over his head. If I'd have been wise, I would have bolted for the kitchen the moment I saw the stormy expression on his face, but in my defense, my brain always seemed to malfunction around Deputy Anderson.

"Uh… hi," I stuttered as he made his way to the counter, a frown permanently etched into his features. "You okay?"

"Fine," he grumbled under his breath. "Coffee. Black."

Wow, so he was going full caveman this morning. That was different. "To go?"

"Yep."

Concern tugged at me as I backed away to fill his paper cup to the brim, making sure to give him the largest we had. "You want a muffin or something?" I asked once I snapped the lid on and slid it over.

"Just the coffee, thanks." Another grumble. He reached into his back pocket and pulled out his wallet, tossing a few bills on the scuffed wood between us without a word.

"You sure you're okay?" Don't ask me why I kept pushing. It was more than obvious the guy was in no mood to talk, but his bad mood was worrying me. It was just so unlike him, not that I *really* knew him all that well. I'd just never seen him be so gruff. And it bothered me. I didn't like it. I wanted to see the laidback Derrick again, not the guy currently standing in front of me.

"Like I said, I'm fine."

He turned to go and I stupidly opened my mouth and pushed... again. "Are you really sure? Because if something's wrong I could—"

The moment he spun back around, I realized how wrong I was to keep pushing. "You could what, Chloe? You gonna talk me through it? Be a shoulder for me to lean on? Listen to all my problems?" he laughed bitterly. "Because that'd really be a switch from the ice queen routine you've been throwing my way for the past fucking month. You've been so busy pretending I don't exist I thought I'd become damn near invisible. What? You have some twisted fetish where you're hell-bent on finding some poor, damaged soul that you can heal and make him fall in love with you? Sorry, sweetheart, but I'm not your guy. I said I was fine. Just leave it alone."

I was frozen in my spot, pain and anger coursing through me at such a fast pace the only thing I was able to do was stand there immobile as the tears began to brim in my eyes. I was going to cry. *Damn it*. I was such an ugly crier. And once I started, it was almost impossible to stop.

Seeing the moisture pooling in my eyes, Derrick's own went wide, as if he'd been in a fog as he spat such hateful words at me, not even realizing what he was saying cut into me like a sharpened knife. "Oh, fuck," he murmured, the sullen attitude disappearing in an instant. "Chloe, *fuck*. I didn't mean that. I'm so sorr—"

"Get out," I whispered, the lump of emotion in my throat threatening to choke me.

"Please just—"

"Get. Out. Now," I said between clenched teeth as the tears finally breached my eyelids and began cascading down my cheeks. "And get your coffee from somewhere else from now on."

"I'm sorry. Believe me. Christ, I'm so sorry, I'm just in a shit mood—"

I lifted my hand, not wanting to hear another word. I hadn't thought it was possible for Derrick to break my heart more than he had when he couldn't even remember my name. But I'd been wrong. I told myself before that I wouldn't make that mistake again and I meant it, damn it!

"Fine, you won't leave, then I will. And you better be gone before I come back in here."

With that, I spun around and shoved through the swinging door leading into the kitchen, ignoring the concerned faces of my employees as I blew past them and through the back door that led to the stairway to the upper level. Taking the stairs two at a time, I burst into my cozy apartment that sat right above my bakery — I fell in love with the space because of this particular convenience — collapsed onto my couch, and for the second time in just over a month, cried my eyes out over Derrick Anderson.

A man who wasn't worth it.

Never again.

4

DERRICK

I'D SCREWED UP.
No, that was putting it way too mildly.

I was the fuckup to beat all fuckups. I'd stuck my foot so far in my mouth I was at risk of choking on it any second. I needed to fix things with Chloe. And not for the sake of our friendship, because if I was being honest, we weren't really all that close to begin with, not that I didn't *want* to be. I enjoyed her company. I laughed easier when I was around her, and I don't mean *at* her due to her nearly crippling awkwardness. No, I just enjoyed being around her. She was good friends with Noah and Harlow, which you'd think would have made it easier for the two of us to develop a closer friendship, but it just hadn't worked that way.

And I wanted to rectify that. I wanted to apologize for causing the pain I saw welling up in her bright green eyes the last time she looked at me. As she stood behind that counter, the struggle to hold back her tears had been so evident. The small smattering of freckles across her nose glowed as it began to grow red, and her bottom lip trembled slightly. I wanted to try and take all of that away, and hopefully repair any damage I had caused because I really did want to be her friend. The problem was, I had no clue what I was going to say to make things better.

"You know, I'm glad you decided to tag along today," Noah spoke from beside me. "Ethan's probably gonna bail the moment he spots some of his friends, and I can only hold Harlow's purse for so long before my balls begin to creep back up into my stomach."

"Amen, brother," a man standing in line next to us muttered under his breath and I looked over to see him holding a bright pink purse in his hand with the words *Kate Spade* printed on the front of it. He and Noah fist-bumped as we moved closer to the ticket counter, the cool breeze off the water was a peaceful reprieve from the uncharacteristically hot summer we'd been having.

"Hurry up, Daddy!" Eliza shouted from over near the benches where Harlow had chosen to sit and rest her feet, her rapidly growing belly making it nearly impossible to stand in the cramped line for tickets into Pembrooke's annual Summer Carnival on the Boardwalk.

There were two times a year when the normally tranquil boardwalk on Pembrooke Lake was packed with what felt like every town citizen. That was during the three months of summer when the carnival rolled in, and the couple of weeks during winter for the annual Holiday on the Boardwalk. Basically the entire place looked like the North Pole had thrown up on it, complete with a massive, heavily-decorated Christmas tree and stores filled with every holiday decoration known to man.

I waved my hand at my eager daughter, hoping she could contain her excitement for a few more minutes. Harlow looked seconds away from passing out due to heat stroke, and Ethan's nose was buried in his phone. "I'm shocked you talked her into coming," I told him as we inched even closer.

"You kidding me? This was her idea," he scoffed. "Damned woman's gonna be the death of me, I swear."

I looked back at the woman who appeared to be absolutely miserable as she sprawled out on the bench. "Really?"

We took another step closer. "Seriously. She's been obsessed with this damned carnival since I met her. We came every summer back in high school. Even with the pregnancy she refused to miss this year since it's her first summer back. No doubt I'll be hauling my ass down here this winter and freezing my nuts off for the Christmas shit too."

We finally made it to the front of the line. I stepped up to the window and bought all-day passes for myself and Eliza, knowing good and well she'll expect to ride every ride here, and eat her weight in cotton candy and other junk food. My head shot to the side when I heard Noah tell the ticket vendor, "Four, please."

"Four?"

"Oh, yeah," he said as we made our way to the bench. "I forgot to tell you, we're meeting—"

"Miss Chloe!" Eliza yelled, cutting Noah off once we were about ten feet from the bench they were all sitting on. My head spun around and I caught sight of her immediately. That light red hair shone brighter as the sun bounced off of it. The pale skin of her arms and legs were exposed in a pair of khaki shorts and a flowey peach tank top. It was strange, I hadn't really paid attention before, but seeing Chloe standing there, the epitome of summer comfort, I couldn't help but notice she was actually... cute.

Well this day suddenly took an unexpected turn.

Chloe

SHIT.

Shit, shit, shit, shit!

I smiled at the little girl despite my insides having seized up at the thought of seeing her father. It wasn't her fault she was born to an asshole. There was no way I was holding that against her.

"Hey, sweetheart. How are you?"

"Are you going to the carnival with us today?" she asked, too excited to have heard the question I'd just asked her.

I looked at Harlow who just shrugged her shoulders

and looked like she wanted to be just about anywhere else right then. "Well, if you're here with Ms. Harlow then I guess so."

"I'm here with my daddy, too."

Damn it, of course she is. At that very moment, I glanced up and locked eyes with Derrick, cussing myself out in my head for feeling a little flutter from just one look into his eyes. I really wasn't in the mood to deal with his shit today. I loved everything about the carnival, the rides, the food, the atmosphere, the blissful breeze that blew off the lake as we walked around, making the temperature outside feel comfortable instead of hot. Coming here was a tradition I'd held every single summer, rain or shine, and I wasn't going to let him ruin that for me.

"All right," my smile was bright, if not fake, "who's ready to get inside?"

Eliza jumped up and down while Harlow, with a lot of help from Noah, hefted herself off the bench and started waddling toward the entrance gates. Ethan never even bothered to look up from his cell.

I'd maybe gotten three steps when a warm hand wrapped around my elbow, pulling me to a stop. "Hey," Derrick said quietly. "Can I talk to you for a minute?"

I opened my mouth to object just as Eliza, walking next to Harlow, spun around and shouted across the way, "Come on, Dad! All the lines are gonna be long!"

Whew, dodged that particular bullet.

I took a step, but Derrick's hand tightened. "You guys

mind letting her tag along for a few?" he called back. "I need to talk to Chloe, it'll only take a minute."

One of Harlow's brows cocked as she shot me a look that said *you've got some serious explaining to do*. Noah, ever the lovable, clueless man, waved his hand. "We got her. Catch up with you guys in a bit."

Then my friends, the jackasses, walked through the gates, abandoning me with no one for company but a bastard.

"Chloe," he said my name without a hint of anger or irritation, but I couldn't bring myself to glance up from the cracked concrete sidewalk beneath my feet. "Please look at me, sunshine. I owe you a huge apology and I'd rather not say it to the top of your head."

Damn it! Why did he have to be sweet… and funny?

"It's fine," I said to the sidewalk. "Nothing to forgive, so we can go now."

Another step, another tightening of his hand on my arm, refusing to let go. I was really starting to get annoyed with that. I finally tilted my head up and met his remorseful gaze. "Seriously, Derrick. I said it's fine, okay? I forgive you, it's all good."

One corner of his mouth tipped up in a smirk and I *really* wanted to dislike it, I swear I did. I just couldn't. "Why don't I believe you, sunshine?"

"Because you're a self-absorbed asshole?" I asked without a thought then slapped my hands over my mouth, in shock by what I'd just said out loud.

"Thought so," he chuckled, good-naturedly.

"Oh my God," I mumbled behind my hands before pulling them away. "I'm so sorry! I can't believe I said that. I don't know what came over me!"

"You were pissed off," he continued to laugh in that deep, rich baritone of his. "And rightfully so. What I said to you a few days ago was fucked up. I was in a bad mood and took that out on you, and for that, I'm sorry, Chloe. From the bottom of my heart."

It was times like this that I wished I was like Harlow, with her thick skin and take-no-shit attitude. But I wasn't. And somehow, despite being polar opposites, we'd managed to become best friends. I just didn't have it in me *not* to forgive someone. That was why I found myself nodding and offering Derrick a small but genuine grin. "You're forgiven."

And he was, but that didn't mean I wasn't still feeling the sting of that fateful Fourth of July picnic. That was the type of humiliation a woman like me never bounced back from. So, while I might have forgiven Derrick for his cruel words earlier that week, I still didn't know how to be around him, how to act. That rejection was still playing on a constant loop in my head.

We made our way through the gates in companionable silence, or at least as companionable as possible, given the entire situation. We spotted Noah's head standing taller than most of the women and children around him. He looked like he'd rather be anywhere else at that moment, and despite the fact I loved the guy like a brother, I couldn't help but smile at his misery.

"Haven't seen that look in a while," Derrick spoke from beside me, startling me out of my musings.

"Huh?"

"The smile," he grinned back at me as he pointed to my mouth. "Haven't seen you smile recently. I was starting to think that sunshine disappeared."

My lips tilted into a frown as my forehead creased in confusion. "I smile all the time."

"Maybe so," he shrugged as we walked, "but not at me. I'm beginning to miss it."

His words were spoken with such ease, such casualness that he couldn't have possibly known my heart was splintering in my chest at that very moment. Just then, I couldn't think of a pain greater than wanting someone so completely, you felt it in every cell of your body, only to have that same desire go unfulfilled. Unrequited love really was a bitch. And she could go straight to hell for all I cared.

"Miss Chloe, let's go ride the Gravitron!" Eliza yelped once Derrick and I made it to our group.

"Okay," I laughed, peering down at the excited girl, at the same time Noah said, "I'm out. Pretty sure I just got mean-mugged by a six-year old that thought I was cutting in line, I'll be in the beer garden if you guys need me."

"I'm gonna go find my friends," Ethan muttered, eyes still glued to his phone as he wandered off.

"And I'm gonna sit on this nice, comfy bench." Harlow plopped down with a sigh and kicked her legs out in front of her. If you guys ride all the rides in this general area..." she made a circle in front of her with her finger, "...I'll cheer you on from here. Anywhere else and you're on your own."

A giggle escaped my throat as Eliza reached up to take my hand. "Ready?"

"Yep," I answered and turned to look at Derrick, he looked like his puppy had just run away as he watched after Noah's retreating form.

I rolled my eyes at how pathetic men were and told him, "If you want to go with Noah, I'm happy to keep Eliza company."

"You sure?" he asked a little too eagerly.

"Absolute—" and just like that, he was gone, actually shouting, "Hey Noah! Wait up!" as he jogged through the crowd.

With a shrug, I clasped my hand tighter around Eliza's and led her to the Gravitron. Then Pharaoh's Fury. Then the ride that swung you around in a circle from a cable, swinging us out above the lake. Then that damned ride that takes you high up in the air just to drop you over and over again. By the time we finished, I needed a break, or I was liable to revisit everything I had for breakfast earlier that day. Luckily Eliza decided she wanted to ride the carousel, giving me a much-needed reprieve from the stomach-churning rides. I took a seat on the bench next to Harlow and shook her awake.

"I'm awake, Noah, I swear!" she shouted with a jolt as she became conscious of her surroundings. "Oh thank God," she sighed, leaning against the back of the bench with her hand on her chest as I laughed at her. "I thought I'd fallen asleep during sex again."

"*Again?*" I cried as hysterical laughter bubbled from my chest.

"It's this baby!" she insisted dramatically. "It's sucking the life force out of me, I swear."

"Hi Miss Chloe! Hey! Ms. Harlow's awake!" Eliza hollered as she made her way around to our side of the carousel before disappearing once again.

"She's adorable, isn't she?" Harlow asked on a smile.

"She really is." Having kids of my own was something I'd always just assumed would happen one day. I just knew I'd get married to a wonderful guy and pop out our brood. I didn't dwell on it, just always considered it a foregone conclusion. It wasn't until Harlow's pregnancy progressed that I started to think about it more and more. I wasn't getting any younger, and as the years passed by, my single status remained disappointingly in place. Having met Eliza only made that need for a child all the more prominent.

"And she seems to be really taken with you," she grinned, nudging my arm.

I felt my cheeks flush under her gaze. "Really? You think?" I wasn't sure why her confirmation was so important to me, but just the thought of Eliza holding me in a high regard made my chest squeeze.

"Definitely. You're a lovable person."

I looked back at the little girl and smiled, waving back at her as she made another go-round. "And by everything you've told me, she's probably hungry for a woman's attention," I grumbled, the dislike of her mother having grown stronger the better I got to know Eliza.

"That woman," Harlow nearly growled. "Don't even get me started on her. Raving bitch... or at least that's what I've gathered from what Noah's told me. Derrick doesn't really say much about her to anyone else. But I'll tell you this, that woman better pray she never crosses my path."

"I know the feeling," I murmured as I waved again at a brightly smiling Eliza. "I'll hold her down for you."

"You got a deal," she agreed holding out her fist for me to bump.

DERRICK

"**S**O HOW LONG do you have her?"

I didn't bother looking at Noah. I didn't have to; I knew exactly who he was talking about. "Who the fuck knows," I grunted under my breath as I lifted the bottle to my lips and sucked down a mouthful of ice-cold beer. What should have been refreshing, tasted like sand in my mouth as bitter thoughts of Layla bounced around in my head. "She's off in Barbados or something with her sugar daddy."

"Aren't you supposed to get her for a whole month during the summer anyway?"

I let out a sarcastic bark of laughter. "That's what the papers say, but you know as well as I do that Layla takes any opportunity she can to screw with me. She doesn't have time for her most days, but when it comes up on my month-long visitation, she suddenly has plans to take Eliza on some *family vacation*." I said the words callously. "I wasn't going to be the asshole that told her she couldn't go to Disney World because her mom booked the tickets during my month. Layla played it perfectly. If I'd have said no, I'd have been the bad guy."

"Jesus Christ, man. How the hell were you married to her for so long?"

"Not sure, I've blocked out all memories," I chuckled before downing the rest of my beer.

Noah's phone chimed and he pulled it out of his pocket to read the text. "Harlow says she's got a sudden burst of energy. They're on the move, we're supposed to meet up with them by the whack-a-mole booth. Apparently Eliza spotted a giant pink bear she wants you to win for her."

I smiled as I stood and tossed my empty beer bottle into a nearby trashcan. "Sudden burst of energy? Thinking maybe you should find the nearest bathroom and bang her up against the wall. At least then she won't fall asleep on you."

A mother walking by with a herd of toddlers shot me a killing glare as she covered the nearest kids' ears. I gave her an apologetic smile as Noah punched me in the arm. "Bastard. See if I ever lay my troubles on you again."

"Feel free to never cry on my shoulder."

"But…" he sputtered. "That's what friends are for!"

I rolled my eyes as we made our way out of the beer garden and toward the game booths. "I'm thinking Harlow's pregnancy hormones are rubbing off, brother. I'm half expecting you to break out in song or tears any time now."

"If I have to sit through one more screaming fit 'cause I bought regular chocolate ice cream instead of double fudge, I just *might* cry."

"I don't envy your life," I informed him with a sympathetic pat on the head.

"*Pfft*. Please," he scoffed. "I'm married to the hottest woman in Pembrooke who's currently pregnant with our love child. When she's not passing out, the sex is phenomenal. You *wish* you had my life."

"Tied down by an ass load of strings just waiting to strangle the life out of me? No thanks. Been there, got the fucked up t-shirt. I've got no plans of ever going back."

"For Christ's sake, Derrick," Noah grunted, somewhat angrily. "You had a bad experience, who the hell doesn't? Marriage isn't a life sentence if you aren't married to a bitch from hell."

"Language!" another mother close by shouted at Noah.

"Look," I looked across my shoulder at him. "I'm happy for you, man. I really am. Harlow's great. But I've been down that road once already, and I've got no desire to get back on it."

"You know, when the day comes you fall ass-over-elbow for another woman, you can count on me being there to rub that shit in your face."

I chuckled again. "Never gonna happen."

Chloe

49

.   .   .

I STARED UP at the Ferris wheel as it made its slow journey around, the warm sun beating down on my head, no doubt burning the ever-loving hell out of my fair skin. I was sure I'd wake up tomorrow morning with a whole slew of brand new freckles dotting my face and arms.

The woes of being a redhead.

The ride came to a stop as people climbed off and others took their place. I always loved the Ferris wheel. It was the one thing I wanted to ride most whenever the summer carnival came around, but watching it now, as one loving couple was replaced with another, I felt a pang of sadness at not having someone special to ride with. Sure, I could have gotten in line at any point, but considering I was by myself, I'd either have been stuck with a complete stranger, or alone, something that, in my current mood, I just didn't want to deal with.

Yep, I was officially in the throes of a full-blown pity party, and it seriously made me want to punch myself in the face. I was single, so what? So the guy I'd been pining over didn't like me back? Boo-freaking-hoo. "I have a great life," I whispered to myself, refusing to go one more second feeling sorry for myself.

Then I heard it and the mental smack down I'd just been giving myself flew out the window. "There you are."

I looked to the side just as Derrick came to a stop next to me. "Harlow said you wandered off. Thought you might want to see me whack the shit out of some moles to win Eliza a hideous pink bear that's almost as big as me."

A laugh escaped against my will at the image of Derrick toting a giant pink bear around the carnival for the rest of the day. "Good luck with that. Those moles can be tricky little assholes," I said, my eyes, glued to the Ferris wheel.

"Hey," Derrick spoke, drawing my attention to him. "You want to ride?" he asked with a chin tilt toward the slowing wheel.

"Oh, uh… nah," I lied. "I think I've got whiplash from doing the bumper cars with Eliza."

"You sure?" he pushed, his large frame ducking down to get a closer look at my eyes. "'Cause I'll ride with you, if you want."

"Nope." The 'p' popped loudly, my voice sounding way too cheerful even to my own ears. "You should get back to the booths. Don't you have a mole to whack and a pink bear to win?"

One corner of his tilted up in a smirk. "I'm sure if I tried hard enough I could make that seem dirty." The heat on my cheeks had nothing to do with the sun. "You coming?"

"Nah, I think I'm gonna go look for something to eat, I'm feeling kind of hungry. But I'll catch up with you later."

Geez, I couldn't have been any more awkward if I'd tried!

I started to walk away, only to be stopped by a hand on my elbow. When I looked back over my shoulder, Derrick was frowning. "You really don't like me, do you?"

"What?" I asked on a shocked gasp.

"It's all right if you don't, I guess. It's just that I've never been outright disliked by someone and not at least known why."

"Derrick," I said his name softly as I turned to fully face him. "I don't hate you."

"Then what the hell's going on?" he asked vehemently. "I know we've never been all that tight, but I always thought we got along pretty well. Was I wrong for assuming that?"

A headache was beginning to form behind my eyes. "No... Derrick, I like you, okay?" I spoke as I reached up and massaged my forehead with my fingertips.

"Then what's the deal? Hell, at least you used to talk to me, now you hardly even look at me. I'm sorry for what I said at the bakery, Chloe. If you're still upset—"

"It's not that," I insisted.

"Tell me what it is then," Derrick demanded.

"You called me Cathy!" I nearly shouted, sounding just as stupid out loud as it did in my head.

"Huh?"

I'd already come this far, there was no point in stopping, seeing as I couldn't make a bigger ass out of myself than I already had. "At Noah and Harlow's July Fourth party. I came up to you to..." *shit, shit, shit, shit...* "ask you out and you were staring at Tammy Bradford's boobs the whole time and said, *'Excuse me, Cathy, I'll be back in a few.'*" I repeated in my best impression of a man's voice, which was seriously lacking. "Then you walked off," I finished with a shrug, staring at a spot on his shoulder the entire time, unable to meet his eyes.

"You... were trying to ask me out?"

Another shrug.

"I called you Cathy?"

"I just figured you'd never noticed me enough to remember my name. I'd had a crush on you since you moved to Pembrooke, and you didn't even remember my name. It... stung," I admitted sheepishly.

He remained silent for several seconds, and I waited for God to show mercy on me and open a hole beneath my feet. Then, "Ah, *fuck*!"

My eyes darted to his at the heaviness in just those two words. I watched in confusion as he reached up to drag his hands through his silky looking hair, appearing to be thinking really hard about something. "Hell, sunshine. I knew your name. I've *always* known your name." His brow was furrowed as he continued to explain. "I'd just spent the entire night handling a domestic with Carl Sanders and his wife..."

"Cathy," I breathed, knowing exactly whom Derrick was referring to. Carl and Cathy Sanders where notorious in Pembrooke for getting drunk and having the cops called when Cathy had enough of Carl's mouth and popped him in the face with whatever was close by.

"Yeah," he murmured softly. "I was going on almost no sleep, and I guess the fact that both your names start with a C... I just got tangled up."

Well didn't I just feel like a freaking moron. I'd just

basically confessed my feelings for a guy who wasn't inter-ested in me, and admitted to being butt-hurt for *over a month* about something that was a simple mistake. I was an idiot. If the ground didn't open up and swallow me, I was going to dig my own goddamned hole and climb right in.

"Uh... okay."

"Look, Chloe..." Ah hell, he suddenly had that extremely uncomfortable look. You know, the one where a guy's trying to think of the best way to let a woman down without her making a scene in public, or going full on *Fatal Attraction*.

"Derrick, really, it's okay," I started, hoping to cut him off at the pass. No such luck.

"I do like you, honestly. But..." *Damn you, 'but!' Damn you straight to hell!* "I'm just not that guy. You deserve someone who can commit and will treat you like you deserve." Basically, someone I'd hoped for way too long that he'd be. "After my divorce, I'm just not capable of that. I'm flattered, really. It's an honor to know you feel that way about me—"

"*Felt*," I lied, emphasizing the hell out of the tense.

"Huh?"

"I *felt* that way about you, not *feel*. Past tense, not present." *Shut up you moron.* "I mean, it was just a silly crush," I laughed uncomfortably, trying my best to cover up the truth. "But I'm totally over it," I said with a wave of my hand. I might have even snorted for effect. Because I was awesome like that.

His brows shot up on his forehead, those hazel eyes

going momentarily wide. "Oh. Okay, well great. But either way, I just wanted to explain, it's not you. You're great. It's me—"

"For the love of God," I groaned. "Please stop. Seriously, stop. This is probably the second most humiliating moment of my life. Just... stop talking." First place would forever and always go to that time in middle school when I started my period for the very first time... while wearing white jeans — because white jeans couldn't be embarrassing enough on their own. I may or may not have tried to play it off that I stabbed myself with a pencil. Didn't work, of course.

"What was the first?" he asked, an eyebrow shooting skyward.

I groaned again. "I'm going to pretend you didn't ask that, and that this entire conversation *never happened*, okay? I'm just gonna squeeze my eyes closed really tight..." I did, "...and pretend that this whole day was just one big nightmare."

I opened my eyes and looked at Derrick. His expression was far too amused for our current situation. "Nope, didn't work. Hold on, let me try again." I clenched my eyelids shut a second time.

"Chloe," Derrick said, his voice full of poorly suppressed laughter. I opened my eyes with a defeated sigh, my shoulders hunching and my head dropping forward.

"Yeah?"

"Are we okay?" he asked, using the rough tips of his

fingers to tilt my chin back up. It was a smooth move, one that made that overly kind, extra-forgiving part of my personality kick in.

"Yeah," I sighed again. "We're good."

"Great," he grinned. "'Cause I really do want to be your friend, not just a passing acquaintance. We live in the same town, have the same friends, and my daughter seems to really like you. And I trust her judgment."

"You should," I replied. "I'm totally awesome."

"I know," he chuckled. "So what do you say? Friends?" He extended his hand to me while I stood there, trying my best to pretend my chest wasn't cracking in half. Man, being friend-zoned sucked balls!

"Friends," I offered with the closest imitation of a genuine smile I could muster as I took his hand and gave it a firm shake.

He gave my hand a tug and began pulling me along with him. "Fantastic, now that that's settled, let's go whack some moles. My girl needs that ugly-as-shit bear."

If that wasn't an *FML* moment, I didn't know what was.

6

CHLOE

TWO WEEKS HAD passed since my and Derrick's impetuous — at least on my part — agreement to become friends. And in that time, he'd stuck true to his word, determined to treat me as more than the casual acquaintance we'd been for over a year and a half.

He stopped by the bakery daily for a cup of coffee and a pastry if he was in the mood. The only difference was, now, instead of shooting me a wink and heading on his way, he actually sat down and started chatting. Most of the time it was just simple small talk, but he made an effort.

Every.

Single.

Day.

I was miserable and elated all at once, which, let me tell you, was a hard as hell combination to deal with. On the inside, I felt giddy at his attention, because clearly, my inner-self was a boy-band-adoring teenager who loved to squeal incessantly. I was constantly having to remind that inner teenager that we were just friends, that he didn't have those kinds of feelings for me. You'd have thought the damned girl was reliving the breakup of One Direction all over again. It wasn't pretty. But I was coping.

Or at least trying to.

"What about on-line dating?" Harlow asked through a mouth full of food.

"How about you swallow so I don't throw up at the sight of your chewed-up food?" I shot back, stacking the last load of clean mugs so they were ready for use the next day.

"Can't help it," she mumbled, spitting coffeecake crumbs onto the recently cleaned bar top. "You're baking is just *sooooo good*," she finished on a groan.

"Come on!" I laughed, grabbing a cloth and wiping down the spot I'd just cleaned a few minutes ago. "You're so gross."

"I'm pregnant. I'm hungry all the time, I've forgotten what my feet look like, I literally sweat *all the time*, and every time this baby kicks my bladder, I pee on myself a little bit. Your pastries are pretty much the only thing I have to look forward to until this little demon pops out. So you don't get to judge me!"

"You must make Noah feel so good about himself," I giggled.

She gave me a careless shrug, finally swallowing her

food and wiping her mouth with one of my pretty napkins. "Don't change the subject."

"What subject?" I asked in all seriousness, having forgotten what she'd said between having to watch her graze and hearing about all the miseries of pregnancy.

"Online dating!" She smacked her palm on the counter then promptly got sidetracked when she spotted a batch of cookies I'd made, playing around with the recipe, trying to get it just right. "Ooh, cookies!"

"Hey!" I cried when she grabbed one and stuffed the entire thing in her mouth! "I haven't taste tested yet, back off!"

She let out a long, garbled groan as her eyes rolled back in her head. "I volunteer as tribute. I'll be your taste-tester for life. *Oh my God*, what's that flavor? It's like a party in my mouth. Gimme another!"

Smiling at another apparently successful creation, I pushed the plate in front of her. "It's almond extract and cinnamon. It's a new recipe I was thinking of adding to the menu."

"You should totally do it," she sputtered, spitting more crumbs. "And you should make a special batch every single day just for me, you know, because you love me so much."

I rolled my eyes and made a mental note to bake more cinnamon and almond cookies tomorrow morning when Harlow suddenly remembered what she'd been talking about before morphing into a bottomless pit. "So are you going to do it? I bet guys would go crazy over your profile.

You'll have more dates than you know what to do with in no time."

My lips were parted, ready to respond when something outside the bakery window caught my eye. Noticing that my attention had drifted, Harlow spun around on her stool to get a look at what I was staring at. Through the pristinely cleaned glass, Derrick walked down the sidewalk with his arm draped over a tall, leggy brunette. As if sensing our eyes on him, his head shifted to the side, the hand on the woman's shoulder came up in a wave, and he grinned as they continued to pass.

It was a direct hit. *Son of a bitch*! When the hell was I going to get over that guy already?

"So..." Harlow drew out as she spun back around, her eyes full of sympathy. "About that online dating thing..."

"Bring it up one more time, and I'll never make you cookies again."

She let out an affronted gasp and picked up another cookie, staring at it in adoration before looking back at me. "Consider the subject dropped."

A FEW DAYS LATER, the door to Sinful Sweets opened, causing the bell to chime out its typical greeting. When I looked up, my eyes landed on a weary-looking Derrick. His shoulders were slumped in exhaustion as he made his way to the counter, only offering small friendly smiles to the customers he knew as he passed instead of being his usual laid back, charming self. But even visibly rundown and ragged, he was still the most gorgeous guy I'd ever laid eyes on, in his faded jeans and olive-green t-shirt that hugged his muscled frame to perfection.

Pushing the lustful thoughts to the side, I studied the dark circles under his hazel eyes. "You look like hell," I said as soon as he reached me. Shit, I really hadn't meant to say that out loud.

He glowered as he dropped onto one of my cushioned barstools. "Thanks," he muttered dryly before scrubbing at his bristly cheeks. It looked like he'd gone about two days without a shave. It was a *really* good look on him. Damn him. "These night shifts are gonna be the death of me," he groaned, propping his elbows on the counter.

"If you're on nights, what the hell are you doing awake at…" My head shot to the side so I could look at the large clock hanging on the wall, "…seven in the morning?"

The heavy sigh coupled with the unhappy expression on his face told me whatever he was about to say wasn't good. "Layla called and woke me up." I was right. "She says her car won't start and needs me to come pick up Eliza for her first day of school."

My forehead wrinkled as I asked, "She doesn't have anyone closer that could help? Jackson Hole isn't exactly on the way for you."

The look he shot me clearly reflected exactly how he felt about his ex-wife. "And bother someone else when she can make my life a living hell? Now why would she do something like that?"

"I'm sorry," I offered softly, not knowing what else to say in this situation. "If there was something I could do to help I would."

"You can help me plenty by getting me the largest cup of coffee you got, sunshine," he answered with a smile. Even at only half its potency, it was still a sexy enough smile to throw my slightly off kilter.

"Uh… sure. Coming right up." I filled a paper cup to the brim before snapping a lid on the top and sliding it his way. "That's on the house," I informed him when he shifted, reaching for the wallet in his back pocket.

"You don't have to—"

Cutting him off with a wave of my hand, I smiled at him. "I know I don't, but that's what friends do, right?" The smile that statement earned me filled my chest, it was like getting an unexpected gift, and I felt niggling desire to do whatever I could to earn myself another one.

Calm your tits, Chloe, the rational voice warned the squealy teenage girl in my head, earning herself the middle finger.

"I appreciate that." He took a sip of the strong brew and I began restacking a display of muffins I'd already stacked just to give myself something to do other than ogle his throat as it bobbed with each swallow. Terrific, now I was mooning over the guy's throat.

"Yeah, sure," I shrugged, feigning a casualness I never felt in his presence.

Suddenly a sultry, feminine voice spoke up, drawing my

attention away from the perfectly situated blueberry muffins. "Well hey there, Deputy Anderson."

I'd been so enamored with all things Derrick that I hadn't even heard the bell over the door sound when Carla Fitzgerald walked in. *Carla Fitzgerald,* the town bike, only beaten in sluttiness by Tammy Bradford. It took everything I had to suppress the sneer that threatened to curl my lips. She'd never done anything to me in particular, but seeing as she had her surgically-enhanced tits pressed against Derrick's arm in that moment, I instantly hated her.

"Miss Fitzgerald," Derrick answered amiably. He wasn't overtly checking her out or anything, but just the fact his attention was on her and he was grinning, suddenly seeming a lot less tired than when he first walked in, made my skin tingle with annoyance.

"I've been hoping to run into you," she simpered, batting her overly-mascaraed eyelashes.

"Is that right?"

Ugh, kill me now, Lord. Strike me with a bolt of lightning or something!

"Mm hmm," she hummed, running her fake nails over his bicep. "There's a new restaurant having their grand opening in Jackson Hole this weekend. My friend's the hostess and managed to get my name on the list for Saturday night, and I'd just *love* for you to join me." Her voice dropped even lower as she added, "The food is supposed to be better than anything you've ever tasted." Her sensual tone was enough to make me throw up in my mouth a little.

Spinning on my heels, I gave the two of them my back, unable to watch Derrick accept a date with another woman. I knew it wasn't fair to feel hurt when I heard him murmur that he'd love to be her date to the opening. I mean, after all, I was the one who'd told him I didn't have a crush on him anymore, for Christ's sake. But that didn't make the pain feel any less suffocating. My hands trembled as I fiddled with the espresso machine, moving aimlessly in an effort to look preoccupied.

"Hey, Chloe," my assistant manager, Erin called. "Something's wrong with the convection oven again. I think it's finally crapped out.

I could have kissed her. The girl had no clue that she'd just saved me. I seriously needed to consider giving her a raise.

"I'll take a look at it, can you cover for me out here?"

"Sure thing."

I started for the door to the kitchen when Derrick's voice stopped me. "Chloe?"

"Hmm?" I hummed, glancing over my shoulder, refusing to turn all the way around and face him while he still had Carla hanging off his arm.

His brows dipped as those warm hazel eyes scanned over my face. "You okay?"

It was the curse of the ginger; whenever I got overemotional, nearing the point of tears, my face would grow red and splotchy. "Yes," I answered, making sure to keep my voice bright. "Just," I pointed over my shoulder, "this stupid oven. I should see what the problem is. You two enjoy the rest of your day." I graced Carla with a stiff smile before placing my hand on the door, praying to escape.

"You need me to take a look at it?" Derrick asked, stopping me once again.

"Nope, I've got it. Besides, you've got to go get Eliza. I'll see you later, okay?"

I didn't wait to hear if he had anything else to say. Pushing into the kitchen, I looked over at Emily, one of my employees, as she stood, frosting cupcakes. "What happened?"

"The old girl finally bit it," she said, tipping her chin to the ancient oven. Luckily I had more than one back here. "Don't think she'll be coming back this time."

I glared at the piece-of-shit oven at the same time I reached into my apron and retrieved my cell phone. It was quite possible that I wasn't thinking clearly, and that one day, I'd regret my decision, but in that moment, I didn't care. I was pissed at the oven and heartsick over Derrick's impending date. Scrolling through my texts, I found the chain between me and Harlow.

Me: *About that online dating thing... I'm in.*

Her response was instant.

Harlow: *What's your stance on converting to Judaism*

My fingers flew over the screen furiously as I typed.

Me: *Stay away from J-Date.*

Harlow: *You're no fun.*

Knowing she'd have my profile up on every available site by the end of the day, I pocketed my phone and sucked in a deep breath. I had the rest of my workday to get through, I couldn't mope about Derrick any longer — it was time to move the hell on. Once and for all.

On the bright side, I'd be able to take my aggression out on a broken oven later that night. I was thinking a baseball bat, a can of gasoline, and some matches were just what the doctor ordered.

7

CHLOE

"THIS IS RIDICULOUS," I groused as Harlow continued to click away on her camera. "Will you stop already?"

She lowered her camera with a beleaguered sigh and shot me a look that told me she felt that *I* was being a pain in *her* ass, not the other way around. "Will you just be still and cooperate, damn it?"

"Stop taking my picture!" I swatted at the camera in her hand. It was one of my rare days off and I'd planned on coming over, lounging on her back deck and drinking margaritas while she glared in envy as she sucked down her virgin daiquiris. But for the past twenty minutes, I'd been fighting off her ever-present camera as she took picture after picture.

"Come on!" I whined. "Enough already. I look like hell."

"You do not!" she insisted. "And we need photos for your dating profiles so I can finish loading everything."

I let out a groan and collapsed against the lounge chair. "I can't believe I let you talk me into online dating."

"Uh, excuse me," she snapped before sucking on her glorified slushy. "But *you* texted *me* about it. So get the lead out and let's do this already! It's a gorgeous day, I thought we'd do some outside shots."

Propping up on my elbows, I looked down at my ensemble, a raggedy pair of cutoff shorts that were a more suitable length for someone in their *very* early twenties, a navy tank top that I just grabbed from my drawer this morning, without looking, and my ratty converse sneakers that had seen better days. Definitely not picture-worthy. Hell, I hadn't even put on makeup, and my air-dried strawberry blonde curls were pulled in a loose knot on top of my head to tame their wildness.

"I'm pretty sure if you posted a picture of me right now, I might actually break the internet."

"Will you stop?" she scolded, her voice no longer holding a hint of humor. "Come here."

I begrudgingly got to my feet and followed after her, my shoulders slumped in defeat.

Once we reached the bathroom, she put her hands on my shoulders and spun me around. "Don't look in the mirror, look at me," she continued to boss as she reached up and yanked the ponytail holder out of my hair.

"Ow!" I shouted, reaching up to feel for a bald spot. "That hurt, you jerk!" She just shushed me and started running her fingers through my hair, tousling it near the crown of my head. Reaching for something on the counter, she pumped a few squirts into her hand and raked her hands through my hair once again.

"What are you doing?"

"Hush," was her only response. I stood quietly as she brushed a bit of eye shadow the color of deep gold on my lids, only moving when told to look up or down as she swiped a little mascara on my lashes. She finished up with a touch of a pinkish bronzer on the apples of my cheeks. The whole process took all of five minutes so I wasn't convinced she'd made much of a difference.

She pulled me from the bathroom before I had a chance to look at her handiwork and into the bedroom she shared with Noah, heading straight for the closet. Hangers slapped together as she looked at, and disregarded, top after top before finally landing on one of her liking.

"Here," she declared forcefully, shoving the top at me. "Put this on, and don't sass me."

"Harlow," I laughed uncomfortably. "There's no way we wear the same size."

"No sass!" she shouted.

"Fine, jeez." I rolled my eyes and tossed the shirt on the bed so I could pull my own off. The loose fitting racer back tank that declared "Sweet Dreams Are Made Of Me" actually fit me surprisingly well. The only place it hugged was across my abundant chest before billowing out around my stomach, effectively hiding the little pudge I could never seem to work off.

"Huh," I mumbled as I looked down at myself in surprise. "What size is this? I can't believe it fits."

Harlow rolled her eyes at me and reached for the hem of the shirt, tucking a small piece into my shorts at the front. "The way you view yourself is seriously skewed," she informed me. "You think you're some chubbo, but you aren't. You're curvy. That's a good thing, Chlo. Stop beating yourself down all the damned time." Taking my hand, she pulled me back into the bathroom and turned me to face the mirror. "See? Gorgeous."

I gasped. *Wow.* I was more than a little stunned at the reflection staring back at me. My makeup was miniscule but the shadow managed to give my eyes a gold-ish hue, and the bronzer on my cheeks made me look fresh-faced, my complexion almost dewy. It wasn't overtly sexy or anything, but I had to admit, with the curls hanging purposefully wild around my shoulders — in a way I've never been able to pull off on my own — and the makeup, I looked really... *pretty*. And I liked it. *A lot.*

"Huh," I said again, unable to formulate any other words.

"See!" Harlow smacked the bare skin on my shoulder, causing me to cringe. "And the way this top hugs your boobs is *hot*. Now let's go."

She dragged me back into the backyard, pushing me down on the lounge chair I'd been sitting on earlier. I reached for my discarded margarita and took a fortifying sip. I folded my legs in front of me and placed my glass back on the table next to me. "All right. What do you want me to do?" God, I had no idea what I was doing. I didn't know the first thing about being in front of a camera, there was no way I'd be able to actually pose.

"Just talk."

"Huh?"

"Just talk like we were earlier. Act like I'm not here taking pictures of you. Candid shots are some of the best ever. You'd be surprised how great they can turn out. And the best part, they're how a person looks every day."

I gave her statement some thought as the backdoor swung open and Ethan stepped out. "Hey Harlow, I'm going to the movies with some friends. I'll be back by curfew."

"Okay, shrimp. Have fun. Love you."

"Love you too," he chuckled at her nickname for him and turned his eyes to me, doing a brief double take. "Wow Chloe, you look really pretty."

My cheeks pinched almost painfully at the bright smile that crossed my lips. I barely registered the sound of the camera shutter clicking. "Thanks, hon. Have fun with your friends."

He returned my smile, his eyes going a little glazed as he stood there in silence for a few seconds. "Uh... yeah. Thanks," he stammered, giving his head a quick shake. "Um, I-I like your hair like that."

I giggled at the goofy expression on his face and heard the shutter click again. "Thanks, Ethan."

"Oh my God, shrimp! Stop macking on the adult and go meet your friends already!" Harlow razzed, making Ethan's face shine a bright red.

"Shut up," he groaned, turning back to the door.

"And remember," she shouted after him "abstinence is the best way to practice safe sex!" Poor Harlow, I didn't have the heart to tell her I was pretty sure that ship had sailed. Ethan was a sophomore in high school, on the varsity football team, and a good-looking kid. Yeah, I didn't hold out much hope that his virginity was still intact. And if it was, I didn't see that lasting much longer. Harlow told me how the girls at school looked at him. I figured he was pretty high on the totem pole.

"God! You're ruining my life!" Ethan yelled back from inside the house.

"Love you too!" she returned.

"You're horrible, you know that?" I giggled. "That poor kid's going to need therapy for years to come."

"Eh, he's fine," she brushed my statement off with a wave. "Okay, now do what you were just doing with Ethan and act like the camera isn't even here."

"Easier said than done when you point it out like that." I took another sip of margarita, enjoying the way my body seemed to be loosening up under the tequila's influence. I wasn't drunk, or even the slightest bit tipsy, just… relaxed. And I had to admit, the way Ethan went all googly-eyed when he stared at me was extremely flattering.

"I heard Derrick's been driving to Jackson Hole every morning this week to take Eliza to school."

"Yeah," I sighed, hating that Derrick was stuck in such a shitty position because of his ex. That woman really seemed to get off on making his life as hard as possible.

"He comes in to the bakery each morning for his caffeine fix. I feel bad for him. And Eliza. From everything I hear, Layla sounds terrible."

"She is," Harlow agreed. "But on the bright side, I know Derrick loves getting to spend as much time with Eliza as possible, even if he is driving out of his way every morning."

My gaze was focused on the dense line of trees that edged the back of their property in place of a fence. Harlow and Noah's backyard led straight into the woods. As a kid, I'd have probably spent hours out in those woods. I had no doubt their kids would grow up exploring imaginative unknown places out there in the coming years. At that thought, combined with the thought of Eliza, I smiled again and let out a deep breath.

"I'm sure. And I can't blame him. That little girl is amazing despite her shrew of a mother." It wasn't until I turned back to Harlow that I realized she'd been taking picture after picture of me. Pulling the camera from her eye, she stared at the screen, pushing buttons, a knowing grin on her own face.

"What? What are you grinning at?"

"Told you they'd be awesome," she giggled, handing the camera to me. "Once we post these, you're going to have so many date requests you won't know what to do."

I looked down at the photos, completely flabbergasted. "Wow, Low-Low," I breathed. "You're amazing."

"And you're beautiful," she replied seriously. "*That's* why they turned out so well."

"Thank you." As I scrolled backward through each photo, I could pinpoint exactly when each and every one had been taken based on the expression on my face. It was amazing to see how my emotions reflected so clearly on my face. No wonder I was such a shit poker player.

I was smiling serenely in the pictures where I thought about Eliza and Harlow and Noah's future family. My brows were furrowed in the ones where we'd been discussing Derrick's ex-wife. My face was a mixture of slightly embarrassed exuberance when we'd been talking to Ethan. Those were the ones I found the most stunning, where I looked the happiest, the *prettiest,* with my wide, brilliant smile and shining eyes.

"Yep, those are my favorite, too," Harlow announced, her baby belly bumping into my shoulder as she leaned forward to get a look at the small screen. "I think we should use that one," she pointed her finger at the picture I'd just scrolled to. And I had to agree.

"Okay, then we'll use that one."

"Yay!" she cheered, grabbing the camera from my hands just as a loud voice called from inside the house.

"Where's my baby momma!"

"Dear Lord, I'm getting sick of him calling me that," Harlow uttered with a roll of her eyes as the backdoor swung open and Noah stepped through excitedly, like he'd been at sea for a year and hadn't just seen Harlow earlier that morning.

"Wildflower!" He charged her, wrapping his arms around her waist and tilting her backward in a dramatic kiss that caused me to giggle. I ignored the pang of envy at the sight of my best friends being so in love. "I've missed you, baby," he crooned as she giggled in his arms.

"Hey there, sunshine," another voice spoke, yanking my attention from the loving couple as my belly swooped. The sight of Derrick standing in the doorway leading to the back deck, looking magnificent in all his shirtless glory had my mouth going dry.

Why? Why did the bastard have to be *so* good looking? Picking up my margarita, I sucked the last of it down in a hearty gulp. If he was going to be staying, I needed another one. STAT.

8

DERRICK

*H*OLY SHIT.

I'd always thought of Chloe as cute, very pretty, in a girl next door kind of way. But when I stepped into the doorway to the backyard, the sight before me was one I hadn't expected. She looked... well, *hot*. She was the type of woman who wore minimal makeup, and it worked for her, but now... now those big doe eyes of her's stood out, and the way her hair hung down her back in wild, attractive curls... I couldn't quite put my finger on why she appeared so different, I just knew she did.

And the way my dick twitched behind my fly screamed to the fact that it was *not* a good thing. *Head out of the fucking gutter, Anderson*, I scolded myself. Chloe wasn't the type of woman I needed to ogle shamelessly. She was a friend, someone I cared about. She was the type of woman you kept, putting a ring on her finger and surrounding her with a white picket fence and a shit load of kids. And as a man unwilling to give her what she deserved, I needed to get myself in check.

Because she deserved better than anything I was capable of giving her.

"Hey!" She smiled up at me after downing the last of what looked like a margarita.

"Uh… someone want to tell me why Derrick's not wearing a shirt?" Harlow asked. "Or is this a new thing you're starting? Just walking around town shirtless hoping to give all the old ladies heart attacks?"

"Hey!" Noah protested. "Stop looking at his chest, damn it. I look just as good shirtless as he does."

"Your lesser half over there doesn't know the first thing about fishing. He managed to snag his hook in my shirt before casting and ripped a big ass hole in it. It was my favorite shirt, too." I crossed my arms over my chest and flexed my pecs for added effect, just to rub it in the asshole's face. My gaze wandered back to Chloe in curiosity, wondering what she thought about the sight of my bare chest. Her face was down, her eyes studying her empty glass in her hands. I couldn't tell if it was the sun shining on her, but I could have sworn her cheeks looked a little pinker than normal.

"Well if your dumb ass hadn't been in the way, I wouldn't have snagged you," Noah pouted, wrapping Harlow tighter in his arms as she giggled against his neck.

"Yeah? Then what's your excuse for throwing your rod in the lake on a cast?"

He lifted his chin in the air, "There was a bug on it."

"Not helping your case, man," I laughed as I caught movement out of the corner of my eye.

"I need a refill," Chloe said, holding up her glass. "Be right back."

"Bring my laptop with you," Harlow called. "We'll upload those photos."

"What photos?" I found myself asking once Chloe had disappeared back into the house.

One of Harlow's brows quirked up as she regarded me with an expression I couldn't quite read, and one I figured I didn't want to. "We took some pictures to upload to a couple dating websites," she answered casually, as if it were no big deal.

"Dating websites?" Noah and I spoke at the same time. "Woman, do you have any idea how dangerous those can be?" He asked in outrage, voicing the exact thoughts that were suddenly racing through my head. "There are rapists and murderers on those sites! Have you lost your mind?"

"Oh come on!" Harlow scoffed with a roll of her eyes. "It's 2016, online dating is how most couples now-a-days meet. You're being ridiculous."

I didn't bother hanging around to listen to her defend such a fucking *terrible* idea. Instead, I stormed back into the house to find Chloe standing at the kitchen island pouring some light green, slush concoction into her glass.

"Are you crazy?" I spat, earning a startled yelp from her.

"Jeez, Derrick, you made me spill my margarita." Grabbing a napkin, she began dabbing at her top, drawing my attention to the way it hugged her tits. It was at that very moment that I noticed, for the first time, just how curvy she was. Usually her clothes hid her body, obscuring her figure to the point a man's imagination didn't really have anything to go on. But the shirt she was wearing just then showcased breasts that had to have been a generous c-cup, at the least, and the way it flowed against her body, moving *with* her curves instead of masking them, showed she had a nice, tiny waist with generous hips a man could grab onto and...

Son of a bitch! I clenched my eyes closed and gave my head a shake. I could *not* get hard over Chloe, for fuck's sake. She was off limits. Off. Limits.

"Online dating?" I asked, pushing the unexpected twitching behind my fly from the back of my mind and focusing on the issue at hand. "Do you *want* to get murdered and buried in the woods? 'Cause that could happen, Chloe." Yes, I was well aware I sounded completely ludicrous, but it happened! Right? I mean, there was that Craigslist Killer guy. And I'm sure if I looked it up, I could find more.

The sound of Chloe's tinkling laughter cut through my mind as I inventoried all the serial killers I knew about, trying to come up with irrefutable proof of just how bad an idea online dating was. Damn, she really did have a fantastic laugh.

"You're crazy," she giggled. "Everyone online dates."

"Yeah! If they want to be decapitated and dumped down by the river!" I crossed my arms over my chest and leveled her with a look that normally made Eliza squirm. "You're not doing it. That's final. I'm your friend and I want you to live a full, healthy life, preferably with all your body parts still attached." Don't ask me why I was being so irrational over the thought of Chloe meeting a guy or... God forbid, guys online. I didn't have the answer to that, all I knew was I couldn't have stopped my mouth from running in that moment if I'd tried.

"You watch way too much *Criminal Minds*, Derrick, you know that? Nothing's going to happen. It's not like I'd accept an invitation to meet a guy in a dark, secluded basement or something. It would be in a very public setting, at least at first, anyway, until I got comfortable around the guy."

That statement made the hairs on my arms stand on end. "Not happening," I said with finality.

Her face scrunched up adorably as she glared at me, challenge flashing in her green eyes like fire. "Is that right?" she asked with deceptive calm, mimicking my stance, her arms folding over that ample chest.

"Damn straight it is." A slow smile stretched across her mouth, and I should have been scared, I should have heeded the warning that look gave me. Unfortunately, I was a man, therefore stupid to most things when it came to the opposite sex until it was too late.

"Harlow!" Chloe shouted. Yep, it was too late.

"What?" she asked, stepping through the door with Noah on her heels.

"Derrick here just informed me I'm not *allowed* to online date. That he's forbidding it, end of discussion."

"He said what now?" Harlow asked, both brows shooting up on her forehead as she cocked a hip and rested a hand on it. I might not have known much when it came to women, but I know *that* posture did not say good things for my wellbeing.

Glancing over her shoulder, I gave Noah a look, asking for some support seeing as I knew he agreed with me. Unfortunately, I'd picked a betraying asshole as a best friend.

"Dude," he shook his head in disappointment. "You never tell a woman what to do. You make a suggestion, or go about it in a way where you convince her that it was her idea, but you never *ever* flat out tell her what to do. You should know this, Derrick." Then, for good measure, the bastard added, "I'm so ashamed of you right now."

I felt the intense need to punch him in the throat all of a sudden.

"Are you kidding?! You were just saying the exact same thing outside!"

"Nuh uh!" he argued, shaking his head and hiding behind his pregnant wife like a coward. "I *suggested* it was a bad idea! Then I kindly *asked* if she was aware of the odds that one of those men could be a potential predator. Never once did I just *demand* she not try online dating. I'm not a caveman, Derrick," he scoffed. "Unlike *some* men in this room."

"You know I'm gonna shoot you, right?" I asked him, narrowing my eyes in angry slits. "Come on! Be logical!" I called to the room as a whole, throwing my arms in the air.

"It's never a good idea for a single woman to meet a man she's only interacted with on-line. The chances that he's some psychopath are exponentially higher than just meeting someone at say, the grocery store, or something."

"Exponentially," Noah parroted. "Good SAT word, brother." I flipped him off.

"Oh, I'd just love to see the research backing up that claim," Chloe laughed. "So, if what you're saying is true, I should just go out to some bar, pick any random guy who offers to buy me a drink, and go home with him?"

"What? Of course not!"

"But she wouldn't have met him on-line," Harlow added brightly. I felt the beginnings of a migraine starting to creep up.

"Look," I pinched the bridge of my nose, trying to form a rational sentence. "What I'm saying is…" then I was struck by pure brilliance, "…I should screen every single likely candidate so I can run a full background check for any felonies or Class A misdemeanors."

Ignoring my perfectly reasonable suggestion, Chloe spoke up, "And the next time you want to pick up a woman at the Moose and take her home for a roll in the hay, I'll expect you to call me first so I can come down and administer a blood test, you know," she smiled sweetly, even though I could see the evil behind it, "for safety reasons."

"That's not the same thing," I argued.

"Oh, I've got to hear this," Harlow laughed. "And why, exactly, is it different for you than it is for Chloe?"

"Because I'm a man," I answered, instantly regretting

the words that came out of my mouth as soon as they passed my lips. "Wait! No — that's not what I meant to say. What I meant is — I'm bigger. I've got more muscles. I can defend myself if need be."

"I'll have you know, I've been taking weekly self-defense classes for the past four years. I'm more than capable of defending myself."

And because I was clearly on a roll with all the stupid, I laughed. "*Pfft*, not likely. You're a pixie for Christ's sake."

I barely got the last word out when I was suddenly choking on my own tongue, unable to take a proper breath as the kitchen floor came at my face at a startling pace only to be stopped by the force of something slamming into my chest, deflating both my lungs and sending me careening backward.

I gasped for air as I writhed on the floor in pain. "What —" I wheezed. "What just—" I sucked in a breath, getting nowhere near enough oxygen in my collapsed lungs, "happened?"

"You just got your ass handed to you by a girl!" Noah hooted before collapsing in a fit of uncontrollable laughter. "Oh God! You should have..." he stopped to wipe a tear from his eye, "...you should have seen your face! Classic! That was classic! Chloe, do it again so I can record it this time."

As I lay on the kitchen floor, dying, I cursed Noah Murphy. I had no friends.

9

CHLOE

"THIS IS A bad idea. This is a stupid, stupid, stupid idea," I said to my reflection in the mirror as I swiped my hands over my stomach, brushing out any wrinkles in my dress while trying to soothe my frayed nerves at the same time.

"It's not a stupid idea!" Harlow called from my bedroom where she was sprawled out on the bed, scrolling through Pinterest on her phone. "It's a brilliant idea. Time to get on one horse to get your mind off another."

"That's not even a saying!" I argued back, walking out of the bathroom to find her laying on her back, her legs stretched out. "And get your nasty feet off my pillows!"

"They aren't nasty! See?" she shoved her foot in my face when I got close enough to yank my pillows out from under her bare feet.

"Gross! Stop," I laughed, batting her foot away. "God, Harlow," I harrumphed, collapsing onto the bed next to her. "What the hell am I doing? I don't even *know* this guy? We've only been talking on-line for a couple of days, he could be a total creeper."

"Or," she paused long enough to roll to her side and prop her head in her hand. "He could be totally great. You'll never know unless you try. Besides, it's just dinner. And you said you thought he sounded nice when you guys talked. You'll be in a public place so you won't have to worry about him knocking you out to harvest your kidney, and you get a free meal out of it. That's a win-win in my book."

I let out a sigh as I stared up at my ceiling. "Yeah, I guess you're right. I mean, we agreed to meet at the restaurant so it's not like I'm stranded if he turns out of be a psychopath or something."

"Exactly! And hopefully he's taking you somewhere fancy."

I stood from the bed and grabbed my phone from the nightstand. "I don't know, I've never heard of it." I scrolled through the text messages between me and Austin, the man I met on one of the gazillion dating websites Harlow set me up on. "It's some place called The Peak?"

Harlow shrugged and shook her head. "Never heard of it."

"I hope it's good. I haven't eaten all day. I'm starving."

"Why haven't you eaten?" Harlow asked in a stern, motherly voice.

"Because I've been nervous!" I threw my hands up at my sides. "I can't remember the last time I went on a date. I've been crushing on Derrick for what feels like forever. I haven't even *thought* about dating."

Harlow grunted with exertion as she scooted across the mattress and tried to get her big, pregnant self out of the bed. "Listen," she spoke once on her feet, placing her hands on my shoulders, "if worst comes to worst and the food sucks, you can stop at a drive-thru on the way home. And if you're feeling generous, pick up a couple extra cheese-burgers for me while you're at it." I remained silent, waiting for her to say more. She didn't.

"That's it? That's your pep-talk?"

Her forehead wrinkled in confusion. "Who said anything about a pep-talk? I just want cheeseburgers."

"You made it seem like you were going for a big, moti-vational speech! You got off the bed and held my shoulders and everything. What the hell? I'm freaking out here and all you can think about is cheeseburgers?"

"Stop. Freaking. Out." She punctuated each word with a shake, making my teeth clack together painfully. "Your hair looks fabulous, your makeup is flawless, and your body is rocking the hell out of that little black dress. You're hot. I'd totally hit that. Be confident. This guy needs to impress *you*, not the other way around. He's freaking lucky you agreed to go out with him in the first place."

"Now *that's* what I'm talking about!" I shouted, pumped up from her speech. "That's a pep-talk!" She was right, I was a total catch and it was long past time I started real-izing it. I was over being the self-conscious girl, always down on herself, taking the smallest flaw and making it into something I hated about myself. I knew my worth and it was about time I started acting like it. Austin *was* the lucky one.

"Okay," Harlow said with a clap of her hands. "Breath check." I leaned forward and breathed in her face. "Minty fresh. Panty lines?" I spun around, showing her the back of the formfitting dress. "You're good. Deodorant stains?" I tilted from side to side so she could check for any white streaks on my dress I might have missed. "Nope," she declared. "You're golden, pony boy. Now get out of here or you're going to be late. Jackson Hole's a twenty-minute drive. Go on, git!" she finished with a hard smack on my butt, sending a sharp flare of pain through my skin. Rubbing at the offended cheek, I shot her a glare as I made my way out of the bedroom.

"And have fun! Don't get pregnant on the first date, it's bad form! I'll just let myself out after I'm done ordering movies from on demand!"

As I climbed into my car, I laughed, knowing damn good and well she wouldn't be able to get past the password I set up on the parental controls after the last time. No way in hell was I shelling out *another* hundred bucks in On Demand movie rentals because of her.

"I'M A CATCH, he's the lucky one. I'm a catch, he's the lucky one. I'm a catch, he's the lucky one," I repeated as I climbed from my car and headed across the street toward The Peak.

From the outside, it looked really nice. Fancy, upscale, and judging from the number of people waiting outside, the food must have been outstanding. My stomach rumbled in thanks. I wasn't sure how much longer I could go without food.

"Chloe?" I heard a man call my name once I reached the sidewalk outside the restaurant. Plastering a smile on my face, I watched as Austin — or at least I was pretty sure it was Austin, based on the one and only picture I'd seen of him — came toward me. He looked different than his picture, not outrageously so, but enough that the difference was noticeable.

He told me he was a nutritionist and personal trainer so I knew he'd more than likely be in shape, but it looked like he'd packed on at least another twenty pounds of pure muscle since the picture he'd posted on the website. And most of that seemed to be in his neck. Seriously, his traps almost went up to his ears. It was disconcerting to look at. He wore a nice button down and black slacks, but the closer he got, the more I feared for the durability of the seams. He looked like one wrong move and he'd Hulk right out of his clothes.

"I knew that was you the minute you walked up." He smiled, placing his hands on my upper arms and leaning in to kiss my cheek. It was a polite, friendly gesture, and I immediately felt like an ass for judging a book by its cover. So he was overly muscled, so what? It was part of his job, right? It was bound to happen. That didn't mean he wasn't a nice guy, and despite the muscles, he was cute, *really* cute.

Blonde hair, smiling brown eyes, and nice, straight white teeth. *I could totally work with this*, I told myself as he placed his hand on the small of my back and guided me through the crowd of people.

"Wow, this place is packed," I stated as we pushed through the front door and attempted to squeeze through the swarm to get to the hostess station.

"Yeah," Austin spoke loudly to be heard over the crowd. "It's opening night. Apparently it's a pretty big deal. Grand opening celebration and all that."

My back went stiff at that. *Oh God*, I prayed. *Please don't let this be the same place Derrick's coming to with Carla.* What were the odds that Jackson Hole was having two grand opening celebrations for two brand new, super trendy restaurants on the exact same night? I really didn't like those odds, but I prayed that was the case.

"May I help you?" the hostess asked, her pitch black hair slicked back in a severe yet stylish bun. With her sharp features and piercing blue eyes, she would have been stunning... had she not been staring down her nose at us in disdain once we got to her, as if she were above interacting with mere mortals.

I never understood why high-end restaurants hired people like that. It didn't give the atmosphere a feeling of class, it just made you feel like you were trapped in a room for an hour-and-a-half with the mean girls in high school. Not something I was a fan of.

"Uh, yeah. Table for two?" Austin spoke, leaning in to be heard clearly.

"And the name on the reservation?"

"Oh..." His cheeks grew flush as he reached up and scratched the back of his neck, testing the limits of his shirt sleeves. "I don't... I mean, I didn't make a reservation."

Okay, he didn't make a reservation at a restaurant that he knew would be buzzing, for a date *he'd* asked me on. Don't get me wrong, it wasn't a deal breaker necessarily, but it didn't really show his dedication when it came to planning something either.

"Sir," the hostess snorted with derision. "This is opening night, as you can see, we're quite full already."

"Oh, that's okay. We don't mind waiting." Austin smiled down at me as my stomach let out a low growl, or maybe that was a cry of agony at the thought of having to wait any longer. Seriously, what did a girl have to do to get a bread basket, for crying out loud?

The hostess's face pinched in an unattractive scowl. "I'm sorry, sir. We're booked solid for the next two months. Might I suggest the Applebee's down the street? I'm sure they'll have a table for you."

At that moment, I couldn't decide if I wanted to slap the resting-bitch-face right off her or leap over the station and kiss her for her suggestion. Yes, I was *that* hungry. Applebee's sounded *fantastic*.

"Austin," I started, placing my hand on his arm. His expression was a mixture of embarrassment and agitation; I couldn't help but feel bad for the guy... even though he was the one who didn't make reservations. "It's okay. We

can just go somewhere else." I smiled up at him to show it
wasn't a big deal.

He turned back to the hostess and that red on his
cheeks darkened, this time, in frustration, not embarrassment. "You mean to tell me you don't have one single table
you can sit us at? Really?"

"That's *exactly* what I'm saying. Now, if you'll kindly
step aside—"

"I will *not* step aside!" Austin slapped his hand down on
the top of the hostess stand, causing me and bitch-face to
jump. "I want to speak to your manager. Now."

I put pressure on his arm, first hoping to calm him
down, but also because I wasn't sure he could even feel my
touch through the six extra inches of muscle wrapping
around his bicep. "Seriously. I love Applebee's. We can
just go—"

"What are you still doing here?" he bit at the woman.
"Didn't I ask to see your manager? Go," he waved his hand
like she was a dog. If I were a betting woman, I'd lay my
money on this being 'roid rage at its finest. No person was
that big without chemical assistance, it just wasn't natural
to have legs for arms. It was safe to say a second date
wouldn't be happening. Harlow's suggestion of bailing
early and grabbing drive-thru was looking more and more
appealing with every passing second.

"Chloe?"

Oh, God. Why me? What did I ever do to you?

I clenched my eyes shut, hoping against hope that I was

just hearing things, that the noisy crowd around us was playing tricks on my ears, no such luck.

"Chloe? That you?"

"Derrick, hey," I said with false enthusiasm as I looked over my shoulder at him and *Carla*.

Derrick's grin was much more open and enthusiastic than mine was, and it was a struggle to ignore the way my stomach fluttered at the sight of it. It didn't mean anything other than he was happy to see a friend. He had another woman on his arm, after all. And besides, I was no longer Sad Sack Chloe, who moped around feeling sorry for herself. I was on a date. With Austin. Who was lucky I agreed. I just wouldn't think about the fact that said date already seemed to be going horribly wrong.

"What are you doing here?" he asked with genuine curiosity as he leaned — *away* from Carla — and placed a feather light kiss on my cheek. I couldn't help but notice the way Carla's eyes narrowed into angry slits as she took me in, top to toe, before she looked at the hostess and blew her a kiss. In everything that had been going on, I'd forgotten she mentioned she was friends with Bitch-Face, and that's how she'd gotten the table.

"I'm... uh, well," I coughed uncomfortably as Austin turned away from the bitch-faced hostess and noticed we had company. He placed his hand possessively around my waist in a way I did *not* like as he gave Derrick the same look Carla had just given me. "I'm actually on a date."

Derrick's gaze bounced between me and Austin, and I

wasn't positive, but if the tick in his jaw and the pulsing vein in his forehead was anything to go on, he was *not* happy. And I wasn't too proud to admit that gave me a little thrill.

"A guy from the internet?" Derrick asked through clenched teeth.

I ignored his question, choosing instead to get introductions out of the way. "Um, Derrick, this is Austin. Austin, my friend Derrick. We were actually just leaving. Turns out we couldn't get a table." I reached back and took Austin's hand, not in an affectionate way, but in one that would hopefully spur his ass to move. Derrick's gaze honed in on our clasped hands before he shot a look at the hostess.

"They can sit with us."

"What?" I squeaked.

"What?" Carla snapped.

"What?" the hostess sneered.

"Derrick," Carla purred, placing her hand on his chest as she batted her eyes up at him. This is supposed to be a really romantic place. Don't you want it to just be the two of us?"

Ignoring her question, he looked back at Bitch-Face. "Does our table seat four?"

"Well..." she sputtered. "Yes, but—"

He cut her off. "Perfect. Then we'll all fit. We're ready to be seated now."

Bitch-Face collected our menus and led us all back to the table. It was official, I was in hell.

10

CHLOE

*T*HE SEATING ARRANGEMENTS at our small round table were less than ideal, with me sandwiched between Austin and Derrick and Carla staring daggers at me from across the table. And the tension couldn't have been any worse if my parents had somehow materialized out of thin air and told the story of the time they walked in on Brandon Adame and me grinding against each other while fully clothed.

"So, Austin," Derrick started. *Oh damn.* "What is it that you do?"

"I'm a personal trainer and nutritionist," he answered brightly. I smiled over at him just so I wouldn't seem like a bitch. Just because I had no intention of going on another date with Austin... *ever...* didn't mean I needed to be rude.

Derrick picked up his glass of water and took a sip "So, you spend your days working out and telling people what to eat." It wasn't a question. "Explains the muscles," he finished, his voice dripping with condescension.

"I help people discover their very best selves," he defended. "It's really fulfilling work. What do *you* do?"

Oh sweet Lord, here we go. Where was our breadbasket? I swear to God, I saw a few tables with them as we walked through the dining area.

Carla chose that moment to lean in and place her hand on Derrick's thigh, looking up at him adoringly as she answered, "He's a deputy at the Pembrooke Sherriff's Department. Such admirable work," she finished on a sigh. I struggled to keep from rolling my eyes.

I chugged down some water as the animosity between Derrick and Austin continued to grow, thickening the air to an uncomfortable level. Derrick was really taking the whole "protective friend" thing too far. Spotting our waiter a few feet away, I slammed my glass down on the table and waved him over excitedly. My stomach made a gurgling sound in approval.

"Excuse me, hi, yes. Is there any way we can get one of those breadbasket thingies?"

"Certainly, ma'am. I'll have that out right away."

My stomach protested. "You know what? Make it two, thanks."

"Chloe," Austin said, leaning over and touching my hand gently, his face soft, I thought he looked sweet... until he opened his mouth. "Do you have any idea how many calories are in a piece of bread? I always warn my clients away from eating such things. Maybe it's best you wait for

SWEET SUNSHINE

the main course, that way you don't gorge on useless calo-ries." Carla made a choking noise from the other side of the table and I glanced over to see her smiling smugly behind her water glass. I shot her a look that screamed, *"You can just go straight to hell, you skinny slut!"* before turning back to Austin.

Typically, a comment like that would have offended me, hell, it might have even made me cry, but *he* was the lucky one to have me in his presence. And no way in hell was I going to be offended by a man who literally had no neck.

Before I could open my mouth to reply, Derrick chimed in. "I think she looks fantastic. A woman with curves like hers shouldn't watch what she eats, it gives a *real* man something to hold onto."

I flushed scarlet red as Carla slammed her water glass down on the table. When my wide, astonished eyes met his, he was smiling down at me, and I felt it all the way to my bones. I felt that unwanted flutter again, the same one I'd been feeling ever since he moved to town, and I had to shake my head to get rid of the daze a simple smile from Derrick put me in.

Luckily, the waiter chose that very moment to place two baskets of warm, delicious smelling bread on the table. Without batting an eye, I grabbed one of the rolls and took a huge bite, facing Austin the whole time as I hummed in approval.

"So good," I groaned through a full mouth, just to rub it in. Screw him and his "useless calories." I *loved* carbs and that was never changing. I owned a bakery for Christ's sake.

As Austin scowled, Derrick took a roll for himself and passed the basket to Carla. "Oh, no thank you," she simpered. "I've cut all gluten from my diet."

"Of course you did," I muttered quiet enough she couldn't hear me.

"I have to fit into a bridesmaid dress next month, and if I'm not careful, I'll get a little pooch." She leaned back in her chair and placed her palms on her flat stomach while poking her boobs out all at once as she looked at Derrick through her long, false eyelashes. I couldn't hold my eye roll back that time.

The conversation grew stilled and awkward as we each placed our orders, and it certainly didn't help when the waiter asked if we'd be dividing the check and Austin nodded, waved his finger between us, and said, "The two of us are separate, thanks."

Just freaking wonderful, the guy had a short temper, didn't bother making reservations, and wasn't even planning on paying for the dinner *he* asked *me* to? I'd already decided there was no way in hell he and I were a love match, but did Karma really hate me so much that I had to not only suffer through a terrible date, but do it with Derrick and his Barbie doll in tow? I hated Karma. She could kiss my ass.

I grabbed the waiter's sleeve as he began to walk off and pulled him to me. "I'll be needing wine. Lots and lots of wine. I don't care what the hell it is, just make it red and make it fast."

"And put it on my check," Derrick chimed in. "I'll be paying for the ladies tonight."

My embarrassment officially knew no bounds.

When our server came back with a glass of red wine, filled to the top, I made a mental note to double whatever Derrick tipped him. He was a good man.

The only saving grace through dinner was the fact that I'd already managed to down a glass and a half of wine. The tightness in my shoulders had begun to melt away and I had that pleasant floaty feeling from the slight buzz.

"So," Carla gazed dreamily up at Derrick as she sipped her wine and pushed her side salad around with her fork. That's right. She was one of *those* people. She ordered a freaking side salad for a meal and barely ate it. I, on the other hand, had already devoured my filet, and didn't feel a bit bad about it. "That wedding next month I was telling you about? How'd you like to be my date?" She placed her fork down on the table and walked her fake nails up his arm. "I'd make it worth your while. I already have a room at the hotel. It's supposed to have a Jacuzzi tub. It's amazing what those jets can do."

Oh gag! I was pretty sure I threw up a little bit. I wanted to laugh as Derrick sputtered into his glass, thrown off. If I had to guess, it wasn't the sexual innuendo that threw him for a loop, it was the suggestion of a wedding date. In all the time I'd been watching Derrick, I noticed one thing. He didn't commit... *ever.* That much was obvious to every woman in Pembrooke.

Granted, it still hadn't done anything to lessen my crush on him, but it was the truth. Oh, he dated, *a lot,* but out of all the women he'd been seen around town with, none of them lasted more than three dates. And I was pretty certain he never went to weddings with any of them.

"Uh..." he cleared his throat uncomfortable as I watched on with morbid curiosity. "I'm not sure that's possible. I have my daughter every other weekend, so..." he trailed off. Then, poor Carla, said the absolute wrong thing.

"Can't you just switch weekends or something? Or maybe cancel just this one time? I mean, my family's going to be there."

With that, I noticed that the tick had returned to Derrick's jaw. "Yeah, because it's as easy as switching shoes," I muttered sarcastically behind my wineglass.

"What was that?" Carla asked, narrowing her eyes at me.

Maybe it was the wine giving me a false sense of courage, or maybe it was just the fact that I was *so* over feeling sorry for myself, or worrying about other peoples' opinions, but whatever the case, I couldn't tone down my disdain as I answered, "I'm sorry, you must not have heard me, what I said was you make it sound as easy as switching out shoes. That's his daughter you're talking about, not some inanimate object. And maybe it's just me, but it seems a little presumptuous of you to suggest he switch weekends, or cancel all together, when you haven't even gotten through your *first* date yet." I let out a loud bark of laughter. "I mean, that really takes some brass ones. I've got to hand it to you," I lifted my glass in her direction. "That's some hardcore confidence you've got there, thinking you stand above a man's own flesh and blood. Can't be easy thinking that highly of yourself."

"No one asked you," she spat back.

"Oh, don't get your hair extension in a twist," I giggled at my own joke. Okay, so maybe I was a little more than buzzed after all. "I was just offering my opinion on the subject."

As I sucked down the last of the wine in my glass, she crossed her arms under her overinflated boobs, pushing them so high they were in danger of spilling out of her dress. "Well, no one here cares about your opinion."

"I do," Derrick cut in his heated gaze on her, and not the good kind of heat.

"Uh... am I missing something here?" Austin asked and I shushed him, waiving my hand in his face. Yep, I was *definitely* a little more than buzzed.

"And for the record, I'd never re-schedule a weekend with my daughter unless it was for an unexpected emergency, and no way in hell would I ever cancel on her."

"But—"

Derrick wasn't finished. "And I'll just say it now, so there aren't any misunderstandings later. And be prepared, because this is going to make me sound like an asshole, but I've found that label is something I can live with if it means

my point comes across clearly. I have no desire, whatsoever, to meet your family. Ever."

Oh, damn. That was so harsh even I cringed. I might
have felt sorry for her, if she hadn't been such a shrew, but
you reap what you sow and all that jazz.

I was contemplating just walking out on everyone at
the table and catching an Uber home. The night couldn't
possible go any further downhill than it already had.

Or at least I thought.

"Hello, Derrick," a feminine voice said from behind me.
I looked back to see a woman who looked like she'd just
walked off a runway standing behind me. Her red dress fit
her lithe frame to perfection without showing off too
much skin. Her blonde hair was so shiny it looked like
gold, *actual* gold! She had perfect cheekbones, perfect
posture, just… perfect freaking everything. But then I
noticed her blue eyes, and whatever was lying behind them
was something ugly. And they were currently pointed
directly at Derrick. If I hadn't thought the evening could
grow any tenser, I'd been wrong. With her sudden appearance the air felt downright arctic.

Then Derrick said her name, and I understood the
sudden frostbite.

"Layla."

*Ladies and gentlemen, we've just entered the seventh circle of
hell.*

11

DERRICK

*M*Y NIGHT COULDN'T have possibly gotten any fucking worse. First, there was the douchebag Chloe was on a date with. The asshole was hopped up on so many steroids his dick was probably Oompa-Loompa sized, I couldn't even begin to wrap my brain around what the hell she'd been thinking.

Then Carla had to go and drop the wedding bomb. As if her being a grade-A bitch to Chloe wasn't already enough to solidify her place on my *never again* list. I'd always been honest, most would say to a fault, but, despite what most people — women in particular — thought of me, I didn't actually *enjoy* being a first-class dick. But sometimes it was necessary. Case in point, Carla.

And the icing on the shit-filled sundae that was my night? My raging bitch of an ex-wife, standing less than two feet away from me.

"What the hell are you doing here?" I bit out between clenched teeth.

She let out a condescending *tsk*. "Now, is that any way to speak to the mother of your daughter? Are you going to introduce me to your friends?"

My mouth opened, the bitter words I was dying to hurl at her ready to bounce right off my tongue when I suddenly felt something on my hand. Looking down, I saw Chloe's small, delicate hand clutching mine in a tight grip. The words dried up in my mouth before they even made their way out.

"Hi," she said kindly, shocking the hell out of me by smiling politely up at Layla, aka, the fucking devil. "I'm Chloe, it's nice to meet you."

Her hand not currently wrapped around mine reached out to Layla in a friendly attempt at a handshake. Layla glared at it as if it were diseased before her hateful stare landed on our touching hands. "Uh... well, I just have to tell you, you have an amazing daughter," Chloe continued. I had to give her credit; she really was making the old college try. I wanted to tell her it was pointless, that Satan was incapable of accepting or giving kindness to anyone. "I've had the pleasure of meeting Eliza several times and she's absolutely wonderful."

Layla's lips curled derisively. "Chloe." She sneered. "I know who you are."

"This will be my one and only warning," I spoke in a low, threatening voice. "You will never speak to her like that again." Both her and Chloe looked at me with equal expressions of *"Holy shit, what'd he just say?"*

"Well isn't that just lovely," Layla sneered. "It's bad enough you're subjecting our daughter to your... *women*, but actually have the nerve to defend her to me? All I've heard about since you took her to that stupid carnival is how wonderful *Chloe* is!"

The woman in question, the one Layla was talking about like she wasn't even there, opened her mouth to speak, but I cut her off, standing from my chair. "Maybe that's because she finally realized what it was like to have a positive female role model in her life for *once* in nine goddamned years." I stepped closer to her. "And you're making me repeat myself, Layla. What the hell did I just say about how you talk about Chloe?"

My ex-wife was never one to back down from a challenge so I wasn't surprised when her eyes narrowed into furious slits as she seethed in a hushed voice. "I won't allow you to try and play family with one of your *whores* around Eliza. You think you can try and replace me? I'm her mother."

"Excuse me!" Chloe snapped from her chair. "We're not even together. I'm with this guy!" She threw her thumb over her shoulder to Austin who looked about two seconds away from fleeing the scene. "And he's on a date with her!" One quick glance at Carla showed she wasn't too far behind the roided out dick-head.

"And maybe," I continued, ignoring Chloe's little outburst, "if you acted like a fucking mother once in your miserable life, Eliza wouldn't be looking to someone else to fill that role."

"Uh... guys?" Carla spoke when neither of us did anything other than glare for several seconds. "People are starting to stare."

"If you think I'm going to let you parade your slut around Eliza, you've lost your damned mind," Layla whispered harshly.

"You know," Chloe piped up after downing more of her wine. "I'm getting *really* sick of being called a whore and a slut. Like, for real."

"You've got no right telling me how to raise my daughter when she's with me," I ground out. "It's Saturday night, Layla. It's your goddamned weekend! Care to explain where my daughter is right now?"

She crossed her arms over her chest, her haughty expression pushing at every one of my buttons. "She's with my sister. I'm enjoying a night out with friends. Despite what you think, I *am* allowed to have a life, you know."

I could feel the blood coursing through my veins beginning to boil. "Yeah, you can have a life. Every. Other. Fucking. Weekend. When Eliza's in Pembrooke with me. When it's your weekend, you spend time with her."

"You know," she smirked, "It's amazing that you think I have to listen to anything you have to say. I stopped having to listen to a word you said when I left your sorry ass."

"Oh, sweetheart," I chuckled sarcastically, "You know damned good and well I was the one that left your ass 'cause I was sick and tired of fucking a dead, frigid fish every night."

She sucked in an outraged gasp. "You sorry son of a bitch!"

Austin stood, reaching into his back pocket and throwing some bills on the table. "You know what, I think I'm gonna get out of here. I just remembered, I have a... thing..."

"Yeah, yeah," Chloe waved him off. "Run along. And while you're at it, do me a *huge* favor and lose my phone number. M'kay? Thanks, bye." Like the punk-ass he was, I saw Austin move away from the table out of the corner of my eye.

"Excuse me," the server interrupted, stopping next to my stand-off with Layla. "Is there a problem here?"

Chloe answered before anyone else. "Nope, no problem. We're actually ready for our check if you wouldn't mind."

"Certainly."

"Oh!" she reached for the money on the table and handed the bills to the waiter. "And this is for the other gentleman's check. You know, the one that kind of looked like a gorilla?"

"Yes, ma'am," the server grinned.

"If there's any change left, feel free to keep it.

"Thank you," he tilted his chin up at Chloe before turning to Layla with a knowing expression. "Ma'am, may I help you back to your table?"

She might have been a bitch, but Layla wasn't stupid,

she knew a dismissal when she saw one. I was leaving our server a fat tip; that was for damned sure. Not saying another word, Layla shot one last hideous look in my direction before stomping off to whatever gutter she'd dragged herself from.

As I turned back to the table, I noticed Chloe stand on wobbly legs. "Well," she sighed heavily, obviously feeling the effects of her wine. "You two enjoy the rest of your night. Pretty sure I'm going to go home, climb in bed and pray that, when I wake up, this whole evening will have been nothing but a really bad nightmare."

"Whoa," I clasped her arm as she tried to pass. "No way in hell you're driving, sunshine."

"*Pfft.* I'm perfectly fine."

"Yeah?" I found myself grinning for the first time since my succubus of an ex-wife walked to our table. "Tell that to the bottle of wine you downed. I'm taking you home."

The server reappeared with our check and I deftly slid my wallet from my back pocket, placing more bills than necessary in the small black folio, but the man deserved it. It was the least I could do.

"But—my car..."

"Carla can drive it back," I answered deftly.

"Uh, what?" I looked over to an incredulous Carla, no longer caring if she thought I was the world's biggest asshole. There was no way I'd ever subject myself to a second date with that woman. Hell, I was already regretting agreeing to the first. "I had wine, too, you know."

"You had a glass," I told her. "And you didn't even finish it."

"But—but..." she sputtered, trying to come up with a solid argument, despite the fact it was pointless. My mind was made up. "Can't she just take a cab or something? This is supposed to be *our* date!"

"Yeah, it was. And now it's over. Now, I can't imagine you're the type of person who'd actually put the wellbeing of someone else in jeopardy by, say, putting them in a cab with a stranger when they're highly intoxicated." Yep, I wasn't above guilt-tripping, not one damn bit.

"I'm not *that* drunk," Chloe argued, folding her arms over her chest and wrinkling her brow in an adorable pout.

I ignored her. "And I certainly wouldn't want to believe you'd rather Chloe get behind the wheel of a car after drinking when you could easily do her the kindness of driving her car home so I can put her in my truck and we *all* make it back to Pembrooke safely." I squinted my eyes and tilted my head as I went in for the kill. "Or am I completely wrong about you?"

"Fine," she said through clenched teeth, throwing her napkin onto the table. "You know, this probably has to be the worst date I've ever been on."

"Hasn't been a cakewalk for me either, sweetheart," I deadpanned. Chloe let out a little hiccuping giggle and I knew she was drunk enough that she was going to be hurting come morning.

I kept my arm firmly around Chloe's waist as I guided her through the busy restaurant. Holding her body next to mine was the complete juxtaposition to how it felt when Carla clung to me on the way here. Carla was all sharp, narrow points, while Chloe was warm, lush curves that molded to me as we walked. I didn't feel any bone when I placed my hand on her, just the smoothness of her waist dipping in before those intoxicating hips flared out. She had a woman's body, through and through, and I wanted to kick myself for even noticing how good she felt against me.

"Where's your car, sunshine?" I whispered in her ear. Was I closer than I needed to be in order to speak to her? Hell yeah. But I seemed to have lost all control over my body when it came to her, and the way she shivered against me as I spoke had my arm hugging her even closer to my side. My pants had grown uncomfortably tight as my erection strained against the fabric. For Christ's sake, I felt like a goddamned teenager unable to control his boner around the pretty girl. It was pathetic.

"Uh," she cleared her throat as she pulled against my arm. I could either refuse to let her put any space between us — like my body wanted to do — and risk some seriously fucked up mixed signals, or I could loosen my hold, allowing her the space she seemed to need from me. I went with the latter, even though every inch of me rebelled at the loss of her warmth. "I'm there," she answered, pointing to a small, two-door Honda.

"Keys?" I asked quietly, closely, unable to help but close the distance whenever the chance arose.

With a small, shuffled step to the side, she dug in her purse until she unearthed her keys and handed them to a butt-hurt Carla. Turning her face toward mine as Carla climbed in and started the car up, those bright green eyes shone up at me, just a hint of glassiness thanks to the wine. "I should — I should probably ride with her."

"You're riding with me," I insisted, my tone sounding a little too direct, even to my own ears. *Jesus*, what the hell was wrong with me? I couldn't seem to think straight and all the blood in my body was rushing to one particular area. Since walking into The Peak and seeing Chloe dressed to the nines, something inside me, some protective instinct had scratched and clawed its way to the surface, only growing stronger and stronger as both Carla and Layla spit their hatefulness at her. I couldn't stand to watch it.

"But—"

"I don't want you alone with Carla."

She stared, mouth open, eyes wide for a few seconds. "You think I can't defend myself against *her*? Please," she snorted. "I could take her."

"I have no doubt about that, killer," I chuckled. "But fact of the matter is, she's been a bitch to you all night long."

"Only because I crashed your date!"

"If I remember correctly, I was the one who insisted. You didn't crash anything."

Her face grew contemplative as she stared up at me. "Yeah. Yeah, you did kind of push in. What was up with that? Were you just itching to have the world's most uncomfortable date or something?" She snorted again, and damn if I didn't want to lean down and kiss her cute mouth.

I needed to get my shit together, and fast, or I was going to do something to screw up our friendship — and why the hell did just thinking that word suddenly leave me feeling bitter?

"What can I say? I'm a masochist like that." I guided her to my truck and had to help her into the cab, I wasn't sure how much more my poor, high strung body could take. I needed a cold shower and a couple minutes alone with my palm before my head exploded.

I walked around the hood of my truck and climbed in, twisted the key in the ignition and put it into drive, only to be hit with the realization I had no clue where Chloe lived. Suddenly, my dick wasn't the problem anymore. No man alive could maintain an erection once he recognized what a shitty human being he was. I'd known Chloe for a year and a half, I claimed to be her friend, and all this time, I didn't know anything about her. Hell, I didn't have the first clue where she lived.

I coughed awkwardly, drawing her attention. "Are you, um… are you sober enough to give me directions to your place?"

The glimmer that was just in her green eyes moments ago got swallowed up by something else. Her usually open expression closed down as she spoke in a small, pained voice, "You don't even know where I live?"

"No," I admitted, my tone apologetic. "I mean… well, I just never really thought about it."

"My apartment's right above the bakery," she said in a flat, emotionless voice as she turned to look out the window. I couldn't have possibly felt any lower if I'd tried.

"Well that's convenient, huh?" I asked way too enthusiastically.

She didn't look at me. "Yep."

"I didn't even know there was an apartment over the bakery."

"Mmhmm," was all I got in return.

The whole drive back to Pembrooke was made in uncomfortable silence. I'd finally felt like I'd taken some big steps forward when it came to Chloe, and after tonight, I couldn't help but think that I'd just put myself back at square one.

12

CHLOE

*T*HE POUNDING ON the front door pulled me from a fitful sleep. Rolling over, I glanced at the alarm clock before burying my face in my pillow and letting out a muffled cry. It was eight in the morning. On a Sunday. One of my only days off this week. I wanted to sleep until well past noon. I *needed* it.

"Go away," I groaned into my pillow, praying whoever was at my door would eventually just give up and leave me in peace.

"Chloe! Open up!"

"Damn it," I hissed, dragging myself from the comfort of my bed. "I swear to God," I cursed as I pulled the door open. "If you weren't pregnant, I'd kick your ass."

Unconcerned by my threat of violence, Harlow pushed past me and waddled into my living room, collapsing on my couch with an exaggerated huff. "Well, if you'd answer your phone, I wouldn't have to drive my ever-widening ass over here and beat your door down."

I shot her a withering look as I rounded the couch and headed for the kitchen, in search of a cup of coffee. I was one of those people who desperately needed caffeine in order to function. "It's eight o'clock! Of course I didn't answer my phone. I was sleeping. Like a normal person."

"Yeah well, Noah's spawn won't allow me to sleep anymore, so I figured I'd come over here and share the love."

I glared over the eat-in breakfast bar that separated my kitchen from the rest of the apartment. That was one of my favorite things about my place. Everything was open and airy. The building had been around since the early nineteen hundreds, and despite countless renovations, it still held a lot of the original charm along with the modern amenities a person this day in age couldn't live without. My apartment spanned across three of the shops below, leaving me with more than enough square footage. The wood floors were original and three of the four walls were exposed brick, giving the space a rustic feel I absolutely adored. The entire place was an open concept with the exception of the bathroom, my favorite room in the place. Everything in there had been updated, from the black and white subway tile to the amazing claw foot tub. My bathroom was every woman's dream.

"Don't you have a husband you can torture instead of me? I didn't realize being your best friend meant I had to share in your misery."

"Well, now you know," she waved her hand dismissively. "Besides, I've tortured poor Noah enough. If this baby doesn't come soon, he's liable to be elected for sainthood just for putting up with me, then I'll *never* hear the end of it. The more I stay out of the house, the less ammunition he'll have to hold over my head in the future."

I smiled despite the fact I was still exhausted. "So what you're saying is, you're playing the long game."

"Exactly." Harlow grinned wickedly as I took a seat next to her on the couch. "A wife should *never* allow her husband the upper hand. That's a part of the vows no one knows about."

"Well thanks for the heads up." I sucked down a gulp of my coffee, hoping it would help me to feel somewhat human again.

"*Sooooo*," she dragged out clapping excitedly. "Tell me about your date! I want to know *everything*."

I rolled my eyes to the ceiling and dropped my head to the back of the couch. "It was a complete disaster," I started. She held on to my every word as I told her about the worst date in the history of bad dates, everything from Austin's assumed steroid use, to Derrick showing up with Carla and turning the evening into the double date from hell, to Layla's unexpected and unwanted appearance. By the time I was done, her mouth was hanging open in disbelief.

"Wow," was all she could say for several seconds.

"Yep. So obviously the excess wine was necessary."

"So, let me get this straight. He actually made Carla drive your car home while he drove you?"

"One of the fewer highlights of the evening, but yes."

"And she didn't key it or slash your tires?"

My back shot straight as I looked at Harlow with wide eyes. "I don't know. I haven't been out to check it. Do you think she would?"

Harlow snorted. "Carla Fitzgerald, are you kidding? Hell yeah, I think she'd do something like that."

My mug hit the coffee table with a loud *thunk* as I bolted from the couch, out the door, and down the steps to the small parking lot at the back of the building. A cursory inspection showed that there wasn't any external damage, at least none that I could see.

"Anything?" Harlow asked from the landing as I made my way back up the stairs.

"Not that I noticed, but I won't know if she cut my brake lines or anything until I actually get in and drive it."

"Nah," she said, following me back into the apartment. "Cutting brake lines would take smarts Carla isn't capable of. I think you're safe for the time being. Just don't get caught alone in a dark alley with her or anything. You're spunky, but that woman's a straight up hair-puller."

"Duly noted," I sighed as I sat back down, closing my eyes against the headache pushing at the backs of my eyes. I really hated hangovers. "I just want to forget last night ever happened. It had to have been one of the most bizarre things I've ever been forced to live through."

"Well, I hate to say it, seeing as he made you cry and all

so I have no choice but to want to gouge Derrick's eyes out, but it's a good thing he was there last night. At least you weren't stuck paying for your own meal. He seems to be taking this whole friends thing to heart, huh?"

"Seems like it," I answered, thinking back to how he hadn't even remembered where I lived the night before. It shouldn't have hurt my feelings as much as it did, I know that. But it was just more proof of the fact that, after spending a year-and-a-half pining over the guy, I really *had* been pretty invisible to him until recently. No woman likes hearing something like that. But I was determined to push that out of my head. I'd made a decision last night and I was going to stick to it. Derrick and I were friends and I was happy with that. So it wasn't a love match, so what. At least I had another person in my life who'd have my back. He'd proven as much the night before. I was moving past that phase of my life. This was a whole new Chloe. A take-no-prisoners woman who was open to new experiences, and refused to settle for less.

The world was my oyster, and I was going to shuck the hell out of it.

ONE OF THE things that Pembrooke shared with all small towns across the country was its love for football. Everyone in town worshipped at the altar of the Pembrooke Bulldogs starting with the scrimmage games until the end of the season. There was an electricity in the air that made the excitement so infectious that even people such as myself, who didn't care much for sports couldn't help but get sucked into the fanfare.

That was why, despite the fact I hadn't been feeling all that well most of the day, I found myself rounding the stadium bleachers that seemed to hold every person in town, including Pastor Mike, the minister of our Baptist church, while I was in search of Harlow. It might have just been a scrimmage game, but I never missed when they played at Bulldog Stadium, sick or not, and with Ethan playing for the second year in a row, I wasn't about to let the start of a pesky little head-cold stop me.

My eyes were scanning the sea of people when I somehow managed to hear a loud, familiar voice yelling over the din of noise coming from the bleachers.

"MISS CHLOE! OVER HERE!"

My head shot sideways toward the fence line that separated the field from the stands and a huge smile broke out across my face at the sight of Eliza jumping up and down, waving her hands in the air frantically. Her excitement to see me was enough to make me forget I wasn't feeling all that great — at least temporarily.

I made my way to the small group at the fence, where Eliza was standing next to Harlow as she spoke to Noah over the waist high chain link. "Hey there," were the only words I'd been able to get out before Eliza's tiny frame barreled into me, knocking the breath from my chest as she wrapped her arms around my waist. I returned her hug with a small laugh as I sucked in tiny breaths in an attempt to re-inflate my lungs.

"I feel like I haven't seen you in *forever*," she said dramatically, making it sound like it had been years as opposed to a little over a week. But I was flattered, nonetheless. I adored the ground Eliza walked on, so knowing she felt the same warmed me from the inside out.

"Well I'm glad you're here," I answered, running my fingers through her dark, silky hair. "I've missed you. Did you come with Ms. Harlow?"

She shook her head animatedly. "Nope. Daddy always brings me to the Bulldog games on his weekend. He went to get peanuts and popcorn. It's our tradition."

"That sounds like a fun tradition," I said, trying hard not to give in to the ingrained desire to look for Derrick whenever I knew he was close by. I was still a work in progress.

"Hey, Chlo," Noah spoke.

I cocked my eyebrow playfully. "Noah. Aren't you supposed to be coaching?"

"And miss a chance to neck with my smokin' hot wife?" he asked, shooting me a cheeky wink.

"What's necking?" Eliza asked, her gaze darting between Noah and Chloe.

"Ask your father," Noah answered quickly as Harlow and I shot him varying looks of *shut the hell up*.

"Ask her father what?" The deep timbre of Derrick's voice sent a chill up my back — or maybe it was the fact that I was starting to feel a little feverish, either way, I felt the effects of his sudden presence.

"What necking is," Eliza answered innocently as she snatched the bucket of popcorn from her father's hands. It was almost impossible to choke back the laughter at the murderous glare he gave Noah.

"Hey, Murphy!" A man shouted from the field, fortunately for Noah, drawing our attention. As he jogged our way, it was almost impossible to miss how attractive he was, even from a distance.

"Holy damn, who's that?" Harlow mumbled under her breath, giving voice to exactly what I'd just been thinking. He was good looking, no doubt about it. I didn't think he ranked quite at Derrick's level of hotness, but damn if he wasn't close.

"Guys," Noah spoke, pulling us from our obvious perusal, "This is our new assistant coach, Fletcher McMillian. Fletch, this is my wife Harlow, Derrick Anderson and his little girl Eliza, and Chloe Delaney."

Fletcher looked at me with a grin that probably made women across the globe swoon. "Nice to meet you, Chloe."

"You too, Fletcher," I smiled back.

"All my friends call me Fletch." His smile positively devastating as he reached over the fence to shake my hand.

"So does that mean we're friends?" Holy shit! Was I flirting? I was totally flirting! How the hell had that happened? It was his smile, it had to be. No woman in her right mind could be immune to a smile like that, whether she wanted to or not.

"Well I certainly hope we can be." Another blinding smile. Holy crap, the women in this town were so screwed.

Noah's voice cut into whatever crazy voodoo Fletch was working. "Chloe here's the one that runs that bakery I was telling you about. Best coffee and pastries in Wyoming."

"Is that right?" he asked. His rough palm was warm as it enclosed mine in a strong, firm handshake. "Well, I'll have to get over there as soon as possible. I haven't been in Pembrooke long enough to really look around, but Noah's been telling me I need to make Sinful Sweets one of my first stops."

"You won't be disappointed," Harlow chimed in, a devious glint in her eye as she talked me up. It wasn't until she asked, "Does your wife not bake?" that I realized she'd just jumped on a golden opportunity to matchmake.

"No wife," he replied, and I wasn't sure if it was my foggy head causing me to see things, but I could have sworn his gaze shot back to me as he continued with, "I'm single."

"*Really.*" The sideways look Harlow shot me couldn't have been more obvious. There was no reason for her to throw in, "What a coincidence! So is Chloe." Not that it stopped her, to my utter mortification.

"I'd say that's definitely a lucky coincidence," Fletcher returned, causing my blush to grow almost painful as my eyes went wide.

"Aren't you guys supposed to be doing something right now?" Derrick cut in, pulling my gaze from Fletcher at the harshness in his tone. "It's the first game of the season and

JESSICA PRINCE

all. Shouldn't you be giving the boys a motivational speech or something?"

"He's right," Fletcher answered. If he'd registered the bite in Derrick's words, he didn't let it show. "It was great meeting you, Chloe. Hope to see you around sometime soon."

"Oh, uh. Y-yeah. I mean, yes." I cleared my throat awkwardly. "I look forward to it."

Noah and Fletcher headed off and the rest of us turned to take our seats on the bench right behind us. I couldn't help but notice Derrick's frown as he sat down on the cold metal bench next to me.

"Miss Chloe, I think that guy likes you," Eliza giggled from my other side.

"I think she's right," Harlow added.

I couldn't be sure if my ears were deceiving me, or if it was just the noise of the crowd around us, but I could have *sworn* I heard Derrick growl.

13

DERRICK

THE SOUNDS OF the crowd cheering and yelling around me were muffled by the blood rushing through my ears. And believe me, no one was as shocked by the intensity of my reaction to Chloe flirting as I was. I knew I was attracted to her. I knew I *wanted* her, but as the desire to pummel the dickhead on the field continued to grow, my brain kept repeating *"Mine, mine, mine. Hands off, limp dick,"* over and over again.

But that wasn't really the case at all, was it?

Chloe *wasn't* mine. She couldn't be. Because I couldn't give her what she wanted. I'd tried the white picket fence thing already. It just wasn't in the cards for me. If I'd been completely rational at that moment, I'd have been happy for her. I was her friend after all, right? I should have *wanted* her to find someone she could be happy with, someone who'd put a ring on her finger and give her a family.

So why was I having so much trouble keeping my shit together?

It was a moot point anyway. She'd already told me she was over her crush, so why would I think she'd even be interested?

Every time that Fletcher asshole turned around and shot Chloe a smile or a wink, I found myself clenching my hands into painfully tight fists. *All my friends call me Fletch.* What a douche. And what kind of name was *Fletch* anyway. I'll tell you, it's an asshole's name. And that asshole just turned around and winked a-fucking-gain!

"Daddy?" I felt a poke on my arm but was still in too much of a murderous daze to register. "Dad!" The slap on my shoulder finally seemed to break the spell.

"Huh?" I turned to look at Eliza who was leaning past Chloe, the bucket of popcorn extended my way.

"You okay, Dad? I've been trying to get your attention for, like, two minutes."

I pasted a fake smile on my face as I looked down at her. "I'm good, baby girl. Just focused on the game, I guess."

She shrugged casually, never thinking to question me. "You want some popcorn? I'm full."

I took the bucket from her, my smile turning genuine. "Thanks, honey." As I pulled back, my arm brushed against the front of Chloe's shirt, just a feather light touch of her breasts against my forearm, but it was enough to make my skin tingle and for her to suck in a sharp breath, sitting up straight at the contact. My eyes shot to hers to see her studying the play happening on the field with an intensity even the most avid football fans wouldn't give a scrimmage game, and I couldn't help but smile, because I knew, I *knew* she'd been affected by just the barest hint of my touch against her breasts.

"You okay?" I asked, trying to keep the lust from my voice. Christ, I'd barely gotten a feel, but I could still tell her tits were fantastic.

"Uh huh," she nodded, not taking her eyes off the field.

Unable to resist, I leaned in a little closer, holding the bucket of popcorn in front of her. "Want to share?" I asked quietly, using the excuse of the loud crowd as reason to speak close to her ear.

"No thanks," she turned to me and grinned, and I noted that it didn't quite meet her eyes. It wasn't until her whole body shivered and she hugged her arms tightly around her, that I noticed her normally peaches-and-cream complexion looked much paler than usual.

"Hey, you all right?" I asked, studying her face.

When she shook her head, sending those strawberry blonde curls ruffling in the breeze, I could smell the faintest hint of vanilla in the air. God, she always smelled like what she'd baked. It was enough to drive a man crazy. She shivered again, pulling my head out of the gutter. The sun had set, making the temperature outside comfortable, but seeing as it was still summer, it was impossible she could actually be cold. "I'm good. I just think I'm getting a little head cold or something. Nothing some over the counter meds won't knock out."

Reaching up, I placed my palm across her forehead, it

was a parental instinct I'd acquired after Eliza was born. "Jesus, sunshine, you're burning up."

"I'm fine, really," she replied, batting my hand away. "I'll take some meds when I get home. I'll be better by morning, I promise."

"Hell no," I objected, a strong protective feeling suddenly coursing through my blood. "You shouldn't even be here right now. Come on." Standing, I grabbed her by the arm and began to pull.

"What the hell are you doing?" She stared at me in shock, digging her little heels in indignantly. "I said I'm fine, Derrick. I'm not leaving until the game's over."

"What's going on?" Harlow asked, our argument having drawn her attention.

"Can you watch Eliza? I'm taking Chloe home. She's running a fever."

"Oh for God's sake," she rolled her eyes and laughed obnoxiously. "I'm not running a fever. I'd think I'd know if I was really sick." Another shiver. *Damn stubborn woman.*

Harlow reached over and felt her forehead. "Uh, sorry to break it to you, sweetie, but you totally are. You shouldn't have come if you weren't feeling good, babe."

"Okay, fine!" she relented, *finally*. "But there's no need for you to leave," she told me. "I drove myself here and am capable of getting myself home."

"You shouldn't drive when you're sick, Miss Chloe. It's not safe. Something could happen to you." Eliza replied firmly, her face set sternly. I was suddenly contemplating letting her paint her room pink like she'd been begging to do for over a year.

"Honey, nothing's going to happen to me," Chloe smiled at her sweetly. "It's just a head cold.

"What if you pass out?" Eliza railed.

"I'm not going to pass out. I promise."

"What if you need to puke but can't pull over in time?"

"I'm not going to puke." I could have sworn Chloe was trying to stifle a laugh.

"But what if you *have* to all of a sudden? One of my friends at school felt *totally fine*, then just started puking out of nowhere! What if you do that?"

I wasn't positive, but I thought all the talk of throwing up was making Chloe look a little green.

She threw her hands up in the air. "Okay, I give up. I'll let your dad take me home, will that make you feel better?"

"Yep," Eliza answered with a pleased smile, tossing a handful of popcorn in her mouth. Yeah, safe to say one of the rooms in my house was going to look like Pepto Bismol.

"You behave for Ms. Harlow," I warned my daughter. "No going crazy, deal?"

"Deal." Standing from the bench, she wrapped her arms around Chloe's waist. "Hope you feel better, Miss Chloe."

"Thank you, baby," she said in a quiet voice. The tone of her voice and the way she ran her fingers through my daughter's hair made something in my chest ache. It was a feeling I'd never experienced before, and I didn't have a fucking clue how to deal with it.

"Feel better, hon," Harlow said. "I'd hug you, but... you know, germs and stuff."

"Love you too," Chloe deadpanned as I placed my hand on the small of her back and began leading her away.

"This is ridiculous," she grumbled as we made our way through the parking lot, still being stubborn even though her body had begun trembling. I thought I'd actually heard her teeth chatter. "I'm more that c-capable of d-driving my own c-car."

"Uh huh," was all I muttered in return. Watching her shake with fever next to me set something off inside me. I couldn't stand the sight of her not feeling well, and despite all her arguing, how miserable she was feeling was written all over her pale face. That protective instinct I'd been feeling earlier boiled over at the sight of it and, without giving it any thought, I stopped moving long enough to hook my elbow behind her knees and haul her up into my arms.

"What are you doing!?" she yelped, her arms instinctively wrapping around my neck. "Put me down, I can walk!"

"Just humor me, okay?" I grunted, willing my body to behave at the same time my pants began to tighten uncomfortably. Yes, she was sick and I wanted to take care of her, but I couldn't deny how amazing her lush little body felt in my arms just then. "You're shaking like a leaf. Just let me help you."

With an indignant huff, she stopped struggling and held on as I made my way to my truck. I placed her on her feet in order to retrieve my keys from my pocket and unlock the door, but something in me wasn't ready to let her go just yet. So instead, I kept my arm locked firmly around her waist as I pressed the key fob and beeped the locks. I held on until the very last possible second when she climbed in and I was forced to shut the door. I knew I needed to get over whatever was happening right then, I just wasn't sure how to do that. I was seeing her differently all of a sudden. I *felt* differently, despite the fact I was well aware nothing could *ever happen* between us.

It's because she's sick, I kept telling myself.

"Thank you," she whispered once I'd backed out of my spot and exited the parking lot.

"For what?" I asked, keeping my eyes on the road instead of looking at her like I wanted to do.

"Bringing me home. I could have asked Harlow to take me. I'm sorry you had to bail on Eliza."

"Eliza adores the ground you walk on." I caught myself smiling genuinely when I pictured my little girl's face every time Chloe came into the room. "She probably would have thrown a raging tantrum if I let someone else take care of you."

Chloe laughed and, despite being sick, the sound was still reminiscent of tinkling bells, just as it always was. I glanced over to see her head resting against the passenger window, her eyes closed. "She's special, Derrick. You're so lucky to have her."

How Chloe felt about my daughter caused that squeeze in my chest to return ten-fold. For nine long years I'd hoped and prayed Layla would pull her head out of her ass and view the perfection that was our Eliza the way Chloe did. But as more time passed, I became increasingly worried that was never going to happen.

And I feared what that would do to Eliza.

How much more would she flourish with someone like Chloe in her life? I shook the thought out of my head as soon as it popped up.

"Thank you," I replied, my voice sounding raspier than normal. "I know just how lucky I am to have her. And you're welcome for the ride. I don't like seeing you sick."

Her voice was softer, more tired as she replied with four words... four words that left my stomach feeling sour... four words I thought I'd always be happy with, but for some unknown reason, had me white-knuckling the steering wheel.

"You're a good friend."

Why the hell did the word *friend* have me cringing like I'd just heard nails on a chalk board? And better yet, what the hell was going on in my head?

14

DERRICK

*A*s Eliza and I walked into Sinful Sweets the next morning, I went on instant red alert. Chloe wasn't behind the counter. She hadn't responded to any of my texts this morning asking how she was feeling, which was why I'd insisted on showing at the bakery for breakfast in the first place. Not that Eliza argued.

"Hey Erin," I called, recognizing Chloe's manager at the espresso machine.

"Deputy Anderson." She gave me a shy, flirtatious smile that I'd usually feed off of, but she was Chloe's employee and flirting back with her — even though it would have been completely harmless — just felt… wrong. Besides, my mind was fully focused on one thing, and one thing only.

"Is Chloe in the back?"

"Oh!" That seemed to have snapped Erin out of whatever she'd been thinking about that had her cheeks turning pink as she stared at me. "No, actually, she's out sick today,"

The young woman's forehead wrinkled as she frowned. "I think that might have been the first time she's *ever* missed work. She must be feeling pretty terrible."

My gut twisted at the realization that Chloe must have been feeling worse than she was the night before. "Do you have a key to her place?" I asked the young manager. "I want to go check on her, see if she needs anything."

"Oh, um… yeah, but it's supposed to be just for emergencies. But I guess this constitutes as one, huh?"

"I'd say so. If she asks, I'll just throw Harlow under the bus and say she let me in."

Erin laughed and pulled a key from her apron pocket. "Okay. There's a stairwell in the hall if you go through the kitchen. You can go that way instead of taking the outside stairs if you want."

"Thanks, I appreciate it." I turned back to Eliza, who was comfortably sitting on one of the barstools. "You okay here for a few, baby girl? I'm just gonna run up and check on Miss Chloe for a minute."

She looked at me with a calculating little girl grin. "If I can have a cupcake for breakfast, I'm totally cool."

I narrowed my eyes. "You get *one* cupcake. If I find out you snuck two, you can kiss that pink bedroom goodbye." I turned back to Erin and stressed, "She gets *one* cupcake."

Erin turned to Eliza and I heard in a conspiratorial tone as I headed around the counter, "We'll just have to make sure to give you one *big* cupcake, huh?"

Eliza giggled and I caught myself smiling even as I rolled my eyes and pushed through the door into the kitchen, ignoring the curious stares as I made my way up to Chloe.

As I slipped the key into the lock, my chest squeezed. It wasn't that same, enjoyable feeling from the night before. It was something uncomfortable and unsettling. "Chloe?" I called as I pushed the front door opened and stepped across the threshold. "You here, sunshine?" No answer. I made my way farther into her place, my gut twisting at her lack of response. The apartment was open so I was able to see the sheet of her unmade bed, a mangled mess, half on, half off the mattress.

"Shit," I muttered, that twisting in my gut growing exponentially, panic setting in. "Chloe. Where the hell are you?"

A moan sounded through the apartment, behind the only door in the entire apartment. Rushing in that direction, I shoved the door open and froze in place at the unsuspecting sight of Chloe curled up in a ball on the bathroom floor near the toilet.

"I threw up," she slurred in a small voice.

"Oh, baby," I said quietly as I fell down to my knees beside her. The rush of relief coursing through my blood at the realization she was okay warred with a concern I'd never felt for anyone but Eliza before. "I can see that." Reaching up, I flushed the toilet and guided Chloe to sitting. Her skin was still uncomfortably hot to the touch as I brushed her matted hair from her damp forehead. "We need to get you up, sunshine. I need to get you to the hospital."

"No." She batted at my hands weakly. "No hospital. I'll be fine."

Despite the ticking in my jaw at her stubborn behavior, I somehow managed to speak in a calm voice. "Chloe, you have vomit in your hair and you're still running a fever. This isn't a goddamned head cold."

"No hospital," she continued to argue. "They smell funny."

Somehow, by the grace of God, I managed to refrain from commenting that they couldn't smell any worse than she did right at that moment. As I helped her off the floor I came up with another idea, because despite the fact I couldn't seem to get my head straight where this woman was concerned, I knew there was no way in hell I'd be able to leave her apartment knowing the condition she was in. "Fine, no hospital. But your only other option is to come home with me. Either way, you're leaving here, whether I have to throw you over my shoulder or not."

"Derrick," she sighed.

"Chloe," I growled in a warning tone. Then, miraculously, the fight washed out of her. "Fine. But I need a shower. I can smell myself."

"You need help or you think you can do it yourself?"

I wouldn't have thought it possible, seeing as she was running a fever and, from the looks of it, had just thrown up the entire contents of her stomach, but she still managed to shoot me a killing look as she answered, "I can do it. Go away."

I failed at masking my chuckle as she gave my chest a

pathetic shove. "Fine. I'm gonna run down and tell Eliza what's going on. I'll only be a second. You sure you're all right by yourself?"

"Yes. Just need to get clean." Then she slammed the bathroom door in my face.

Chloe

THE SHOWER HAD HELPED, but hardly. My head felt like it was about to fall off my shoulders, and my entire body felt like I was moving through cement. That, coupled with the jaw-clacking chills and pain radiating throughout my entire body made me less than happy as I pulled the bathroom door open and came to a halt at the sight of Derrick rummaging through my underwear drawer. To be fair, I'd always been a *horrible* patient when I was sick.

"What the hell are you doing, perv? Stop touching my underwear!"

"Relax, crazy," he responded, turning from my drawer to a bag he must have found in my closet, and tossing the clothes inside. "I'm packing you a bag so you have everything you need at my place..." he trailed off as his eyes came up and landed on me. "Fuck me," he groaned in a pained voice as his gaze raked up and down my towel-clad body. I tried to tell myself that the goosebumps were from the fever and not his penetrating stare, but God knew I was lying.

"Uh…" he stumbled before grabbing something off the bed and extending it my way. "You should get dressed," he waved the yoga pants and t-shirt at me. "You don't want to get any sicker."

I took the clothes from his hand and made my way back into the bathroom. Once I finished dressing and tying my damp hair in a knot at the top of my head, my energy was tapped out. Dropping down onto the closed toilet seat, I squeezed my eyes closed, trying to stop the spinning in my head and the rolling in my stomach. I couldn't remember the last time I'd ever felt so sick.

There was a faint knock on the bathroom door, followed by Derrick's low, enticing voice. "Sunshine?"

"Hmm?" I hummed, keeping my eyes closed as the door creaked open. It wasn't until I felt the rough pads of his fingers skimming from my temple to my jaw that I opened them and met his warm hazel eyes, filled with so much concern.

"Let's get you out of here so you can rest, sweetheart."

All I could do was nod, so I didn't have it in me to protest when he scooped me up into his arms and carried me from the bathroom. "My purse," I said… or at least I think I did. My mouth moved, but I wasn't sure if I was actually forming words or not.

"I got it," his chest rumbled against my cheek as he spoke. "I have everything you need. Just relax and let me take care of you."

As my eyelids fluttered shut and I snuggled into the heat of his chest, the last thought I had before my body fell into sleep was: It was nice to finally have someone to take the burden off my shoulders for once.

I HAD NO clue how long I was out. I didn't recall anything after Derrick lifted me off the toilet seat and carried me through my apartment. I opened my eyes to the sound of voices and had to blink some of the fog away. The bed I was in was *huge*, the mattress plush and felt like a cloud. Definitely not my own. Not that my mattress was anything to sneeze at, but it didn't hug my body, that was for damn sure.

"You sure there's nothing else you can do for her?" *Derrick's voice.* Then I remembered Derrick's ultimatum, either go home with him so he could take care of me, or go to the hospital.

"She's gonna be just fine, son." I finally got my bearings enough to notice Derrick and Dr. White standing a few feet away from me. I'd known Dr. White my whole life. He was the town doctor and, in a town as small as Pembrooke, made house calls on a regular basis. His name was fitting, considering the shock of white hair on his head and the full-on Santa beard he sported. He had a gentle, friendly demeanor and everyone in town loved him, even the small kids who were afraid of needles but forced to go in for their annual vaccinations. You couldn't look at the man

139

who was a cross between St. Nick and Colonel Sanders and not love him.

"Give her the Tamiflu when she wakes up, Tylenol for the fever, and keep her hydrated. She'll be back to her normal self in no time."

I blinked my eyes as Derrick's chest rose and fell with a large sigh, almost as if he was relieved to hear what Dr. White was saying. Then, "Thank Christ for that. Woman's stubborn as hell when she's sick. I lost count of how many times I wanted to wring her neck."

Now I *know* I heard that right. "Uh, laying right here, you know," I grumbled. "I can hear you."

Dr. White laughed. "You act like he's lying. Known you all your life, Chloe. A ray of sunshine on most days, but when you're sick, you're a downright pain in the ass, girl. Horrible patient."

"Thanks," I deadpanned, or at least tried my best, seeing as I still felt like crap and had trouble concentrating on much else. I pushed myself up to sitting and rested my back against the headboard.

"Try not to give Deputy Anderson too hard of a time, Chloe," the doctor told me, earning himself a scowl. "I know you're in a hurry to get better, so rest and meds. Don't overdo it, or I'll stick you in the hospital just for fun."

He wasn't joking, either. Sure, Dr. White was sweet, but if a patient didn't take their wellbeing seriously, they got to see a whole new side of the old man. A side I wasn't too keen to see, so I gave him a muttered, "Yes, sir."

"Tamiflu twice a day for five days, with food. You can

quit the Tylenol as soon as your fever breaks and stays down. Water and sleep. I'll be checking on your progress with Deputy Anderson since I know you well enough not to trust you as far as I can throw you."

"I can feel the love from here," I frowned. "Stop, it's too much. You'll make me cry."

Dr. White laughed again and turned for the door, Derrick following behind. "I see what you're saying about being a horrible patient," he said in a not-so-quiet voice.

"Can still here you!"

"Didn't say it quietly, sunshine," he shot over his shoulder as he walked the doctor out. Once alone, I let my eyes scan my surroundings. I'd never been to Derrick's house before, and what I saw definitely wasn't what I would imagine for a single guy living alone, child or not. The walls were painted the softest dove gray to contrast the dark navy bedding on the king-sized bed. The bedframe, dresser, and nightstands were all made of a dark, rich cherry wood, almost the same color as the wood flooring. And he had a massive cream-colored area rug — *an area rug*, for crying out loud — that stretched from under the bed, all the way across the room, stopping just feet from the stone hearth of the fire place.

The room was impeccably decorated, and I thought to myself, if this was what the guest room looked like, I couldn't imagine just how amazing the master bedroom was. But none of those details — stone fireplace included — were the most stunning feature. That went to the view beyond the glass French doors on the far left wall, beyond the cozy little deck built off what looked to be the side of the house. Nothing but forest and mountains as far as you could see.

It was absolutely breathtaking.

Derrick's view was what people all over the country traveled to our tiny mountain town to see. You couldn't look at a view like that, all lush and green, and not be moved by it. It was tranquil, peaceful, nature at its most beautiful, and I instantly fell in love with it.

"I brought you some toast, sunshine" Derrick said, pulling me from the amazing sight beyond the French doors. "Doc said you had to take the meds with food, so—"

"Derrick... the view," I sighed dreamily.

"Yeah," he smiled, his eyes following mine out the doors. "No such thing as a bad morning when you wake up every day to that."

Wait... "This is *your* room?"

The mattress dipped under his weight as he sat on the bed, his back to the fireplace so he was facing me. "Yep," he answered, sitting the plate of toast on my lap and reaching up to press his palm to my forehead. He held it there for longer than necessary to gauge a person's temp before those rough fingertips skated down, down, down, past my temple all the way to my collar bone. It was the type of touch you expected to feel from someone who wasn't simply a friend. "Only two other rooms in this place. One's Eliza's, and the other's an office, slash gym, slash storage room. Didn't think you'd appreciate sleeping on the futon in there."

"But... but..." I sputtered. "Where are you sleeping?"

"On the couch."

"Derrick!" I cried. "You can't sleep on the couch. Don't know if it's lost on you, but you're not exactly a small guy. I'm tiny! Like, *really* tiny! I'll take the couch and you take your huge bed back."

Derrick's laughter shook the bed in a way I had no doubt I'd have thoroughly enjoyed had I not felt like I'd been run over by an eighteen wheeler. "To put your mind at ease, no, it's not lost on me that I'm not a small guy. Which is why I bought myself a massive sectional I knew I'd be comfortable sleeping on, seeing as I have a tendency to pass out on the couch watching TV more often than not."

Okay, so that was a valid argument. But still!

"But still," I continued to argue, "I don't feel right taking your bed."

"Did I or did I not tell you to relax and let me take care of you?" he asked in a tone that brooked no argument, while at the same time, something I couldn't quite read flashed in his hazel eyes. "Seeing you lying on your bathroom floor is something I never want to have to witness again." The way he said that caused chills to snake along my spine.

"So you're staying here, you're taking the bed, you're eating the damned toast so you can take your pills, and you're done arguing, got it?"

"Got it," I replied instantly. My momma didn't raise a door mat, but she taught me one very important lesson growing up. Pick your battles. And from the determination painted across Derrick's face as he all but growled his words, this wasn't a battle I needed to win. So I picked up the toast and began to chew slowly, hoping my stomach would cooperate. All the while trying not to analyze the way that Derrick was staring at me, almost like he didn't recognize me.

Shit, I needed that Tamiflu to kick in fast so I could get back to my regularly-scheduled programming. The longer I stayed in Derrick's house, surrounded by all things *him*, the harder it was going to be to go back to being his friend.

15

CHLOE

*C*HILLS THAT WRACKED my body woke me from a fitful sleep. My eyes opened to the dark room, only lit by the moonlight pouring in through the glass doors. The view I'd appreciated so much just hours ago was the furthest thing from my mind as the fever I thought I'd broken earlier came back with a vengeance.

With a groan, I pushed up and shuffled across the bed in an attempt to reach the bottle of Tylenol on the nightstand. My hand landed on the cold wood at the same time my head fell back down to the pillow. It felt like my own body was fighting against me, too weak to do something as simple as hold my own damned head up.

I smacked my palm against the top of the nightstand as I blindly searched for the pill bottle, letting out another pained groan as my fingertips hit the plastic, sending it skittering to the ground.

"Damn it," I cursed, trying to will my limbs to actually

cooperate. I really was a shit patient. I had already managed to convince myself I was knocking on death's door, throwing myself a pathetic pity party as I did a mental calculation of how I'd divvy up all my belongings between my loved ones. I'd just decided to hell with it when the bedroom door came swinging open.

"Sunshine?" Derrick's deep, sleep-gruff voice broke through the silence of the room. "You okay?" I let out another groan and felt the bed dip under his weight seconds before his hand rested on my forehead. "Shit, you're burning up."

He fumbled around near the nightstand for a moment before soft yellow light filled the space. I was hit right then by the sight of a chiseled, shirtless Derrick, wearing nothing but a loose fitting pair of sleep pants that sat low on his waist. The sight would have overwhelmed all of my senses had I not been delirious with fever. From the rattling sound, he'd located the Tylenol bottle on the floor and popped it open. He shook two capsules out, snagged the glass of water and leaned over me. "Open up. You need to take this to break the fever."

I didn't bother arguing. My lips parted far enough for him to dump the meds into my mouth, and, with his now-free hand, he cupped the back of my neck and lifted me up high enough to bring the water glass to my lips. I sucked it back and let out a sigh as he lowered me back to the pillow.

"When I die," I started on a whine, "my recipe book for all my pastries is in a box on my closet shelf."

"Sweetheart, you aren't dying." I could hear the smile in his voice, but I'd already squeezed my eyes closed.

"Don't argue. This is important," I said as my body trembled against the chills of my fever.

"All right," he said, his voice telling me he was simply humoring me, despite me being completely irrational. It was amazing how, even on my deathbed, I was able to read all of that from just those two words.

"When I die," I repeated for dramatic effect — like I said, I was a horrible patient, so sue me, "whatever you do, don't let Harlow get ahold of those recipes. She's a *terrible* cook. It would be sacrilegious."

The mattress shook with his laughter. "I've heard stories."

"Unless you've been forced to live through it, you can't possibly understand."

"Ethan and Noah told me all about Thanksgiving. I have a good idea," he muttered, bringing up a dinner that still gave me nightmares. How one person could not only screw up but desecrate food in such a way, was beyond me.

"I still wake up screaming sometimes," I whispered, shivering at the memory.

The light in the room was extinguished and, just as I thought Derrick was going to stand to leave, he surprised me by sliding down the bed, his body warm against mine as he wrapped an arm around my waist and pulled me into him.

"What are you doing?"

147

"You're shaking," was all he said in response as he whipped the covers over us.

"So you're... cuddling me?" I asked incredulously.

"I'm keeping you warm." His soft words whispered across the skin of my neck, eliciting another tremble for a totally different reason. Judging by the way Derrick's arm tightened around me, he felt it and thought it was another fever chill. *If only he knew.*

"You don't have to," I attempted lamely, even though his body pressed flush against my back helped to not only ward off the worst of the chills, but also relaxed me. "You could get sick, too."

"Hush, Chloe," His chest rumbled against my back, and as I shifted just slightly, feeling his skin against my arm, I was reminded that he was barely dressed, and that, only moments ago, I'd gotten an eyeful of all the wonder that was his body. And I didn't even feel good enough to appreciate it.

"Derrick?" I asked, starting to feel sleep pull me under. I could say with all honesty that, what came out of my mouth next was strictly due to the fever, but I'd only be telling the partial truth.

"Yeah, baby?"

I shivered again, *loving* the way he called me that. It was the second time I'd heard that word fall from his lips in regards to me, and I felt it all the way down to my bones.

"When I'm better and can fully appreciate it, will you walk around without a shirt on?"

His laughter shook both of our bodies. "Whatever will

help you get better faster, sunshine." And just as sleep tugged me under, blacking out everything around me, I could have sworn I felt something like lips press against the back of my neck.

"AND THEN SARAH WAS LIKE, 'You can't come to my birthday party 'cause you're friends with Lilly Mathewson!' And I was all, 'well, I don't want to come to your stupid party anyway. And Lilly's way cooler than you!'"

I stifled my smile as Eliza rattled on at an alarming speed, her gaze focused down on my toes that she was working diligently to paint a bright, sparkly pink that she just *knew* would help to make me feel better as she told me all the latest elementary school drama.

I'd been sequestered to Derrick's bedroom for the past thirty hours, and even though I was starting to feel more like myself, the damned man gave me a look that promised punishment, then pointed in the direction of the bed every time he caught me out of it. After waking up wrapped in his arms earlier that morning, I'd been doing everything possible to convince him to let me go home. Unfortunately, nothing worked.

Last night and this morning proved to be too much for my normal frame of mind. Having him hold me — basically snuggling with me all night long — made the friendship boundary we'd put in place all the more blurry, and my poor, confused heart skip several uncomfortable beats.

Staying there wasn't healthy for my sanity.

Luckily I'd had Eliza to keep me company for the past few hours, helping to keep my mind off the horde of butterflies taking up residence in my stomach. We'd watched Disney movies, I'd let her brush my hair, and now I was getting my own personal pedicure from the world's most adorable nine-year-old.

"So Lilly's your best friend then?" I asked. "Is she nice?"

"Yeah, she's super nice," Eliza answered sincerely, just before her shoulders slumped. "But Mom says I have to be friends with Sarah too."

"Why's that?" I asked, unhappy with the way the light seemed to fizzle out of Eliza so quickly.

"Because," she shrugged, "she said Sarah's mom and dad got money and Sarah's one of the popular girls in my class, so if I wanna be popular too, I gotta stay friends with her." Her hazel eyes, identical to her father's, came up and met mine, her gaze sad as she said, "And she won't let Lilly come to our house for sleepovers 'cause she said I don't need to hang out with a kid whose dad is the school janitor. I can only be friends with Lilly at school, which sucks, 'cause she's my best friend."

I *really* hated that woman. But it wasn't like I could show that in front of a little girl. I worked to school my features even though my heart was breaking at the sight of her sadness. It might not have been my place to offer up my advice, but I couldn't just sit there while her own mother filled her head with things that could turn her from the bright, caring girl she was into something tarnished and ugly.

"Honey," I said in a soft voice, "I'm going to tell you something my mom told me when I was little. We're all born with empty places inside of us that are meant to be filled up by people who make us happy and who make us feel good about ourselves. Those places are special, because if you pick the right person to fill it, they help you to be whole. If Lilly makes you happy and you feel whole around her, then you hold on to that as tight as you can because those are the types of relationships that last forever."

"Is that what Ms. Harlow did for you? Fill up one of your empty places?"

"Absolutely," I smiled widely. "And we'll still be friends until we're old and gray and lose all our teeth."

Her happy giggle warmed something in my chest that had gone cold at the sight of her sorrow. "Then you'll look like Granddad when he doesn't have his teeth in!"

"Your granddad doesn't put his teeth in?" I asked, finding myself laughing as well.

"He only pops them out for special occasions," Derrick's rumbling voice announced, and my and Eliza's gazes shot to where he was standing, one shoulder propped against the door frame. "Isn't that right, baby girl?" He winked at his daughter and my belly quivered.

"Yep. Like Christmas and my birthday." She giggled again before turning back to me. "Granddad is Daddy's father. He lives on a ranch in Montana with goats! We go there every year for Christmas and Spring Break 'cause that's when my birthday is."

"That sounds like fun, sweetheart. I've always wanted to visit a ranch."

"You should come with us next time!" she clapped glee-fully. "Can she Daddy? Can she?" She spun back around to face me before allowing Derrick a chance to answer. "You'd love it so much. It's so pretty there! You have to come!"

"Oh, uh…" I shot a look at Derrick to see one corner of his mouth hitched up in a smirk.

"*Pleeeeeeeease*," she begged.

"How about we discuss it when it's closer to our next trip?" Derrick finally said, offering up a solution that fortu-nately placated and excited Eliza, at least for the time being.

"Okay!" she agreed.

"Time to go pack, baby girl. Your mom will be here soon."

She stood on her knees and moved toward me, wrap-ping me in a hug and muttering, "Bye Miss Chloe. Hope you feel better."

I returned the hug, holding tight. "Thank you, baby. I'll see you soon."

She made her way across the bed, but I didn't miss the way her head drooped, or the sigh she released as she followed orders. I wanted to scoop her up and keep here there with me forever, but I knew it wasn't logical.

After Eliza disappeared through the door, Derrick moved closer to the bed. "How you feeling, sunshine?"

"Stir crazy," I answered, trying to ignore the way my skin tingled at his closeness. "But at least I have pretty toenails," I added, wiggling my toes on top of the comforter for him to see.

The lines around his eyes crinkled as he smiled at my feet before turning his face back to me. "That you do, sweetheart. Prettiest toenails I've ever seen."

"Eliza has a gift. If college doesn't work out, you should offer to pay for her to train to be a nail tech."

"I'll keep that in mind," he chuckled, and my stomach flipped at the sound.

I needed to get *out* of there. Especially if Eliza wasn't going to be in place as a buffer any longer. "Derrick, I haven't had a fever again all day, and the Tamiflu seems to be working. I really think I'm fine to go home." It was an argument we'd already had earlier in the day.

His face grew firm as he leaned in close. "Told you this morning, sunshine. You're staying here until you finish your full five days of meds. I'm not willing to risk you relapsing."

"You're being unreasonable!" I cried, pounding the mattress with my fist.

"If being concerned about you and wanting you to get better is unreasonable, I can live with that," he shrugged casually and stood to his full height.

"Derrick," I growled in a warning, but his attention turned toward the French doors.

"Bitch is here," he muttered under his breath and I turned to watch a sleek black Mercedes come to a stop at the edge of his driveway. The door opened and Layla stepped out, dressed as though she'd just stepped off the runway, complete with killer heels, painted on jeans, and a tight top that showed way too much cleavage for a woman picking her daughter up from her ex-husband. The outfit was more suited for trolling the bars for a one-night stand.

I let out a sigh as I watched her strut up the walkway. "I really hate that woman," I muttered under my breath.

I hadn't realized Derrick heard me until his deep laugh resonated through the air, and I turned back to see he'd leaned close once again. "Be right back, sweetheart. Don't even think of getting out of this bed."

Then he did something that shocked me completely speechless while rendering me immobile at the same time. Cupping the back of my neck, he pulled me up just enough to press a kiss to my forehead, then he turned and sauntered out of the room like he didn't have a care in the world.

Yep. I needed to get the *hell* out of there.

16

DERRICK

$\mathcal{I}$ COULD SEE the confusion written on Chloe's face as I walked from the bedroom. I wanted to offer up *something* to help her understand what was going on between us, but the truth was, I didn't have a fucking clue myself. I just knew the pull to her was impossible to ignore. What's more, I didn't *want* to ignore it.

That was a conversation we needed to have in the very near future, but at that very moment, I had more pressing matters to deal with. Such as my bitch of an ex-wife filling my daughter's head with bullshit that could potentially damage her down the road. As I made my way down the hall, my fists clenched, my jaw ticked, I struggled to rein in the fury I wanted to unleash on the woman. The conversation I'd just overheard Eliza and Chloe having had my body locked up tight.

A knock sounded on the front door, but I took my time,

refusing to rush to let the she-devil in. Was it childish to make her wait, knowing it would piss her off? Yes. Was I above such childish behavior? Fuck no. Not when it took everything I had to keep from raining hell down on Layla. There was another knock, this one louder, more aggressive. I hit the front door, waited a few more beats until she started pounding again before finally opening it.

"Took you long enough," she huffed impatiently, her eyes narrowed in an ugly glare.

"Eliza!" I called over my shoulder. "Your mom's here, baby girl. Time to go."

Layla moved to step across the threshold, only coming to a halt when I didn't move out of her way. "What? You're not even going to let me in?"

"Got no reason to," I answered blandly as Eliza's footsteps sounded through the house. It was a totally different sound than what I heard every time I went to pick her up. Those steps were always rushed as she hurried through Layla's massive house in Jackson Hole. My girl was always excited to spend the weekend with her dad. Now, well, they were much slower, as though she was doing everything she could to stretch out the few remaining minutes she had with me.

"I need to talk to you," Layla huffed.

"Coincidence," I informed her. "I need to talk to you, too. But we can do it out on the front porch."

She snapped, "Are you serious right now?"

"As a fucking heart attack." I kept my voice low as Eliza

rounded the corner into the living room and headed our way. "Give me a hug sweetheart." I leaned down to her level as she placed a kiss on my cheek and wrapped her arms around my neck tightly.

"Love you, Daddy."

I returned the hug. "Love you too, baby girl. See you in a few weeks, okay?"

"Okay."

"Eliza, go wait in the car," Layla told her. No hug, no warm greeting after not seeing her own flesh and blood for nearly three whole days. It made my blood boil.

"Yes ma'am," Eliza mumbled. "See you later, Daddy."

"Okay, honey."

She leaned back through the door. "Bye, Miss Chloe!" she yelled back into the house. "See you soon!"

I heard Chloe's sweet voice call back, "Bye, baby!" but I didn't take my eyes off the woman standing in front of me, suddenly fuming at the sound of Chloe's voice coming from inside my house.

Eliza barely made it down the front walk, out of earshot, when she seethed, "Are you fucking kidding me with this shit, Derrick?"

I took a step forward, effectively backing her up so I could close the front door, both of us standing on the flagstone landing right outside of it.

"None of your business who I've got in my house, Layla."

"I told you—" she began to rant, but I cut her off.

"You don't want to push me right now," I warned. "I don't give a flying rat's ass what you told me. I said it's not your business, so let it go. Now, what's this I hear about you trying to dictate who Eliza's friends with?"

The woman actually had the nerve to roll her eyes. "Oh my God, *that's* what you want to talk to me about? Christ, Derrick, it's not even that big of a deal."

"It's a huge deal! You're filling our daughter's head with shit that's going to screw her up in the future. I don't give a damn if that Sarah girl's popular or if her parents are so fucking rich they wipe their asses with hundred dollar bills! You will *not* tell *our* daughter who she can and can't hang out with. That shit stops now."

For the first time in all the years I'd known her, Layla didn't fight back, and that instantly set me on edge. But it was her following words that sent up red flags and warning sirens.

"Fine. You're right."

"Say what now?" I asked, shell-shocked by her immediate acquiescence.

"I said you're right." The earlier anger was wiped from her face, replaced by a look that had my blood running cold. "I hate fighting with you over every little thing when it comes to Eliza's upbringing," she said softly, looking up at me through her fake eyelashes, appearing almost reticent. "It would be so much easier if we were on the same page, don't you think?"

My voice was laced with skepticism as I answered, "Whatever you say, Layla." I took a step back, my hand reaching behind me for the doorknob, ready to cut whatever this bullshit was that she was pulling off at the quick. "Have a good day. I'll see you when I come to pick Eliza up in two weeks."

"Wait!" Layla called as I started to turn my back on her. "Harold and I broke up!" she said on a rush.

And there it was. I turned back to her, arms crossed over my chest. "And you think I care about this because…?"

"He broke up with me because he said he couldn't play second best to you anymore." A sound like screeching tires echoed in my ears, nearly drowning out the rest of what she was saying. "He knew I wanted my family back, that I wasn't really happy with him, and he couldn't take it anymore. I hate that I broke his heart, but I can't deny that he was right, Derrick." She stepped into me, placing her hands on my chest as she gave me a doe-eyed expression. "I screwed up. I messed up our family. But I'm still in love with you. I want you back, baby."

I don't know how long I stood there, at a total loss for words before my brain finally began to function once again. "Let me get this straight," I said, reaching up and wrapping my fingers around her wrists so I could pry her talons off me. "Your gravy train left the station, probably kicking your ass to the curb, and you actually think I'm stupid enough to believe some bullshit about you wanting your family back?"

She snatched her hands back, working to make her face appear wounded. "It's not bullshit, it's the truth!"

"Woman, you've lost your damn mind!"

"It's because of *her*, isn't it?" she shot a snarled look at my front door. "That's why you won't even consider it! *We're* your family, not some slut you've been banging for a couple of weeks! You never would've been so cruel to me if you hadn't met *Chloe*."

My head fell back on a loud laugh, and it was my turn to ask, "Are you fucking kidding me with this shit?! This has nothing to do with Chloe, other than she's ten times the woman you could ever be! You forget, Layla, I was married to you. I know exactly how you think. You don't want your family back. You're scrambling for a Plan B because you lost your free ride. You've got no job, no skills, and no one else to do any of the heavy lifting. If you think you're going to use our daughter as a pawn in whatever fucked-up game you're playing, you've got another thing coming."

Her chest heaved as she sucked in air. "This is all her fault!" she shouted, jabbing her finger at the house.

My voice dropped to a menacing tone as I said, "You don't talk about Chloe. You don't even *think* about her. This isn't about her. This is about *you* being a manipulative bitch. And so help me, if you step over the line where Eliza's concerned one more time, I swear to God, woman, I'll drag your ass to court so goddamned fast it'll make your head spin. You don't have your sugar daddy's money to hide behind anymore, I'm done letting you manipulate her. This shit ends today, do you understand me?" When she didn't respond I snapped, "Nod your head if you're hearing me, Layla."

She gave me one jerky nod in acknowledgment.

"Good, now get the hell off my porch and get our daughter home." She turned on her heels and began stomping off, but I wasn't done. "Oh, and Layla?" She snapped her head over her shoulder, eyes full of fire and hatred. "I find out you took your shit out on her," I pointed to her car, "I'll bury you. That's the only warning you get. Your drama doesn't touch her."

She didn't utter another word as she finished the walk to her car, got in, slammed the door, and backed out of my driveway, but I knew she got me. The fear was written all over her face. Karma was finally paying the bitch back and she had nothing to fall back on.

I let out an exhausted sigh as I reached up and rubbed the back of my neck, waiting until her taillights disappeared before going inside. Just like all the other times I'd been forced to deal with Layla, I was left bone tired and weary.

"Uh, you all right?" I heard as I walked into the house, closing the door behind me. My head came up to find Chloe standing at the mouth of the hall in nothing but a pair of sleep shorts and a baggy t-shirt. She shouldn't have looked so damned beautiful, especially considering how sick she was, but damn if I didn't have to struggle against getting hard at her adorable, rumpled look.

"What'd I say about getting out of bed?"

"I heard yelling," She shrugged and leaned against the wall, arms crossed over her chest, no doubt trying to hide the fact she wasn't wearing a bra. I didn't tell her it didn't matter. My imagination was active enough all on its own, and now that I saw her as something more than just a friend with cute girl-next-door looks, I couldn't keep my head out of that damn gutter.

"You look better," I said as I made my way toward her, ignoring her initial question. "You're not as pale as yesterday."

"Yep." She stood up and fidgeted from foot to foot as I stopped directly in front of her and placed my palm on her forehead. "No fever," she replied. "And I'm feeling a thousand times better."

I felt the muscles that had been tense just seconds ago begin to loosen as I grinned down at her, knowing exactly what she was going to push for, and knowing I wasn't going to allow it. It was unbelievable how just a few seconds with Chloe managed to erase the foul stench that clung heavy in the air any time Layla was around. Usually the woman would ruin my entire day in just a handful of minutes. But not now... not this time. And the only difference was the sunshine standing before me.

"You're not going home," I told her, feeling my grin stretch into a wide smile as she blew out a huff and stomped her foot.

"I have to go to work, Derrick!"

"I already called Erin and told her you'd be out today and tomorrow. No sense in arguing about it. She and the rest of your staff told me to pass on their well wishes. Quite the supportive team you got there."

She let out an adorable growl and stomped her foot

once more before spinning around and storming back into the bedroom, slamming the door behind her.

I laughed as I headed for the couch, plopped down, and flipped on the TV, feeling lighter than I had in years.

All because of sunshine.

17

CHLOE

I WAS DREAMING. I had to be. There was no other logical explanation for what was happening to me.

And it was the Best. Dream. Ever.

Something pulled me from the deepest recesses of sleep, and as I blinked my eyes open to the sight of the darkened room, my sleep-addled brain was still too drowsy to figure out what had woken me. As I stared out of the French doors, nothing but black blanketing the forest ahead, my whole body tensed at the realization that the tingles I'd been feeling thanks to the erotic dream I had of Derrick weren't abating.

Then I realized why.

"Derrick?" I asked on a gasp as his large hand spanned against my belly, pushing me further back into him.

"Shh," he whispered in my ear, just before pulling the lobe between his teeth and biting down.

"What are you d-doing?" My voice broke as a shudder worked its way up my throat.

"What I've been dying to do for what feels like forever," was his bewildering answer. I didn't understand what was happening. We were supposed to be friends. *Just friends.* Yet, for the past few days he'd been acting like he wanted more from me. I couldn't wrap my head around what was going on.

When the hell had he started wanting me? Until a few days ago I had no idea he'd even noticed I was a woman.

"I don't..." I breathed as his tongue left a trail across my tingling flesh. "I don't think—"

"Don't think," he rumbled. "Just feel, baby. Christ, you undo me." He bit down on the tendon that ran from my neck down to my shoulder.

I moaned as the sting of pain sparked into something that made my blood run hot and my stomach clench. As he rained open-mouth kisses from ear to shoulder and back again, my hips involuntarily rocked back, pressing against the hardness of his erection. He groaned against my skin and I shivered as he continued his toe-curling assault. I'd never had a man pay such attention to that particular spot on my body, and it was driving me mad. It was as though every single nerve ending in my body was located *right there*. What he was doing to me made it impossible to control the needy sounds that fell from my lips. I was so turned on that rationality had flown out the window. There wasn't tomorrow or the repercussions it could hold, there was only here... only *now*.

His voice was gravelly as he said, "So fucking sweet," against my shoulder before biting down again.

"Mmm, *Derrick.*" I rolled my hips, pressing harder against his cock, desperate for *something*, some friction to help ease the pressure building between my thighs.

With a low, rumbling growl, one hand twisted into my hair, pulling my head back so hard my scalp stung, while the other snaked from my stomach to my breast and squeezed. I loved it. *All* of it. I went mindless with pleasure, nothing mattered but what Derrick was doing and how it made me feel. I couldn't think, I could barely *breathe* the craving was so intoxicating.

"Oh God." I rocked and rocked and rocked my hips back as he let go of my breast just long enough to reach under my t-shirt and palm it without any barrier.

"Love how you light up for me," he moaned, thrusting his hips forward. "Are you wet, sunshine?"

"Derrick," I whimpered as his hold on my hair enabled him to twist my head any which way he wanted so he could continue to feast on my skin. "I need…"

"What, baby?" Another bite from him, another groan from me. God, it was like he was ravenous for me. "What do you need?"

"*More,*" was all I was able to get out.

In a blink, I was on my back, my top whipped over my head as Derrick loomed above me, his hips forcing my thighs apart as he settled himself between them. His mouth claimed mine in a brutal, dominating kiss.

"Mmm, Chloe." His moan vibrated through his chest

and into mine as he trailed kisses along my jaw. "What are you doing to me?"

"I-I don't know," I panted, fisting his hair as my back arched beneath him, pressing my breasts into his firm, solid chest.

He slid against me, his rigid length pushing against where I needed it the most. At the pressure of his cock grinding against my core, my head fell back against the pillow, a low, guttural sound coming from deep within my throat.

"You drive me fucking crazy," he murmured as his lips moved lower and lower. "I can't get you out of my head, no matter how hard I try."

His tongue flicked my straining nipple, shooting pulsing waves of pleasure to my center, making me even wetter, more desperate. With each lash of his tongue, my body writhed against his, searching for something to send me over the edge, into the abyss.

"Oh, God. Don't stop doing that." I let out a cry when his mouth pulled away.

He moved back up my body, his lips close to my ear when he whispered, "Tell me you want me inside you." My mouth opened to follow his command only to get stuck in my throat. He let out a pained moan as his hips undulated against me. "Say it."

"I—" my brain chose that very moment to reengage, pushing back the pleasure coursing through me and pulling rationality to the forefront of my mind. This wasn't me. I couldn't do this with all the uncertainty that loomed between us. I wasn't one to ever judge a person on their choices, but I also wasn't the kind of person who could have meaningless sex. Maybe it was the romantic in me that still pined after the fairytale ending, but I knew if I slept with Derrick and it turned out it was just a heat of the moment thing for him, I'd be crushed.

"Wait. Wait, wait, wait." My palms spread wide on his bare chest, giving him a tiny shove back, even as my body screamed at the loss of his weight.

Derrick's voice was soft, laced with concern as he lifted up slightly so he could look down at me. "What's the matter?" I shook my head back and forth in confusion. The pads of his fingers ran along my forehead, moving the hair off my face and tucking it gently behind my ear. I had to clench my eyes closed at the soothing action.

"Chloe?" he asked when I said nothing. "Baby, look at me."

I couldn't. I shook my head again in answer. I couldn't get my spiraling thoughts under control. I struggled to calm the war raging inside of me, I registered his movement just seconds before the light on the bedside table clicked on.

"Sunshine. Open your eyes."

I managed to peel my eyelids open and looked up at him as he rested on his haunches between my still-spread thighs, his shaft straining against the blue cotton of his boxer briefs. It wasn't until I caught his gaze skating along my chest before snapping back to my face that I realized I was still topless, exposed.

169

"Uh…" I pulled the sheet across my breasts, holding it against me like a shield. "Can you… could you hand me my shirt?"

He leaned over the edge of the bed and snatched my shirt off the floor, passing it my way. I pulled it over my head in a rush as I scooted back on the mattress until my back rested against the headboard.

"Tell me what's going through your head," he said, moving closer to me, closing the space I'd just put between us, the space I desperately needed in order to think clearly.

"I—" my voice cracked on the emotion suddenly clogging my throat. "I can't do this if it's… if it's not going to mean anything to you." I watched as his eyebrows formed a deep *V*. "You think this wouldn't mean anything to me?"

I released a pent up breath as I ran my hands over my face agitatedly. "No. I mean yes! God, I'm not saying this right!"

I shivered at the contact when his hands landed on my shins, rubbing in soothing circles. "Just relax, sunshine. It's just me. Take a deep breath and get it out." I did as he instructed, inhaling deeply through my nose and blowing it out past my lips. "Can you…" I pointed down at his hands that had managed to make their way up my legs. "It's hard to think straight when you're touching me like that." I gave him a shy grin. He smirked in return as he held his palms up.

"Not touching you," he chuckled. "Now tell me what's happening in that gorgeous head of yours."

"You said I deserved a man who could commit to me."

He flinched as I reminded him of the conversation we'd had in front of the Ferris wheel. The same conversation that managed to crush any hopes I'd had of us being *more*. "What's changed between then and now?" He let out a long sigh as he ran a hand through his hair and cupped the back of his neck. The sudden deflation in his shoulders caused my head to tilt as I studied his face closely. "Or has nothing changed at all?"

He paused. Then, "Chloe…" he sighed again, and I had my answer.

And it gutted me.

"I understand your reasons for shying away from commitment," I informed him, my voice hard as I fought the sting building behind my eyes. "I've *met* the reason, and I can't fault you for your choices, Derrick. But you know me." That was what hurt the most, honestly. "You know I'm not capable of giving you what you've had from the other women in town." I paused as my anger built and my heart splintered apart in my chest. "You *know* me."

"Sunshine—"

"Admit it!" I snapped. "Admit you knew I wasn't like your other women."

I watched in morbid fascination as his eyes widened just slightly and the realization of what I was saying caused the color to bleed from his face. "I knew, sunshine. But that's not what—"

I jumped from the bed, unable to stand being so close to him. "Did you, or did you not climb into be with me tonight with the sole purpose of getting into my pants?"

God, I didn't want the answer to that.

But I needed to know. I needed the truth.

"That wasn't all this was!" He insisted.

"You wanted to have sex with me." It wasn't a question.

"Yes," he ground out.

"And afterward?"

"I…" he trailed off, momentarily lost for words before finishing with a ragged, "I don't know."

My chest heaved with every labored breath I took. "You said you wanted to be my friend because you cared about me."

"I do! I do care! Fuck, Chloe!"

"Then tell me you didn't come in here to use me like you've used every other willing woman in Pembrooke." A few tears broke free and I quickly batted them away, only to have more fall in their place. "I need you to tell me that, because I've been in love with you since I met you." His chest expanded as he sucked in air, his expression like I'd just slapped him. "I accepted you at your word when you said you weren't able to give me what I needed, and I agreed to be your friend because I'd rather have that from you than nothing at all. So I need you to tell me you weren't using me. I need you to say it, because the thought that you'd have such little respect for me hurts worse than you could imagine."

He moved toward me, his face ravaged as he tried to reach for me, but I moved out of his grasp. "Sunshine…"

My voice shook as I said, "Just tell me the truth."

"You told me you didn't feel like that anymore," he

stated frantically, continuing in my direction. "You said it was a crush and you were over it!"

"I lied," I whispered brokenly.

"*Fuck!*" He began pacing in front of the fireplace, his hands fisted in his hair.

He still hadn't told me what I needed to hear. But it wouldn't have mattered anyway. I would have known it was a lie. He could have tried to paint over the truth with sweet, placating words, but in the end, the outcome would have been the same.

My heart was broken, once again.

"At least answer one question for me," I demanded, surprised at the strength in my words despite my tears. "Would we have still been friends come morning, or would I have been discarded like the rest of them?"

"You aren't like the rest of them," he said quietly, shaking his head as he stared me in the eyes.

"That's not an answer."

"I don't know! I don't know, Chloe. My head's a fucking mess when it comes to you. I don't know what I'm doing or what I want to happen. I can't fucking *think* straight when you're around."

I was officially done.

"I know this is your house and you're going to do what you want to do in the end, but I'd appreciate it if you'd get out of this room."

"But we need to talk about this."

"I'm all talked out," I said with a defeated shrug. "I'm exhausted and feel like shit. I just want to sleep." It was a lie, but I knew playing the sick card would work. Derrick was nothing if not insanely protective.

"We'll talk in the morning," he proclaimed, his shoulders squaring as his chin came up like what he'd just said was definitive. "You'll get some sleep and we'll talk this through in the morning. Everything's going to be just fine, Chloe. You'll see." I stood, frozen in place as he came close and pressed a tender kiss to my forehead. "Rest, baby. Then we'll talk."

It took ten seconds for my feet to come unglued from the floor once the bedroom door closed behind him, then I was a flurry of motion, dumping all of my stuff into my duffle bag haphazardly as I snatched up my phone and dialed.

I spoke as soon as the line connected. "I'm so sorry for calling this late," I managed to get out just before the sobs broke loose, "but can you come get me? Please?"

18

DERRICK

*H*OLY SHIT, WHAT *did I just do?*

That sentence had been the only thing floating around in my head since walking out of Chloe's — well, technically *my* — bedroom fifteen minutes ago.

I froze.

When she asked me what would happen between us come morning, if we'd still be friends, I completely fucking froze. And I hated myself because the tears in her eyes and the pain etched across her beautiful face were all my fault. All because I'd been too much of a coward to admit there was something between us, something so much more, and it terrified the shit out of me. There was no way in hell she'd have been discarded. She'd managed to burrow herself under my skin, and I was starting to come to grips with the fact that she was there to stay. Hell, I *wanted* her there!

But did I *say* any of that?

Fuck no.

I locked up and managed to break her heart in the process, even though that was the last thing on Earth I ever wanted to do.

I needed to fix things between us *now*. I couldn't wait until morning. I knew pushing when she was sick was a shitty thing to do, but I couldn't let her fall asleep thinking I wasn't totally and completely fucking in this with her. She had to know the truth. I stood from the couch, prepared to grovel like my life depended on it — which felt about right considering the tightness in my chest — when the glow of headlights poured into my living room through the opened curtains, lighting up the once dark space. I made it to the door just as a knock sounded.

"Noah?" I asked once the door was opened. "What the hell are you doing here?"

The hairs on the back of my neck stood on end at his stony expression. "Man. What'd you do?"

With that one quietly spoken question the blood in my veins ran ice cold. "No," I stated with finality once it dawned on me why he was at my house at such an ungodly hour.

"Don't have much of a choice man." He gave me a pitying look. "Can't force her to stay."

"I'm ready," Chloe's voice sounded through the room, stabbing straight through my chest like a goddamned knife.

"You're not leaving."

Panic. Bone chilling panic began coursing through me as she moved closer to the door, eyes focused on her feet as she moved, refusing to look at me. "Please move," she said quietly once she stood a foot away.

"Chloe, look at me."

Nothing.

"Please, baby. Just look at me." I was begging. Christ, I'd never begged a woman for anything in my life. Not even Layla when we were married. But I wasn't above doing anything and everything in my power to get her to hear me out. "I'm sorry. Look, we need to talk, okay? I need to explain—"

She cut me off. "I want to go home."

"Sunshine, you're not leaving," I whispered. I reached up to touch her only to have her head snap up, eyes narrowed as she glared. Her normally gorgeous jade eyes were so full of pain and anger, I felt it all the way down to my bones.

"Fine!" she snapped. Her little hands hit my chest and she shoved with all her might, rocking me back a foot, just enough clearance for her to make it through the open door.

"Goddamn it!" I shouted, darting out after her, oblivious to Noah's wide-eyed stare as his gaze darted between us. "You're not fucking leaving!" I latched on to her upper arm and tried to pull her against me. Despite her struggle, I was convinced, if I could just touch her, hold her, kiss her, I

177

could calm her down enough to make her see reason. But she wasn't having any of that.

"Let. Go." Luckily her kick went wide, missing my shin by a couple inches. I couldn't imagine how badly that would have hurt had she actually connected with my leg. I loosened my hand just enough for her to pull free as I tried to keep away from her flailing foot.

Before I had a chance to grab her again, Noah was in front of me.

"Just give her time to cool off," he spoke. But my gaze was riveted to the tiny woman with strawberry blonde curls walking away from me. My lungs felt like they were being squeezed in a vice. I couldn't get enough air as she closed herself in Noah's truck.

"I can't," I croaked.

"Look, just let her sleep it off for a few hours, all right? There's no reasoning when they get like this. It's like talking to a brick fucking wall, brother."

"I need her to let me explain."

"Don't we all." He patted my shoulder compassionately before adding, "Welcome to the club, you poor son of a bitch."

I finally pulled my attention off his truck and looked down at him. "Huh?"

"You're sprung my friend. Wrapped around her little finger. In other words, officially fucked. Sucks feeling like you aren't in control of shit anymore, doesn't it?"

All I could do was stand there as he turned and made

his way to the truck that was going to take Chloe away from me.

"I'm screwed, aren't I?" I asked his retreating back.

"Absolutely!" he answered far too cheerfully. The bastard.

Chloe

FOR THE FIRST time in my life, baking wasn't helping calm my frayed nerves. From the moment Noah dropped me off at my place, I'd been in the kitchen, mixing, icing, decorating, you name it, and nothing had helped.

"Uh…" Erin murmured from her place a few feet away as I banged on the espresso machine like it owed me money. "Are you *sure* you should have come in today?"

"Yep!" *Bang.* "I told you, I'm fine." *Bang, bang.*

"But Derrick said—"

"Derrick's an idiot!" She took a step back at my banshee-like yell. People sitting at the tables enjoying their breakfast and coffees paused to stare. "Sorry," I grumbled before sucking in a calming breath. The last thing I needed to do was bite my employees' heads off when they'd done nothing wrong. "I'm just tired. I didn't get any sleep and the stupid delivery guy called this morning and informed me the new convection oven isn't coming in for another two days."

She still sounded hesitant as she shuffled toward the kitchen door. "Well, I'll uh… just let you get to it," then she made her escape like her ass was on fire.

"You're just a regular ray of sunshine this morning, aren't you?"

I shot a heated look over my shoulder at Harlow, who'd shown up at Sinful Sweets as soon as the doors unlocked an hour and a half ago. "Don't you work?"

"Nope." She made an annoying popping sound on the "p". "Maternity leave is in full effect. Now you get to see my smiling face every day until I push this little bundle of joy out of my body *Alien* style." She gave her belly an affectionate rub.

"Lucky me," I deadpanned.

"You know, you can't avoid the subject forever—"

"Watch me," I interrupted, refusing to tell her what went down between me and Derrick that warranted a rescue call at the butt crack of dawn.

"Chloe," she said in a warning tone just as the bell over the door rang.

"Oh, sorry," I fake winced. "Looks like you'll have to wait, I've got a new customer."

She crossed her arms with a "*hmph*" and pouted as I turned to see who had just walked in. "Fletch!" I said in surprise, choosing to ignore the shit-eating grin that suddenly spread across Harlow's face, as well as her mumbled, "Well this morning just got a lot more interesting."

"Chloe," he smiled sweetly as he took the barstool next

to Harlow, turning to offer her a nod. "Harlow. How are you lovely ladies this morning?"

"Well I'm twenty-months pregnant," Harlow answered, "so every time I sneeze, I pee myself. And its allergy season. How do you *think* my morning's going?"

"For crying out loud," I rolled my eyes, "not everyone needs all the gory details of pregnancy, Low-Low." I gave a startled-looking Fletch an apologetic smile.

"But if cooking another human being in my belly for months doesn't give me the right to say whatever the hell I want, then what will?" she asking indignantly. "Surely pregnancy gives you certain perks. Why else would women do it?"

"Um... for the joys of bringing a baby of their own into the world?" Fletcher asked on a laugh.

Harlow waved him off. "Oh, what the hell do you know?"

I turned my attention to Fletch. "Ignore her. Pregnancy makes her cranky. What can I get you?"

"Well, since I hear you've got the best coffee in Pembrooke, why don't we start there?"

"On it," I smiled my first genuine smile of the day. "Black?"

"That'd be perfect. To go, if you don't mind."

I set about making his coffee, pouring it into a travel cup and snapping a lid on before sliding it his way. "First cup's on the house. Hopefully you'll like it enough to come back. Then I'll start charging you."

He smiled again. God, he had a really great smile. "I

appreciate it. I'm sure it's as good as everyone says. But I actually came in here for another reason. Coffee was just a bonus."

"Really?" Harlow and I both propped our elbows on the bar, leaning in closer, me because I was curious, her because she was a nosey pain in the ass.

"Um, yeah." His cheeks turned just a touch pink as he reached up and scratched his jawline. "I was wondering if maybe you'd like to have dinner with me one evening."

I stood straight, caught off guard by his unexpected offer.

"Oh," I said.

"Like on a date?" nosey-ass Harlow asked.

"Well," Fletch chuckled, "if she's interested. If not, we'll just call it a meal between friends. But for the sake of full disclosure, I'm kind of hoping dinner has more of a first-date vibe to it."

My mouth dropped open, but before I had a chance to respond, a low, menacing voice spoke up.

"She's not interested."

All three pairs of eyes shot to where Derrick was standing, just a few feet away from us. I hadn't even heard the damn bell of the door!

"Ooooh." Harlow practically clapped with glee. Damned woman really needed to get a life.

"For the love of God!" I snapped, throwing my hands wide. "Does no one work in this freaking town?!"

Derrick ignored my dramatics and stated, "I need to talk to you."

"Well I'm busy, so unless you came in to buy coffee or pastries, I've got nothing to say to you."

"Um... are you two together or something?" Fletch asked.

"No!" I answered at the same time Derrick shot, "Yes."

"Have you lost your mind?" I shouted at him. "We are *not* together!"

Derrick's eyes stayed firmly rooted on Fletcher as he confided. "We're just having a little fight, you understand."

Fletcher actually nodded in understanding.

"For Christ's sake! We are *not* together!" I cried, drawing the rapt attention of every single person in the bakery.

"Yes, we are."

"No. We. Are. Not!"

"This is better than Maury," Harlow breathed, grabbing a cookie from the display case and munching down happily.

I pointed at her. "You're paying for that!"

"You know," Fletcher started as he stood to his feet, "I should really get going. Thanks for the coffee, Chloe. I'll see you around." He turned to Derrick and held out his hands. "Sorry for the misunderstanding, man."

"It's okay." They shook hands amicably, then Fletch headed for the door, waving over his shoulder as I yelled, *again*, "We aren't together!"

Derrick rounded the bar, heading straight for me. "What are you doing? You can't be back here!" I yelped as he closed the distance.

"I said we needed to talk."

"Well I don't want to talk to you!" I argued.

"I made a mistake last night," he continued, still on the move. "I let you leave thinking I didn't want something more with you. That couldn't be further from the truth."

I couldn't do this. Not again. The man had already shattered me twice before, there was no way I'd survive a third time. "Too late."

"It's not too late," he declared, desperation flashing in his hazel eyes as he stopped only an inch away.

"Guys?" Harlow spoke, but I was too consumed with the man before me to pay attention.

I shook my head, fighting back the tears that threatened to fall. "I can't be like all your other women," I whispered. "I *can't*."

"I don't want that," he insisted, reaching up and cupping my cheeks.

"Uh… guys?" God, she was an annoying pregnant woman.

"Well what do you want, Derrick? Because I can't do this with you anymore!"

"Everything." That one word was spoken with such reverence that my lungs froze, my heart stuttered in my chest. "Watching you walk away last night was fucking unbearable. I won't do that again, sunshine. I can't. I want to give you everything you want."

Neither of us spoke or moved for what seemed like an eternity as we stared at each other, me in shock and him in determination.

That was, until Harlow shouted, "Guys!"

"What?!" we both snapped at her.

"No biggie or anything, but either my bladder just exploded or my water broke. And seeing as I just peed five minutes ago, I'm thinking it's the latter."

19

CHLOE

I COULDN'T REMEMBER ever being so exhausted in my life.

The moment Harlow announced her water broke, full chaos ensued. She'd insisted Derrick drive her to the hospital right then, refusing to wait for Noah because, in her words, "He'll lose his shit the moment you call, and the last thing I need is to deliver this baby in a ditch because he's driven us off the road!"

She wasn't too far off the mark. He *had* lost his shit, running around the hospital like Harlow was the first woman on the face of the planet to have ever given birth. It was the longest thirteen hours of my life. That was for damned sure. I handled making all the necessary calls to let people know Baby Murphy was on the way, ran to get ice chips, and took Noah's place at her bedside to hold her hand when she kicked him out for, and I quote, "doing this to her." And she did that *a lot*.

Around hour seven, her friends from New York, Navie and Rowan, had shown up and Rowan helped Derrick keep Noah from completely spiraling out while Navie and I tended to a sometimes murderous Harlow. Poor Ethan looked like he was going to pass out when the doctor came in to check her dilation.

In all the hours spent at the hospital, Derrick and I hadn't had a chance to say more than two words to each other about what had gone down at the bakery earlier that day, and even with everything going on around me, I still hadn't been able to get what he'd said out of my mind. I yo-yoed back and forth between excitement that he'd meant it to dread that he actually hadn't. That, coupled with the birth of baby Lucy was enough to cause me to crash the moment Derrick loaded me in his truck to drive me home.

It wasn't until I felt him lifting me from his truck that I woke up.

I blinked my eyes open, taking in the dark sky and trees surrounding me. "Where are we?" I asked on a yawn.

"My house."

That woke me up all the way. "What?" I yelped, my spine going stiff as I wriggled in his hold. "Why didn't you take me home?"

His arms tightened around me. "Because we need to finish our conversation, and now that Noah's a little occupied, there's no chance of you running away again."

"Put me down," I demanded hopelessly. "I'm more than capable of walking all on my own, Derrick."

"I would, but you see," he started with a tone far too casual for my liking, "you have this nasty habit of taking off before I can fix the situation."

As we reached the front walk, he hefted my weight like it was nothing, freeing one hand to unlock the front door.

"Yeah, well, you have a terrible habit of making me cry. Sorry for not wanting to stick around for that."

He kicked the door shut behind us, still refusing to release me as he moved through the house, down the hall, and into his bedroom. The moment my feet touched the ground his hands were on my face, palms to my cheeks, fingers tangled in my hair.

"I hate that I made you cry." There was so much guilt in his voice that any snarky response I could have made died on my tongue. "I'm sorry that I've ever hurt you, Chloe. It's the last thing I'd ever want to do, because I *do* care about you. And I respect you more than anyone I've ever met."

"Th-thank you," I whispered.

He wasn't finished. "I knew I made a mistake last night the moment I walked out of this room." My heart leapt. Stupid betraying bastard. "I was coming back in here to fix it when Noah showed up. You never even gave me a chance to apologize for what happened."

God, I really didn't want to hear his apology or how he regretted everything that took place in his bed before it went so *so* bad. I tried to pull away from him only to have his fingers tighten in my hair, making my scalp sting.

"Look, you don't have to apologize, okay? We got

carried away. It was a mistake. I forgive you, all right. I just..." I clenched my eyes closed and finished softly, "I just don't want to talk about it anymore."

"You think I'm apologizing for kissing you?"

My eyes popped open to find him looking down at me in confusion. "Well... yeah."

"Christ, Chloe!" He barked, his hands falling from me like I'd burned him. "Did you not hear a goddamned word I said this morning?"

My mouth hung agape like a fish in desperate need of water as I watched him begin to pace. "But... but."

"Layla made my life a living hell for years, Chloe. Fucking *years.*" He seemed to be on a tear so I stood silent and let him vent, hoping that whatever he was getting to on the other side of the story about his bitch of an ex-wife was something good. I was *really* sick and tired of crying.

"When I finally managed to get myself out of her twisted bullshit, she decided to use my daughter in order to keep manipulating me. When she couldn't control me through money or sex, she started using Eliza."

I reached out to touch him, whispering, "Derrick," but he was lost in his own head.

"Ten years, Chloe. Ten years I've been stuck with this bullshit, having it weigh on me so heavy it's hard to breathe sometimes. The *only* thing that made that misery worth it was Eliza. So when the divorce came through, I told myself never again. No way in *hell* was I ever putting myself *or my daughter* in the position to be manipulated by some calculating bitch again."

He raked his hands through his hair before laughing humorlessly. "She doesn't even want her. Did you know that? Her own fucking daughter. All Eliza is to her is a pawn in her fucked-up game. She's destroying my little girl, and I can't do a goddamned thing about it!"

At the anguish on his face, I moved. I couldn't just stand there while he hurt over his daughter. "I'm sorry," I said, wrapping my arms around his waist and burrowing my face against his chest. "I'm so sorry that you have to deal with such an awful person. And I'm sorry Eliza doesn't have a better mother. But you're wrong about her being destroyed. She's still got you. And as long as you're there to lead her down the right path, she's going to be okay. I promise."

I closed my eyes when I felt his arms wrap around my body, holding me tightly against him. "Thank you," he said softly, his lips against the crown of my head.

I pulled back just enough to look in his eyes. "And I get it, I swear. I understand why you hate the idea of another relationship. It makes sense, knowing what you've had to deal with for so long. I can't fault you for not trusting—"

"I trust you," he said, putting a finger over my lips to silence me. "I trust you, sunshine. And you're the first woman to make me realize it could be worth it."

My head jerked back. "What could be worth it?"

His thumb caressed my bottom lip. "Commitment. I haven't met a single woman in ten years that's given me faith in settling down again. Not until you. I've felt it since the first moment I saw you with Eliza. How you give my girl something she's needed for so long, how sweet and caring you are, how she looks at you like you hung the moon, that all means more to me than you'll ever know. I'm just sorry it took me so long to pull my head out of my ass."

My throat felt thick. "W-why do you say that?"

"Because. If I'd been a smarter man, I could have had this a year-and-a-half ago."

His lips came down on mine in a kiss much softer than the night before, but full of so much more meaning. As his tongue swept forward, seeking entry, I stood on my tiptoes and wound my arms around his neck, meeting the kiss head on. He tasted like coffee, the addictive flavor making me moan and press against him, spurring him into a sudden frenzy.

His fingers returned to my hair, holding tight as he moved my head to the side for better access to my mouth. The kiss grew heated, hungry. Tongues wound together, teeth nipped at lips, ragged groans. It was the best kiss I'd ever had, and when he pulled away, I cried at the loss. That was, until his mouth came down on my neck, licking and biting just like he had the night before.

God, the man was talented with his mouth, and as I panted for air, everything in my body tingled with arousal.

"When we wake up in the morning," he licked my neck, "everything's going to be different." He bit down near my collar bone. "Better." His tongue traced a wicked path along my ear. "I'm going to fuck you again, then I'm going to make you breakfast."

"Oh God." I don't know what had me hotter, the thought of him inside me or of him cooking for me.

He pulled back, the hands in my hair forcing my glassy eyes to meet his. "This is real, sunshine," he spoke reverently.

"Okay," I nodded breathlessly.

"I'm going to take you on dates. We're going to make plans with my daughter. I'm not saying it's always going to be perfect, I know I'll fuck up down the road, but I want to try with you. I want to give you what you want. I want you to be a part of mine and Eliza's lives."

"I want that too," I managed to choke out.

"And if this stays good, I'll give you that white picket fence, baby."

I wouldn't cry. I wouldn't cry. *Damn it*! I could feel my eyes welling up. He couldn't possibly know how much saying that meant to me. But I was happy enough just being *with him*. I didn't need promises for the future like that.

"Why don't we just start with taking this a day at a time for now?"

"I'm cool with that." He grinned down at me. "As long as I'm inside you in the next ten seconds, I'm cool with anything."

A teasing smile spread across my lips as I took a step back, my hands at the hem of my shirt as I repeated his words, "I'm cool with that."

The second the shirt cleared my head, he was on me. I never knew clothes could be removed so quickly! In the blink of an eye, we were both naked and my back hit the mattress. What started off soft and sweet had taken a quick turn to frantic. We couldn't kiss enough, couldn't touch enough.

"Need you," I moaned as he sucked one of my nipples into his mouth, flicking the tight peak in a way that had my back arching up, desperate to get closer.

My thighs opened and he settled in, the thick head of his cock skating through my wetness. "I've been dying for this," he ground out, pushing forward just an inch.

"Wait! Wait!"

His head dropped down on what sounded like a whimper. "Not again, baby. Please don't do this to me. Not now. Not when I can fucking *feel* you."

"Condom," I exhaled, trying not to smile at the agony in his voice. *I* did that to him. I was the one driving him that crazy. "I'm not stopping you, we just need a condom."

His head came up, hazel eyes meeting mine. "I'm clean, Chloe, I promise. I'd never put you in that position."

What was he saying? Was he actually suggesting…? "I'm clean, too, but—"

"Are you on the pill?"

I nodded.

"Do you trust me?"

I reached up and caressed his face. "I do. But do *you* trust *me*? Derrick, I don't want you doing anything you're not completely comfortable with."

In response, he pushed his hard length the rest of the

way into me, making me moan long and loud. "I trust you with everything," he grunted. "Everything, sunshine." His hips picked up pace, thrusting so deep I felt him fill every single inch of me. My head shot back, eyes screwed closed as I fisted his hair. I'd never felt so full in my life. "Nothing between us."

"Oh, God, Derrick." My hips lifted to meet his as he pumped into me. "Don't stop. Just like that."

His mouth came down and I met his lips, our tongues mimicking our hips as he drove his cock into me harder and harder.

"This is real," I panted against his mouth, needing reassurance before falling over the edge into a release so strong it scared me.

"It's real, baby." He bit my bottom lip before licking the sting away. "So fucking real."

With that, I went over, my nails digging into his skin as I clenched around him, crying out his name. I came for what felt like hours, until spots started dancing in front of my eyes. Just as I started coming down, I felt his hand slide between our sweat soaked bodies, his thumb pressing against my clit as he rubbed tight circles.

"One more, Chloe. Give me one more."

My head thrashed back and forth. "I can't. Too much, Derrick. Oh God, it's too much!"

"Just one more, baby." He pressed down hard just as the head of his cock hit that spot inside me, setting me off like a firework. I screamed as he pounded into me once, twice, three times before burying himself deep and growling out his release, filling me up.

The last thing I remembered after coming down from the best sex of my life was him placing a soft kiss on my temple and whispering, "Best I've ever had."

Then I was out.

20

CHLOE

*T*RUE TO HIS word, after our first night together, he'd woken me up with his mouth—the very *best* alarm clock in the world — and then made me breakfast after giving me two glorious orgasms. It had been three blissful days and, other than work, we'd been inseparable, and even then he'd find whatever chance he could to stop by the bakery for a few minutes a couple times a day.

As I squeezed my eyes closed and tipped my head back, I let the water rinse the shampoo from my hair, unable to keep the happy smile off my face. It'd been firmly in place since I'd woken up in Derrick's bed earlier that week. Even the ungodly hour wasn't enough to dampen my mood.

The sound of the shower curtain scraping against the rod sounded just before cold air hit my wet body. "Agh! Cold!" I shouted, my eyes shooting open to find Derrick in all his naked glory climbing into my tub. The sight was mind-altering, really. It made my mouth water and my body quiver... but I was already running late.

He gave me a wicked grin. "Sorry about that. Let me warm you up."

"No, Derrick," I said with a laugh as I tried to dodge his hold in the small confines of the claw foot tub. "I'm already late! This is the second morning this week."

He reached for me. "It should be illegal to wake up so fucking early. It's not normal, baby. Way I see it, I'm doing you a favor by keeping you in bed longer."

"Maybe if I was actually sleeping!" I giggled, goose-bumps breaking out across my skin. "But I've had less sleep in these past three days than is healthy, Derrick. And it's all your fault."

He looked at me with a smirk and nipped my bottom lip. "You're welcome."

"If you don't keep your hands off me, then the cupcakes won't get baked. If the cupcakes don't get baked, the people of Pembrooke will revolt!"

"Let them," he mumbled, his fingertips digging into my waist as he pulled me flush against him and began kissing my neck.

I moaned with pleasure before giving him a pathetic shove, barely moving him an inch. "If they revolt, I'm blaming it all on you."

His head came up, his eyes narrowed in playful slits. "You wouldn't."

"Watch me. I'd throw you right under that bus and not feel bad about it."

"Evil woman," he said in a raspy voice, going back to my neck, knowing damn good and well that spot was my weakness. "Good thing you're too damned cute for me to stay mad at."

It was all too much, sensory overload. His smell, his touch, his mouth against skin as his erection dug into my belly. I don't know why I bothered fighting it, we both knew I'd cave.

And that was exactly what I did.

We stayed in the shower until the water ran cold, then moved to the bed for round two. In the end, I didn't get down to the kitchen to start baking until a quarter after five.

And I didn't regret it a single bit.

"Look at you." I glanced over my shoulder to find Erin and a few of my other employees staring at me with shit-eating grins on their faces as I iced the latest batch of chocolate and espresso cupcakes. "You're all glow-y. Some-one's getting some!" she sing-songed.

All I could do was grin because she was *not* wrong. "Pretty sure I pay you guys to do more than stand around and give me shit," I said, but I did it with a smile.

"See!" Erin cried. "You're even smiling when you're trying to be a hard-ass! It's three o'clock, you've been on your feet all day, and you're *still* smiling! No wonder he calls you *sunshine*," she winked.

I rolled my eyes as Kristen, one of the girls that worked the register up front pushed the door to the kitchen open. "Hey, Chloe. There's a woman up front asking to talk to you."

"Really?" I asked, standing from my hunched over position. "You know who she is?"

Kristen shrugged. "Never seen her before. She just asked to talk to the owner."

"Huh. Okay. I'll be right out." I handed the piping bag over to one of my pastry chefs and went to wash the icing from my hands, curious as to who was asking for me. The moment I pushed through the door to the front of the bakery, I got my answer. And I was *not* happy about it.

"Layla," I offered congenially even though all I wanted to do was reach across the countertop and slap the resting bitch face right off of her. "What can I do for you? Do you need coffee? Something to eat?"

"The only thing I need from you is to leave my husband alone," she blurted out, none too quietly.

Okay, I attempted being nice even though the woman standing before me was probably the only person on the planet who made me contemplate homicide, but if she wanted a fight, I was down for that, too. Onlookers be damned.

"I'm pretty sure you mean *ex*-husband. Because the last I heard he couldn't stand your manipulative, self centered ass."

"You don't know what you're talking about," she spit

out, her pretty face twisted with so much hatred and anger it made her look ugly.

"Really? That's funny, because I'm pretty sure I'm dating him seeing as we've been in the same bed the past three nights."

She let out an indelicate snort. "Please, just because he fucks you doesn't mean you're together, you ignorant little girl."

I leaned in closer, propping my hands on the wooden surface between us. "Oh, I know that. I'm talking about the fact he told me I'm the first woman he's met who's ever made him consider commitment after, and I'm para-phrasing here, so forgive me, 'living a decade of fucking misery.'"

Layla's top lip curled up. "You're nothing but a home-wrecking slut!"

"And you're a shrew who was too self-absorbed to see she had a good man for ten years! And what's worse, you're *still* clueless to what you have because you treat your daughter like she's nothing but a game piece! You don't deserve either of them and I can't wait for the day when it's all ripped out from under you. Eliza's a brilliant little girl and you should be *counting your blessings* that you're lucky enough to have her. Instead, you're too consumed with being a greedy bitch to see what's right in front of you! If you don't get your shit together, Layla, you're going to lose her too. And that just makes me sad for you, because you're too stupid to see what you've got."

"You stupid bitch!" She lunged, but I'd been prepared

for it. With the bar between us, all I had to do was take a step back to get out of her reach, leaving her to make an even bigger fool out of herself as she tried to scramble across the waist-high counter in too tight clothes and impossibly high heels, making the feat impossible.

I rolled my eyes. "Your pathetic attempt at threatening me isn't going to work, so you might as well just quit wasting my time and yours and get the hell out of my bakery before I call the cops and have them remove you. And trust me," I glared, "I'd love nothing more than to do just that. I'm willing to do *anything* to help Derrick build a case against you for full custody if you don't get your shit together."

At that, all of the color drained from her face and her body went lax, sliding off the countertop until her heels hit the floor.

"Uh, everything okay here?" I turned to see Noah standing a few feet away, his body drawn tight like he was ready to pounce if need be.

"Hey!" I smiled, coming around the bar to give him a hug. "What are you doing here?"

"Harlow had a craving for cookies and when I offered to bake them myself, she threatened to dismember me in my sleep." I laughed and one corner of his mouth hooked up, but he didn't quite smile, his eyes sliding back to Layla in concern.

"Everything good?" he asked, looking back at me.

"Yep." I turned to face Layla. "She was just leaving."

Having composed herself after my last well-placed hit,

she glared at me as she hooked her purse over her shoulder. "This isn't over," she warned as she walked past.

"It's so fucking over it's not even funny," I told her. "And if you ever step foot in my bakery again, you won't like what happens." She turned to stomp out, but I wasn't finished. "Oh, and Layla?" I paused until I had her full attention. "You can rest assured that I'll be telling Derrick about this little exchange." I waved my hand around to encompass the room and all the customers sitting in fascinated silence. "Coming into his girlfriend's place of work and threatening her?" I shook my head, giving her a pitying look. "Not smart, honey. *Really* not smart. Especially when your daughter's school got out thirty minutes ago and it's a twenty-minute drive back to Jackson Hole. Wonder how a judge would feel if he knew you made your own child wait outside her school just so you could stir up drama?"

"Probably wouldn't be too pleased," Noah offered, throwing an arm around my shoulders in a show of solidarity.

"No one asked you!" she bit out.

"You're still standing here," I said in warning as I reached to pull my phone from my apron pocket. Before I even got it all the way out she was scuttling out the door faster than a woman in heels that high should be able to move.

"You sure you're cool?" Noah asked once she was gone.

I let out a long sigh and looked up at him. "Yeah, I'm good. She doesn't get to me. I just *really* can't stand that woman."

He chuckled. "Think the feelings mutual, sweetheart. And who knew you had it in you to be a badass?" He gave me a light jab in my shoulder. "I'm seriously impressed, although I have to say, I don't think I'm okay with you and Harlow playing together anymore. She's bad enough as it is."

I shot a wink at him as I walked back behind the counter. "Where do you think I learned it?"

"Damn it! I knew she'd corrupt all the good ones! We need an exorcism, STAT!" I laughed as I boxed up a dozen cookies for him to take to Harlow. "Now, you know you're gonna need to call your man and fill him in on everything that just happened, right? If he hears it from someone else, his head's liable to explode."

"Yeah, I know. I'll call him."

"Good. And Harlow wants you guys over for dinner—" I looked at him with panic etched across my face before he could even finish that sentence. Luckily he held up his hands and exclaimed, "Don't worry. I'm picking up take-out from the Moose."

I breathed a sigh of relief. "In that case, we'll see you tonight." I handed him the box and he gave me a twenty and a kiss on the cheek before heading out. Now to call my overprotective, somewhat moody boyfriend and tell him I'd just had a run-in with his ex-wife from Hell.

What fun.

21

DERRICK

"KEEP STARING LIKE that and you're gonna get her pregnant just by looking at her."

I choked on the sip of beer I'd just taken and turned to glare at Noah, the bastard. I wiped my mouth with the back of my hand and elbowed him in his gut, taking pleasure in how he hunched over and groaned in pain. Harlow and Chloe both looked at us from across the deck. I smiled and waved like it was nothing until they turned their attention back to the baby in Chloe's arms.

"Will you shut the fuck up?" I whisper-yelled.

"Just stating the obvious, man," he grunted, still out of breath from my well-placed elbow to his ribs. "You're looking at her like she's a steak and you haven't eaten in a goddamned week."

There was no denying that. I wasn't sure exactly when it happened, but Chloe had suddenly become something I obsessed about on a regular basis. When we weren't together all I could think about was her. When we were, I couldn't keep my damned hands off her. I was like a junkie needing a fix. I'd gone from anti-commitment to wanting her within my grasp constantly in the blink of an eye. If you had told me months ago I'd actually *enjoy* being so twisted up about a woman, I'd have laughed in your lying face.

But that was then. And as I looked at Chloe holding Lucy, Noah and Harlow's new baby girl, there was no fear, no dread tying my stomach into knots. I didn't worry about the *what-ifs*. I was just happy. Really fucking happy.

And damn she looked good holding that baby.

"She tell you about what went down with Layla at the bakery today?" Noah asked, pulling me out of my own head.

"Yeah," I sighed. "I don't know what the hell I'm going to do about that woman." Anxiety clawed at my insides whenever I thought about my daughter. I'd give anything to have Eliza with me constantly, but I just didn't have what I needed to take to a judge in order to strip Layla of her rights. At least not yet. But the wait felt like it was slowly killing me.

"Man, you should have seen your girl," he tilted his chin toward Chloe, appreciation heavy in this voice. "Didn't know she had that kind of spunk in her. Even *I* was a little scared of her. Sweet, shy Chloe's got some claws on her, brother. And they're sharp as hell. I'm pretty sure Satan's Mistress is still feeling the sting of them."

I wasn't going to lie, after Chloe told me what had

happened, and the boiling rage that turned my vision red finally subsided, I'd gotten hard as a rock visualizing my little sunshine going toe to toe with the she-devil. Hell, I was getting hard now just thinking about it.

"Says good things she'd defend you and your girl like that," he continued. "Woman like that, well, I'd say she's worth keeping around for the long-haul. But that's just me," he shrugged like he thought he was being smooth and I didn't have a clue what he was getting at.

"You aren't telling anything I haven't already realized, man." I looked at him out of the corner of my eye, one side of my mouth hitching up in a grin.

He chuckled. "So you managed to pull your head out of your ass?"

"Yep."

"Thank Christ," he sighed and patted me on the shoulder. "Harlow will be pleased. Now she won't have to shank you in your sleep."

Chloe

I LET OUT a yawn as I walked into Derrick's house, dropping my purse and overnight bag on the couch as I passed. "Lucy's adorable," I smiled through my exhaustion as I thought about the tiny baby I'd just spent hours hold ing. Was there anything on earth that smelled better than a newborn baby?

"She's a little cutie," Derrick agreed as he closed and locked the front door. "You look like you could fall asleep standing, baby."

I hummed and gave him a sleepy smile as I kicked my sandals off. "I probably could."

He moved closer and wrapped his arms around my waist. "Waking up so fucking early can't be good on you, sunshine."

I nuzzled into his chest, basking in his warmth and the concern lacing through his words. I never thought I'd be where I was right in that moment. I'd dreamed of Derrick holding me just like this countless times, but I didn't actually think it would happen. I always considered him out of my reach. To be honest, sometimes I still had to pinch myself just as a reminder that I wasn't dreaming.

"It comes with the territory, honey. A baker's gotta bake."

His hands ran a soothing pattern up and down my back and he spoke against the top of my head, "Maybe if you didn't hold such a tight rein on your employees, you'd see they're more than capable of picking up a little bit of the slack."

I pulled back to look up at him, his arms wound around my waist so I couldn't move completely away. "What are you talking about?"

"You put too much pressure on yourself, baby."

My brows furrowed. "Well, yeah. It's *my* business. My livelihood. If I don't do it, who will?"

"Did the bakery fall to ruin when you were out sick?"

"No," I answered on a glare, making him smile that devilish smile I loved so much.

"Who do you think took care of everything while you were gone those few days?"

"My staff," I grumbled, reluctant to concede his point.

"I know you want to be in control." He reached up with one hand and tucked a strand of hair behind my ear. "I'm not saying you need to let things go completely, but maybe work out a schedule where you're not the *only* one going in at the butt-crack of dawn to prep and bake for the day. I have no doubt your guys would be willing to take on the extra work. They're pastry chefs after all, isn't that what they like to do?"

I opened my mouth to argue but my mind blanked. There wasn't a single thing I could say that he wouldn't be able to rebuff, easily. Because the fact was, he was right.

"I see I'm getting through," he chuckled and I smacked him in the shoulder.

"No need to gloat about it."

"Ah, but there is. You see, if you lighten your load and share some of the early morning hours, I won't have to feel so guilty for keeping you up all night long."

The glower I pasted on my face contradicted the rush of moisture I felt between my legs. *God, he was hot.* "Someone's feeling cocky."

His mouth came down on mine. "And in a few minutes, you will be too."

MY HANDS SQUEEZED the slats of the headboard so tightly my knuckles grew white. I moaned in ecstasy as I threw my head back. I couldn't remember sex ever being so good before.

"That's it, sunshine," Derrick grunted as he pounded into me from behind, one of his hands leaving my hip in order to wrap my hair around his fist. "I want to feel you squeezing me."

"Oh, God. Don't stop Derrick. So close. Baby, so close," I groaned, using the headboard as leverage to push myself back on his cock even harder.

"Does my girl need it harder?" he asked after pulling on my hair so I'd straighten up on my knees, giving him the perfect access to my ear and neck.

"Yes. *Yesssss*," I hissed out when he gave my hair another yank, never once losing stride in this thrusts.

"Want to fuck you hard, baby. You want that too?"

"Uh huh."

I cried out at the loss of him when he pulled out, but the sound was cut off when he suddenly flipped me onto my back, spread my legs wide, and shoved back in. *Hard.*

"Hang on," he warned just as he grabbed hold of the headboard like I'd been just seconds ago and began fucking me so hard I could feel him *everywhere*.

"Oh shit! Oh God. Yes, *yes*! Just like that," I cried as I dug my nails into his shoulders. I could feel my release building, building, building, threatening to crash over me and pull me under.

"*Fuck*," he ground out between clenched teeth. "So fucking beautiful. Christ, sunshine, the way you take my cock… goddamned *perfect*."

My hold slipped on his sweat-dampened skin and I lost purchase of his shoulders, raking my nails on his chest as he continued to thrust, driving me closer to insanity with each one. He must have loved the bite of pain, because he lost all control, his whole body moving as he powered in and out, fucking me like a madman.

"Need you to come," he panted, his hazel eyes a shade darker than normal as he stared down at me.

"I'm close," I gasped. "So fucking close."

"Get there, baby."

"Almost," I whimpered.

"Get there," he pulled almost all the way out before slamming back, "*now*!"

That was all it took. I fell over, yelling his name as the most intense, most powerful, most consuming orgasm I'd ever experienced washed over me. It seemed to last forever. My back arched, my eyes screwed shut, and all I could do was hold on as pleasure rocked through my entire body, clamping my walls down on his cock so hard I was sure it had to have hurt.

"Holy shit," he groaned, his hips pumping one last time

before he buried himself deep and emptied inside me. *"Fuck fuck fuck!* Unh. Oh God!"

Every twitch, every jerk of his erection sent tremors through me until we both collapsed in a panting, sweaty heap onto the mattress.

I had no clue how long we lay there in silence, nothing but the sounds of our short, choppy breathes filling the room, but it wasn't until we'd managed to slow both our heart rates down that he pushed up on his forearms and looked down at me, his eyes warm with something unfamiliar, something I'd never seen in them before as he smiled.

"Next weekend I have Eliza, I want you here with us," he stated matter-of-factly.

My eyes went wide for a moment before I laughed. "Derrick, I think sex might have melted your brain."

He stared in silence for several seconds, just long enough to make me squirm with discomfort, which only brought attention to the fact that he was still inside me. "Derrick?" I asked, uncertainty shrouding me voice.

"I want her to know about us," he said softly.

"You're serious?"

"Dead serious, sunshine." He leaned down and ran his nose along mine. "I told you, this is real. *We're* real. I want her to know you're in my life as something other than just a friend."

"You don't…" I swallowed audibly against the emotion building in my throat. "You don't think it's too soon?"

God, his smile was going to be the death of me. No man

should be allowed to have *that* brilliant of a smile. "Not at all. Besides, she'll be fucking beside herself with excitement."

I giggled. "Yeah. She does kind of like me, doesn't she?"

"I think it's safe to say she more than *likes* you, sunshine."

"I more than like her too," I whispered. My chest squeezed as the words I so desperately wanted to say fought to be released. I knew it was too soon, I knew it would more than likely freak him out, but I couldn't hold them in. I needed him to know how I felt.

"I more than like you too." Okay, so maybe it wasn't the most eloquent way to tell a man you loved him, but I'd kind-of-sort-of chickened out last minute.

He laughed before releasing a sarcastic breath. "Well thank God for that, because I'd hate to tell you I love you and not have you say it back."

I froze and I swear to God, my brain malfunctioned just then. "What?"

His lips brushed against mine softly. "I," *brush*, "love," *brush*, "you."

"Like a... *friend*?" I dragged out, desperately needing confirmation that I hadn't stumbled into some sort of alternate reality where down was up, left was right, and love meant something *totally* different.

"*No...*" One of his brows quirked up. "Like the woman I want to move into my house sometime in the near future so I never have to sleep without her next to me again." I gasped, but he kept going. "Like the woman I see eventually wearing my ring, carrying my last name, and if she's willing, hopefully someday my babies."

"Bab*ies*?" I asked on a sniffle as tears broke free and began making tracks into my hair. "Like more than one?"

"Well how many are you thinking you want, sunshine? I mean, I already have one. Are we talking a football team's worth here? Because I don't know if I have that kind of strength."

I laughed through the tears and wrapped my arms around his neck, pulling him to me. "I was thinking three," I whispered in his ear. "But like you said, we already have one, so I'd be happy with two more."

His head shot up, hazel eyes intense as he stared at me. "*We?*"

I wasn't sure if I was stepping over the boundaries, but he had to know the full truth. "I love your little girl, Derrick. I know I'm not her mother, and I'd never want to try and replace Layla if that wasn't what Eliza wanted. But she's special to me. I want to give her what she needs. I want to be there for her just like I would any child I gave birth to."

"God, you're amazing," he breathed.

"Now, that being said," I continued. "I hate Layla with a fiery passion and even though I hope she gets her shit together for Eliza's sake, I'll still want to throat-punch her on a regular basis. But for you and Eliza's sake, I'll refrain."

"Big of you," he laughed."

I shrugged with a smile. "I thought so."

He kissed me hard, every ounce of his love for me

pouring through that one kiss until he finally pulled back, leaving me breathless as he began to grow hard inside me.

"Again?" I asked with wide eyes.

"Depends?"

"On what?"

"Well," he moved forward just an inch, and it was enough to make me hot all over again. "You haven't *technically* said you love me back."

"I haven't?" I groaned, lifting my hips to try and get some friction going.

He pulled out. "Nope."

"Silly me. Derrick?"

"Yeah, sunshine?"

"I've been in love with you since you moved to Pembrooke, and I never stopped."

Another breathtaking smile. "That'll work."

Oh yes it would.

22

CHLOE

*A*s I PACED the length of Derrick's living room for about the thousandth time, nervously chewing on my thumbnail while I waited, I thought back to the conversation we'd had earlier that morning over breakfast.

"Baby," Derrick's voice shook me out of my thoughts, pulling me back into the present. "You have to relax. You're gonna give yourself an ulcer if you keep worrying so much."

"I can't help it!" I cried, throwing my hands in the air before letting them fall back onto the counter. "I'm freaking out! What if she hates the idea of us being together? What if she thinks I'm trying to take you away from her or something, and she ends up hating me?"

He chuckled and I kind of wanted to punch him. "That's not gonna happen, sunshine."

"But what if it does?!"

"It won't," he replied adamantly.

It did nothing to sooth my frayed nerves. "I think we should wait," I spit out quickly.

He stared at me, a blank expression on his face before going back to the pancakes I'd made us. He shoveled a bite into his mouth, chewed, then swallowed and stated plainly, "No."

"No? What do you mean, no?"

"I mean no. We aren't waiting. We're telling her today once I get her home, and you're going to see all this worrying was for nothing. And I, being the gentleman that I am, won't say 'I told you so.'"

"Ugh!" I shouted. "You're being unreasonable!"

He stood from his stool at the island and carried his plate to the sink, actually taking the time to rinse it and put it in the dishwasher. That almost made me hot enough to forget what I was stressing about and jump him right there in his kitchen.

He leaned against the counter, thick arms crossed over his wide chest, and regarded me with a somewhat bored look on his face. "Okay, I can see there's no talking you off this ledge you've put yourself on, so I'll do you a favor." I actually breathed a sigh of relief, thinking he'd come around to seeing my side of things. That was, until he spoke again. "I'll tell her myself on the way here. That way, when we get back, it'll all be done and you'll see how great she takes the news."

"That's not a favor!" I stomped my foot. I found myself doing a lot of that over the nearly two weeks we'd been dating. God, that man could frustrate the hell out of me. Good thing for him he was so good looking.

He pushed off the counter and headed my way. "Well, that's the best I got baby." He planted a kiss on my forehead and *grabbed his keys. "Now, I gotta go get my little girl. We'll be back in about an hour, think you can get a hold of yourself by then?"*

My answer was to flip him off. He laughed and gave me a peck on the lips before moving away, calling, "Love you too, sunshine," over his shoulder just before the front door closed.

The sound of Derrick's truck rumbling up the drive yanked me back to reality. It was do-or-die time. And don't ask me why I was approaching the situation like a fighter about to climb into the cage, there was nothing about my thought process at that moment that was rational.

Sucking in a deep breath, I forced my feet to move toward the front door. I stepped out into the front stoop and crossed my arms over my chest, giving the truck and its occupants a tiny, unsure smile. Seconds later, the passenger door was thrown open and Eliza jumped out and barreled toward me.

"Miss Chloe!" she shrieked, only coming to a stop once she's plowed into me, nearly taking me off my feet, and wrapped her arms around my waist. "Daddy told me you're his girlfriend!" she exclaimed, leaning her head back to look up at me with happy, shining hazel eyes. "Does that mean you're gonna get married? Oh! Can I be your junior bridesmaid?! I'm too big to be a flower girl, and Lilly said she was a junior bridesmaid in her cousins wedding and it was *so cool*! She got to wear a dress kinda like the rest of the bridesmaids and got to stand up there with the rest of them and everything! When you and Daddy get married I want to do that! Can I, *pleeeeease*?"

I lifted my head, eyes wide as I glanced at a smirking Derrick as he carried Eliza's bag to the house.

I looked back down at Eliza and finally returned her hug. "Uh, sure…" I answered hesitantly. "If we ever get married, you can totally be a junior bridesmaid."

She squealed in delight and pulled away to do a little happy dance that made me laugh. "So you're happy about it?"

"*Totally!*" she yelled. "You're the coolest, and you make Daddy smile like, *all the time*. And now I'll have someone who I can do stuff with like, give pedicures and watch all those movies Dad complains about because he says they're too girly. And you can teach me how to bake!"

Yep, I was pretty sure my heart just exploded. I blinked rapidly, unwilling to turn into one of those weepy women who cried every single time they felt happy about something.

"We'll do all those things," I said in a soft voice, pulling her in for another hug. "And just for the record, I totally think you're the coolest, too."

She pulled back and graced me with a smile that made me love her even more. "I know. I'm just like my dad." With a wink, she ran into the house.

"Don't say it," I warned to Derrick who'd stood there, watching our entire interaction with one hand casually in his pocket.

He shrugged innocently. "Didn't say anything, sunshine."

"You said you wouldn't say it."

"And I haven't." His smirk turned into a full blown grin, and I knew he was fighting to hold it back.

"It's written all over your face, Derrick, you *want* to say it."

"I have no clue what you're talking about."

"Oh please! Your eyes are totally screaming, '*I told you so.*'"

"Yeah, well, that doesn't count."

"Does too!"

Pulling his hand out of his pocket he wrapped it around me and pulled me in for a quick kiss. "Are we really standing here arguing over stupid bullshit? My daughter is psyched and thinks *you're the coolest*. Let's celebrate that."

I melted into him. "You're right."

Another kiss, then he smirked. "Told you so."

"Asshole!"

<hr />

THE WEEKEND HAD BEEN great so far. Eliza and I had painted each other's nails. I taught her how to French braid. We went to Ethan's football game Friday night, and took her over to meet Lucy during the day on Saturday. Other than Noah's surprised choke of laughter, there hadn't been any awkwardness when she looked up at the little bundle she'd been holding and asked when Derrick and I would give her a little sister.

We watched a ton of girly movies and gave Derrick shit whenever he started to complain. He wasn't used to being outnumbered so it was fun to mess with him whenever we got the chance.

I'd been in the best mood when I woke Sunday morning, only somewhat dimmed by the fact that Eliza would be going back to her mother's later that day. But I was determined to make the most out of every single second I had with her.

"Chloe?" That was another thing that had changed. Since announcing that her dad and I were dating, she'd taken to calling me just Chloe, dropping the *Miss* all together. I loved that she was comfortable enough with me that there was no need for the formality any longer.

"Yeah?" I looked over to where she stood by the kitchen island, face a mask of concentration as she worked to pipe frosting onto the marble swirl cupcakes we'd baked together.

"Thank you for doing all this stuff with me this weekend."

I put down my own piping bag and turned full toward her. Derrick had been called in to the station unexpectedly earlier that morning, giving Eliza and me a chance for some solid girl time. The kitchen counters were lined with all kinds of sweets that he'd undoubtedly enjoy once he got home.

"Of course, honey. I had a blast with you. I always do."

She moved on to the next cupcake, but I could tell there was something weighing heavily on her mind. When she spoke again, my heart broke into a million pieces.

"I've never had anything like this before. My mom..."

she trailed off and swallowed so hard I could see her throat bob up and down. "She doesn't really do this stuff with me. She says she's always too busy."

"Oh, sweetheart," I said in the most soothing voice I could muster, while inside, my blood boiled, "I'm sure she'd love to paint your nails and stuff if she had the time."

Eliza shrugged, refusing to meet my eyes. "I guess. She's always going out with her friends. Before her and Harold broke up she was always leaving me with my Aunt Lilith or calling Dad to watch me so they could take trips together and stuff. I didn't really like Harold…" another shrug, "…I don't really like Aunt Lilith either. She's always mean to me and doesn't let me come out of my room when I have to stay over there."

My stomach bottomed out and the hairs on the back of my neck stood on end. "Eliza… does your aunt… does she ever hit you?"

"No." My shoulders slumped on a heavy sigh of relief. I don't know what I would have done had she said yes. I'd have told Derrick, most definitely, but murder wasn't totally out of the question, either. "She's just mean. And her and Mom are always saying nasty things about Dad. I don't like it."

I didn't know what to say. There was nothing I could tell her that would make her feel any better about her own mother's neglect, so I did the only thing I could think of. I closed the distance between us and hugged her tightly, holding my breath until her little arms wrapped around me in return.

"It'll be okay, honey," I whispered, praying to God I wasn't lying.

She pulled back and I caught her wiping a tear from her cheek. It killed. I felt my own eyes welling up as I watched her. "Do you think — can you talk to my dad about me living here with him? I want to stay here. I don't want to have to go back. Will you talk to him for me, Chloe? Please?"

At the desperation in her tone, the wide, solemn look in her eyes, I lost the battle to keep my emotions in check. Tears began pouring down my cheeks, unchecked as I dropped to my knees and pulled her to me. I don't know how long we stood there, just holding each other, but I refused to move until she was all cried out, her little body trembling as she cried into my shirt.

"I know your dad wants you here with him, sweetie, and I know he's doing everything in his power to make that happen. But it won't happen overnight. We just need you to be brave for a little while longer, okay? Can you do that for me?"

She nodded against my neck and I never wanted to let her go.

"Just a little while longer," I whispered, but I wasn't sure who I was trying to convince: her or me.

Trying to take her mind off the heavy burden she was carrying, I placed my hands on her upper arms and pushed her back so she could see my face. "Hey, I have an idea. Why don't we pack some of these sweets up and go surprise your dad at work? We can even stop and get him lunch too. I bet he'd love that. What do you think?"

She only nodded, but she did it with a grin. That had to count for something.

Right?

23

DERRICK

*A*s I PULLED my ringing phone from the pocket of my work pants and looked at the screen, the first thought that crossed my mind was *I am not dealing with this shit.* It was bad enough I was at work on a Sunday. A Sunday when I had my daughter, but I'd be damned if I was going to be put in a bad mood on top of that.

It had been two weeks of bliss with Chloe. She'd had a meeting with her employees and was now only going in before sunup three days a week, splitting the days with her other pastry chef. That meant extra hours where I kept her in my bed and under my body.

Pure Heaven.

She eased some of the worry I carried over Eliza. She made me laugh more than I had in years, and she turned me on like no woman ever had before. Being with her was like a balm for my soul. And my daughter was absolutely in love with her and the idea of us being together.

So seeing that particular name flashing on the screen of my phone was a very unwanted interruption to the bubble I'd been living in.

"What do you want, Layla?" I said in place of a typical *hello*. I leaned back in my chair and propped my feet on the desk in front of me. "I'm at work and I don't have time to deal with your shit, so if you're calling to start drama do yourself a favor and hang up now."

Her response of, "I need to see you," put me even further on edge. I could feel the muscle in my jaw ticking.

"You'll see me when you come to pick up Eliza in a few hours."

"I need to see you *now*," she demanded, ever the entitled brat.

"That's not happening. I'm hanging up now."

Just as I pulled the phone from my ear, I heard her frantic voice carrying through the speaker. "It's about custody!"

My hand holding the phone paused. I sucked in a deep breath, holding the air in my lungs as I tried to calm myself before finally releasing it in a slow *whoosh*, dropping my feet to the floor and sitting up straight. "What about custody?" I asked once I'd brought the phone back to my ear.

"Look, I'm already in Pembrooke, okay? Can we please just meet somewhere and talk? It can even be public! I don't care. I just need to talk to you in person about this."

Did I trust Layla? No fucking way in Hell, but I couldn't

tell if the tears in her voice were real or fake, and when it came to my daughter's welfare, I'd made myself completely clear. I wanted to believe that she wasn't callous enough to actually cross me, especially after my threat, where our daughter was concerned. There was still a part of me that wanted to believe that somewhere, deep inside her, she loved Eliza.

It was for those reasons alone that I agreed to meet her.

"Fine. I'm about to take my lunch break. I'll meet you at the Moose in ten, but I swear to God, Layla, if you're fucking with me, that's it. I'm contacting a lawyer and doing what I have to in order to get Eliza away from you."

"I'm not, I swear! I'll meet you in ten minutes. Thank you so much, Derrick."

I disconnected the call feeling unsettled but not exactly sure why, other than being in the same room with Layla gave me hives. I stood from my desk and slipped my phone back in my pocket before heading out of the station.

Might as well get it over with. That way I could finish up my shift and get back home to my girls. That thought put a smile on my face. As I made my way down Main, walking the few blocks it took to get from the station to the Moose, I was determined not to let whatever conversation I was about to have effect my day.

I had too much to look forward to.

Nothing could touch that.

BY THE TIME I pushed through the door of the Moose, our local restaurant/bar/hangout, Layla was already sitting at a table, twirling a glass of water between her palms nervously.

She smiled shyly and slid a glass in front of me as I took a seat across from her. "I got you an iced tea. I remember you always ordered tea when we went out."

For the love of God, I'd probably ordered tea maybe twice in all the years we'd been together. Just went to show how self-involved she was. "You have ten minutes," was my only reply.

"But I thought you said you were on your lunch break."

"I am," I answered flatly. "And while I agreed to talk with you face to face, I'm not too thrilled with the idea of breaking bread with you. I'll get something to eat once we're done here."

Her face got soft, a look I was pretty sure I'd never seen on her before, as she said, "Derrick, don't be ridiculous. Surely a conversation about our daughter would take longer than ten minutes, and I'd hate for you to have to go back to work on an empty stomach because you didn't have time to eat anything."

Before I could pass on her offer, a waitress suddenly appeared at our table. "Hey, there. Are you ready to order or do you need a few more minutes?"

"Nothing for—"

Layla interrupted. "I'll have the Cobb salad, dressing on the side, no bacon, egg or avocado, (basically all the things that made it more than just lettuce) and he'll have the turkey club." She moved her smile from the waitress back to me and my back went stiff.

"What the hell are you playing at?" I asked in a low voice once our server had moved off to place our orders.

Her eyes went wide, the picture of innocence that I didn't buy for a second. "Nothing! I just didn't want you to go hungry. And I remembered the turkey club was your favorite."

"Cut the shit," I hissed. "I don't like tea, the turkey club has *never* been my fucking favorite, and you're not a nice person. So whatever the hell this is," I waved a finger between the two of us, "it's done. Got it? I came because you said you wanted to discuss the custody arrangement we have. That's *all* I'm talking about. Either get on with it or I'm gone."

"Fine," she whispered. Her shoulders slumped as a sad expression moved across her face. "I was just trying to make things more... peaceful between us."

"Time for that was years ago, Layla."

"You're right," she sighed with defeat and looked up at me, one lone tear trailing down her cheek before she brushed it away. "I've made a lot of mistakes, Derrick, I know that now. And if I could go back in time and change things, I swear I would." Her hand came across the table and rested on mine for a moment before I pulled back.

"What's that have to do with custody?"

"You're a great father. And a good man," she continued,

231

still not getting to the topic at hand. "Believe me, I know what I lost and not a day goes by that I don't regret how I treated you. I hate to admit it, but it took seeing you with someone else to realize…" she trailed off and pulled in a lungful of air, more tears fell from her eyes, "that you're the love of my life. I'll do anything to get you back, baby. *Anything*. Please just give us another chance," she ended on a whisper.

I don't know how long I sat there, my mouth hanging open in shock before I was finally able to move, and when I could, I shot to my feet yelling, "You are *un-fucking-believable*! You know that? Jesus Christ! This is an all-time low, Layla, even for you. I'm leaving."

Her eyes darted from me to the door and back again before she stood in a hurry and did something so unexpected, so bewildering, I froze. In the blink of an eye, her arms were wrapped around my neck, her chest plastered to mine, and she'd yanked my head down in a kiss so hard I automatically tasted blood from where my lip cut on my teeth.

After a few seconds, my stupor wore off and I reached up, grabbing her arms with every intension of shoving her away, when I heard a voice speak one word that chilled me to my bones.

"Daddy?"

I spun around to find Eliza standing in the doorway of the Moose, hand-in-hand with Chloe, both of them wearing equal expressions of dismay at the sight of me and Layla kissing.

"Oops," Layla said, a smile in her evil voice. "Looks like your little girlfriend caught us, Derrick."

I rushed over to them both, afraid if I let loose on Layla, they'd somehow manage to escape before I could explain. "It's not what it looked like," I said, desperation laced through my words as I frantically searched Chloe's face for any hint that she believed me. "I swear to God, baby. It's not what you think. I'll explain everything, I promise, but I need you to take Eliza out of here. Can you do that? Just go outside and wait for me. I'll be there in just a minute."

Chloe blinked, her gorgeous green eyes still clouded with disbelief.

"Daddy," Eliza's distressed voice called my attention to her.

"It'll be okay, baby girl, just go outside with Chloe for a minute. I'll be right there. I promise."

I turned back to Chloe to see her nod in agreement. The relief that flooded me with just that one simple nod was so overwhelming I couldn't help myself, I leaned into her and pressed my lips against hers, only to have her pull away and wipe at her mouth.

"Her lipstick," she whispered at my worried expression. "It's still on your face."

"I'm sorry," I said on a ragged whisper.

"Do what you have to do. We'll wait outside. Then we'll talk."

With that, she turned around and led Eliza out of the restaurant. And I looked back at the bane of my existence, hate turning my vision red.

"You," I said in a low, menacing voice as I stalked toward her, "just fucked up. You think you've seen me angry before? That was fucking *nothing* compared to what I feel now." The self-satisfied smile that she'd been wearing slowly fell as she grew pale. "You're fucked, sweetheart. From here on out all communication will be made through lawyers, so I suggest you do whatever you have to in order to hire one, because I'm about to make your life a goddamned nightmare."

Her throat bobbed up and down as she swallowed audibly. "Derrick—"

"Shut up," I gritted out. "Pick up and drop off of Eliza will be at the Sherriff's station from here on out. You're not to set foot on my property, you understand me? If you do, I'll have you arrested. You just used our daughter in your fucking twisted game for the last time. This evening will be the *last* time you ever take her away from me."

"Are you-are you threatening me?"

"That was a fucking promise, sweetheart."

Without another word, I turned and stormed out of the Moose. My eyes frantically scanned the sidewalks outside until they landed on my girls about a yard away, sitting on a wooden bench outside the hardware store.

"You stayed," I breathed as soon as I got close.

"We said we would," Chloe stated flatly, her eyes focused over my shoulder. I looked back to see what had her attention, only to find Layla had just sauntered out of the restaurant and was heading for her car.

I turned back. "Don't look at her, look at me."

Her gaze snapped to mine before lowering down to look at a rattled Eliza, taking my attention with her.

"Hey, baby girl," I said, lowering down to my haunches so we were eye level with one another, trying my best to infuse a smile in my words. "You okay?"

"Are you... are you and Mommy getting back together?"

"No honey, we're not." At my answer she visibly relaxed. "Then why were you kissing her?"

A quick glance back at Chloe showed she had one eyebrow cocked, clearly as eager for my answer as Eliza.

"Your mom did something she shouldn't have and kissed me when I didn't want her to. What you saw was her making a bad choice. We're not getting back together. I'm with Chloe and she makes me really happy, honey."

She nodded seriously. "Good. She makes me happy, too."

"I need to talk to Chloe in private for a second, baby girl," I said as I stood to my full height and pulled my wallet from my back pocket. "There's an ice cream place right there." I pointed to Blizzard Bob's which was just two doors down from where we were and handed her a ten. "We'll be done talking by the time you get back."

"Can I get two scoops?"

I narrowed my eyes at her sudden smile. "You can have *one*."

She let out a huff and hopped off the bench. "Fine. Be right back." Then she was gone. Once I saw her walk safely through the door, I looked back down at Chloe, who still sat on the bench.

"Bribing your daughter with ice cream. That's a new one for you."

I rubbed the back of my neck uncomfortably. "These were extenuating circumstances."

She uncrossed her legs and stood up. "I bet. You know she totally got two scoops, right?"

One corner of my mouth hooked up at her teasing tone. "I have no doubt about that, whatsoever. My girl's got a sweet tooth."

Chloe returned my grin. "Good thing your girlfriend's a baker." With that sentence, I took my first full breath in ten minutes. "She kissed you." She stated matter-of-factly. "You didn't kiss her back."

"Hell no!" I answered vehemently. "I'd stood up to leave and she must have seen you through the window and kissed me. I swear to you, I didn't want it."

"I know," she said softly. "I trust you, and I know how you feel about her. What's more, I know how you feel about *me*."

"I love you," I said instantly.

"And I love you too. But what I don't understand is why you were there with her in the first place."

I collapsed onto the bench, pulling her down with me and settling her in my lap as I explained. "She called and said she wanted to discuss the custody arrangement. My gut told me it was a mistake, but..."

"But you're Eliza's dad and want what's best," she finished, running a hand through my hair.

"Exactly. Before I even showed up, I warned her that if

she was playing me, that was it. I was getting an attorney and taking her to court."

"And what happened?"

A deep frown spread across my face. "She fucking played me. She's so goddamned manipulative that she used our daughter *again*, after I warned her. She lied and made her play, and now I'm done. I don't know if what I have is enough to get full custody of Eliza, but I'm going for it anyway. That woman is poison."

Her fingertips came up and smoothed the furrow in my brow. "Good. Derrick, she told me today she wants to live with you. I can't imagine there's a judge out there who wouldn't listen to that little girl explain what she wanted and why and not see that you're the best choice."

I squeezed my eyes closed and rested my forehead on her shoulder and I inhaled deeply. "I'm sorry you had to see that today."

"Honey, I'm more concerned for you. You're the one that had to *live* through it."

My head shot up and I chuckled as she smiled down at me. "So you're not mad at me?"

Her face scrunched up adorably as she pretended to give it some thought. "Nah, I'm not mad at you. As long as it never happens again, we're good."

"It won't," I replied.

"Then we're good." She reached up and brushed her fingers along my jaw. "I trust you, Derrick. I mean it. And I love you. I know you wouldn't cheat on me. I'm just sorry you were stuck in that position."

"God, I love you," I breathed, leaning in to give her a kiss.

She pulled back, causing me to frown.

"I'll kiss you as much as you want, honey. *After* you scrub your mouth, preferably with industrial strength soap."

24

DERRICK

*C*HLOE LAID CURLED against me, her face pressed in the crook of my neck as I wrapped my arm around her, trying to let her soft, even breaths lull me to sleep.

Unfortunately, it wasn't working. Three days had passed since the latest stunt with Layla, and the anxiety I felt at my daughter being stuck in that house with her clawed at my gut so painfully I actually felt sick.

It was well after two in the morning and I still couldn't get my mind to calm down enough that my exhausted body could relax enough to sleep. I kept replaying the conversation I'd had with my attorney over and over again, trying to think of *something* that would help my case.

"Mr. Anderson," my newly hired attorney Walter Lancaster started, rubbing a hand along his jaw, "I understand your concerns, believe me. And I'm not telling you what you want is

impossible. I'm just saying that it's going to be an uphill battle. While I have no doubt that everything you've told me about your ex-wife is true, it's harder to prove a person is manipulative to the point that's it's harmful to a child's wellbeing. We could have your daughter testify that—"

I spoke up, interrupting him mid-sentence. "I'm not putting Eliza through that. I won't do it. She's been through enough just living in that house with that woman. I can't make her get up there in front of, not only a judge, but her own mother as well. Isn't it enough that she wants *to live with me? Won't the judge take that into consideration?"*

I left Walter's office feeling even more disheartened than I had when I walked in. I felt like I was failing my girl and there wasn't a goddamned thing I could do about it. I'd never felt more helpless in my entire life. After the conversation with Walter, I'd been so low that nothing could pull me out of it, not even the sunshine in Chloe's smile.

But like the good woman she was, she hadn't pushed, trying to cheer me up when she knew it was impossible. She just let me stew in silence, offering silent comfort in the form of her touch, her kiss. I couldn't have possibly loved her more.

The ceiling fan spun in lazy circles, the moonlight shining through the trees and into the room created wild patterns along the walls that I'd spent the last two hours tracing with my eyes, uselessly searching for sleep.

Chloe's body shifted next to me as she dreamed, curling tighter against me, the feel of her warm skin like the balm it always was. I turned to my side and wrapped both arms tight around her, holding her to me. I don't know how long I laid there, listening to her inhale and exhale, like a soft melody before the loud ringing of my cellphone cut through the serene quiet.

All of my senses went on high alert as I hit the lamp and snatched my phone off the nightstand. A phone call that late at night was never a good thing. I felt Chloe come awake beside me as Eliza's name flashed across the screen, making the hairs on the back of my neck stand on end.

"Baby girl?" I answered.

"Daddy?" I could hear the tears in her voice with just that one word and everything inside me tensed as I shot up and threw my legs over the side of the bed.

"What's wrong, honey?"

"I-I can't find Mom."

"What do you mean you can't find your mom?" I heard Chloe gasp at my words, but I was already off the bed, snatching my clothes from the floor.

"I w-woke up…" she hiccupped on a sob, "'cause I had a nightmare. B-but she's n-not here. I looked everywhere, Daddy. Her car's not in the d-driveway. I'm scared."

I tried to make my voice as calm as possible, even though, on the inside, I wanted to find Layla and wring her skinny neck until her head popped. "It's okay, baby girl. Don't be scared. I'm leaving right now, okay? I'll be there as soon as I can. Don't worry. I'm coming."

"O-okay." Another hiccup.

"Hold on so I can get dressed, all right? And I'll stay on the phone with you the whole time."

"All right, Daddy."

I hit mute and threw the phone on the bed so I could yank my clothes on. Chloe was already up and heading for the dresser. "I'm going with you," she insisted.

"No, baby. You stay here."

"Like hell I am!"

"Listen. I don't have time to argue, sunshine. I need you to stay here. That stupid bitch left my daughter home by herself in the middle of the goddamned night, and she had a nightmare. If Layla so much as shows her face when I get there, it's gonna be ugly. You being with me will just make it worse. Please, just stay here."

Her body slumped in defeat, but I knew she wouldn't fight me. She wanted me to get to Eliza as much as I did.

"Okay, just… hurry. Get to her fast and get her home."

I pulled her against me slamming my lips to hers in a fast, hard kiss. "I will, baby. And once I get her here, she's never leaving."

Her green eyes were wide on her pale, worried face. "Promise?"

"Swear."

I turned on my heels, snatched the phone from the bed, and turned off mute, putting it to my ear so I could talk to my girl while I hurried to her so she wouldn't be scared.

THE TWENTY-MINUTE DRIVE took me less than fifteen. Pulling into Layla's drive, I saw her car was still gone, the garage door open, leaving Eliza even more exposed in the middle of the night with no fucking one there to protect her.

"Okay, honey. I just pulled up," I told her as I turned off my truck and shoved the door open in the blink of an eye. As soon as I hit the steps, the front door was thrown open and Eliza's arms were wrapped around me in a death grip.

"It's all right," I soothed, running a hand down her hair. "Come on, let's get you packed up, okay?"

"Yeah." She sniffled and pulled away, heading back into the house. I followed, and what I saw when I crossed the threshold had my vision going red.

"Baby girl."

Eliza stopped and turned to me. I pointed at the two empty wine bottles sitting on the coffee table. "Are those old?"

She shook her head, another tear falling down her cheek. "Nuh uh. Mom was drinking them before I went to bed. Her words started sounding funny and she got really mad about something, yelling and not making sense, so I went to bed without giving her a kiss goodnight."

That bitch. That fucking goddamned bitch!

She got drunk and belligerent, then got behind the wheel of a fucking *car*, and abandoned our daughter in the middle of the night. There wasn't a doubt in my mind that when I called Walter in a few hours, I'd have everything I needed to strip that bitch of custody completely. She was fucked.

"Come on, sweetheart. We're packing you up."

When we got to her room, she pulled a small suitcase out of her closet and started putting in a few articles of clothing.

"Do you have any more bags, Eliza?"

"Uh, yeah. Why?"

"Get them."

She went back into her closet to retrieve more bags as I started scooping up everything in her dresser and dumping it into the open one on her bed. "Daddy, what are you doing?"

"Everything, Eliza. I want you to pack all of your clothes. You're not coming back here, you understand me?"

Her eyes widened as she whispered, "Really?"

"Yes. I want you to put everything you want with you into those bags. You're moving in with me, starting tonight."

"Okay!" she shouted, sounding excited for the first time tonight since she called me, scared and in tears, before frantically throwing anything she could reach into her bags. We were finished and in my truck about forty-five minutes later. It was amazing what a little girl *insisted* she needed just to function. Her bags were stuffed full, and Layla hadn't shown her face in the time I cleared Eliza's room out.

Not that it would have mattered.

"You really mean it, Dad? I'm really gonna live with you

all the time now?" she asked once we were on the road, heading back to my house, back to Chloe.

"I mean it, baby girl."

She was silent for a few seconds. "Do you... do you think Chloe will move in with us, too?"

I looked at her out of the corner of my eye. "You want her to?"

"Yeah," she answered softly.

I gave that some thought, then landed on what was probably the most brilliant idea in the world. "Then you should tell her that." Because there was no way in hell my woman could say no to my girl. It was a foolproof plan. "And really sell it, baby girl. Maybe throw in a few tears, too."

She giggled as I reached for my cell, resting in a cup holder in the center console to call Chloe and tell her we were on our way. It rang until finally going to voicemail. Maybe she'd fallen back to sleep. Or maybe she was in the shower. No telling.

We were about five minutes from the house when my phone rang. I answered without taking my eyes off the road, thinking it was Chloe calling me back.

"Hey, baby. We'll be there in five."

"Anderson," the familiar *male* voice spoke. I pulled it away from my ear long enough to look at the screen. *Why the fuck was someone from the station calling me?*

"Carlson?" I asked, recognizing the young deputy's voice.

"Man, I hate to have to tell you this, but I need you to get to St. Vincent's as soon as you can."

"The hospital?" Everything inside me grew frigid. "Why do I need to get to the hospital, Carlson?

Then he said the two words that had the power to bring my entire world crashing down around me.

"It's Chloe."

25

CHLOE

I FELT HELPLESS. I was so concerned for Eliza, for Derrick, but I didn't want to call and distract him from taking care of his daughter. I don't know how long I wandered through the house, restless, knowing there wasn't a chance in hell I'd be able to go back to sleep, not that I wanted to. I wanted to be awake when they got home. I'd been a mess of nerves all day long knowing Derrick was meeting with a new attorney, then his subsequent lapse into silence at the not-so-helpful news he got from the meeting, and that phone call had done nothing but twist my already unsettled stomach into knots.

If something happened to Eliza because of *that woman*, I didn't know what the hell I was going to do. All I could hope was that this latest stunt would be the straw that broke the camel's back. I wanted Derrick to have his little girl, and I wanted Eliza to live in in an environment that would make her *happy*.

I just hated that it took something like this to reach that point.

I'd just decided to start a pot of coffee for when Derrick returned, knowing he'd need it, and that he probably wouldn't be able to sleep any more than I could, when my phone went off. The chime was the notification I set up for the security system I'd had installed in the bakery a few years back.

"What the hell?" I muttered to myself before the phone starting ringing.

"Hello?"

"Yes, Miss Delaney? This is Daniel with Security Solutions. It appears the sensor for the front window to your store has gone off. Are you on the premises?"

I propped the phone between my ear and shoulder, thankful I'd gotten dressed after Derrick's call from Eliza. "No, but I'm on my way there now."

"Okay. We're alerting the authorities now."

"Thank you, I'll meet them there." I disconnected the call and was out the door in no time.

Derrick's house was only a few minutes from the bakery, and considering I was the first call, I knew I'd make it there before the Sherriff's department, and seeing as there were no cruisers in front of Sinful Sweets when I pulled up, I was right.

"Shit," I gasped as I parked along the street, climbed out of my car and stepped onto the sidewalk right in front of the bakery. The plate glass windows that made up my entire storefront had all been smashed out.

With my hand over my mouth in complete shock, I made my way to the front door, the glass also broken into a million pieces, and stepped inside, in complete disbelief by what I saw.

Everything was destroyed. The pastry displays, the cake stands that decorated the wooden bar top. Stools were overturned, chairs looked like they'd been picked up and smashed against the walls. Unbelievable damage done in such a short amount of time. My dream, my livelihood, looked like a tornado had gone through it. Tears clogged my throat as I took in the damage. I couldn't believe that someone had done something so heartless, so cruel.

I turned to make my way back outside, pulling my phone from my pocket to inform the police about the break in myself as my mind spun in a million different directions.

Who could have done such a thing?

Why did they target my bakery?

Or was it something personal against me?

Then I remembered.

I dialed 911 on my phone and brought it to my ear as I ran out of the bakery. "911, what's your emergency?"

I was only a few feet away from my car, mouth opened to answer, when the squealing of tires and sudden flash of headlights took me by surprise. The last thing I remembered were the lights so close they blinded me before pain smashed into my body with a force so strong I wasn't sure I'd survive it.

Then everything went black.

Derrick

"DADDY, WHAT'S HAPPENING?"

"I don't know, sweetheart," I answered honestly as the blood roared through my ears. I jerked the wheel, causing my tires to squeal as I pulled into the hospital parking lot. "Just stay close, okay?"

We got out of the truck and, hand in hand, ran through the emergency room doors. There was no one at the front desk, so, not having a clue where I was going, I just started running, Eliza doing the best she could to keep up.

"Derrick!"

I spun around to find Harlow and Noah standing in the doorway of a waiting room, equal expressions of concern marring their faces. "What's happening?" I demanded to know. I needed answers fast. My heart was beating against my breastbone so hard my chest ached. "Where is she? What happened?" I fired off at a rapid pace.

"Calm down, brother. Just calm down," Noah soothed, placing his hand on my shoulder to try to calm me down. But that wouldn't be possible until I had some fucking answers. I couldn't lose her. I just... *couldn't.*

"What happened?" I repeated, the calmness of my voice was a complete surprise considering how frantic I felt.

"We don't know everything," Harlow spoke up. "I'm listed as her emergency contact so we got the call and woke Ethan up to watch Lucy then we rushed right over. All we know is there was some sort of car accident. They rushed her back as soon as they got in. We haven't even seen her."

Car accident. What the hell? Eliza squeezed my hand tight, her little body plastering itself to my side. "Why the hell was she even driving?"

"Anderson."

My head jerked around to find Carlson standing there. "Tell me what's going on."

His eyes moved from me to Eliza and back again. "Think we can talk somewhere a little more private?"

Catching his meaning, I squatted down, eye to eye with my scared daughter. "Honey, I need you to stay here with Harlow and Noah for a few minutes, okay?"

Her bottom lip trembled. "I don't want to leave you."

"Please, baby girl. Just stay with them, okay? It'll only be a few minutes, I promise."

"Hey Eliza," Harlow spoke, keeping her voice light. "I have Netflix on my phone. Why don't we watch a movie while we wait?" I could tell she didn't want to, but she nodded her head and moved to her anyway.

Carlson and I moved out of the waiting room and into the hall, moving down and away from the door.

"What the fuck happened?"

"We don't have all the details yet, but we know that the security system to her bakery went off earlier this morning. The company called her then called it in to us. We were in route but she beat us there, not by much, couldn't have been more than two minutes, but when we were pulling up, we saw her crossing the street. We spotted another car driving erratically and it hit her before she had a chance to move out of the way."

"Are you fucking kidding me?!" I bellowed, raking my hands through my hair. I began to pace as Carlson continued recounted what had happened.

"We don't think the car intentionally hit her. From the looks of it, it tried to swerve at the last second, but it was too late. The driver jerking the wheel last minute is probably the only thing that saved Chloe. She came to in the back of the ambulance. She was in severe pain, and there was some damage done, but she was awake, man. That's the good news."

"Good news? That's the fucking *good news*? HOW COULD IT GET ANY WORSE!" I yelled at the top of my lungs.

Carlson rubbed the back of his neck, pulling in a deep breath. "Derrick, after the car swerved, it plowed straight into a light pole so the driver wasn't able to get away."

"Well that's a silver-fucking lining," I growled. "Where's that bastard now? Tell me you've got him in custody, or so help me God—"

"We have *her* in custody." He paused. "Derrick, it was your ex-wife."

My entire world stopped.

"What?" I didn't even recognize the scary cadence of my own voice.

"We don't have the security footage yet, but I'm willing to bet she was the one that trashed your girl's place, too."

"This has to be a nightmare," I mumbled more to myself than to Carlson as I started pacing once again. "A seriously fucked-up nightmare."

Then I remembered something, the knowledge hitting me like I goddamned sledgehammer. "You get her to blow?"

He shook his head. "She was too out of it. We had to bring her in too, but we had the doctor do a blood test when she got here. Man, she was more than twice the legal limit. So fucking much it had to have been straight booze running through her veins."

I'd never hit a woman in my life. God knows, dealing with Layla as long as I had, she'd test the patience of a saint, but I never laid my hands on her. But right then I wanted nothing more than to find her and choke the life out of her.

Carlson spoke up again. "Just thought you should know, she's been asking for you since she got here."

"Chloe?"

His face grew grim as he shook his head. "No."

I couldn't remember a time in my life where I'd ever felt more rage, more inescapable fury than I felt right then. I was downright murderous. "You keep that fucking bitch away from me. You understand?" I warned Carlson. "I don't give a fuck who she's asking for or what she wants. If I get anywhere near her right now, one of you is gonna have to lock me up, because I'll kill the bitch."

Carlson nodded. "I get you, brother. And I don't blame you one fucking bit. That woman is certifiable."

"Tell me something I don't know. And keep a deputy outside her door. The minute the doctor clears her I want her ass behind bars. Got me?"

"I got you, man."

"Derrick?" I turned to find Noah standing next to an older man in a white doctor's coat, standing near the waiting room door. Turning on my heels, I started in their direction at a fast clip, desperate to know what the hell was going on with Chloe.

Please God, please, just let her be all right. I'll do anything. Just don't take her away from me.

"How is she?" I asked in a panicked tone as soon as I reached them. "Is she all right?"

"All I can say is Miss Delaney is a very lucky woman."

My lungs expanded with that one sentence and it felt like it was the first real breath I'd taken in hours.

26

CHLOE

HE FIRST THING I thought when I woke up was "Sweet mother of Hell, everything hurts." God, even my hair and toenails ached.

I let out a groan as my eyelids fluttered open, only to slam back shut when the bright lights assaulted me and made my already pounding head feel like it was going to split in two.

"How are you feeling?"

I recognized the soft voice as Harlow's.

"Can you—" I stopped talking, not recognizing the rough, gravelly voice as my own. I cleared my throat, which only made it burn worse, and tried again. "Can you turn off the light?"

A faint *click* sounded through the room and everything grew dark behind my eyelids. When I cracked them open again the only light filtering in was from the sunlight coming through the cracks in the blinds.

"Where am I?" I asked, voice still unrecognizable.

Harlow appeared above me, looking exhausted and rumpled. "You're in the hospital. How do you feel?"

"Like I was hit by a truck," I groaned.

"Well, close enough. It was a Mercedes, but tomato, toe-mah-to."

I let out a small laugh only to have agonizing pain slice through me like a dull, serrated knife.

"Oh God, don't make me laugh. It hurts so bad. Why the hell does it hurt so bad?"

"You have a concussion, several cracked ribs, and a broken wrist."

"That's all?" I asked as I hit the button to raise the bed, elevating me just enough so I could see the room around me. "It feels a thousand times worse than that."

Harlow sat on the side of the hospital bed down by my legs. "Well, your body basically looks like one gigantic bruise, and you've got a wicked case of road rash along your left arm, so that's probably a contributing factor.

"Sounds about right," I grunted as I struggled to find a comfortable position. God, my ribs hurt like hell. Even *breathing* caused me pain.

"Silver lining, you're going to look like a bar-brawling badass just as soon as some of the swelling goes down." I knew she was trying to lift my spirits, but the tear that breached her eyelids and made a track down her tired face belied her casual tone.

"Hey," I said softly. "I'm okay, honey."

"I know," she sniffled, wiping across her nose with the

back of her hand, all classy like. "But you scared the hell out of me. Don't ever do that again."

I felt myself smiling despite even my lips hurting. "Deal. I promise never to get hit by another car again."

Her face was still in a pout, but she nodded her head and offered an abrupt, "Thanks."

"Oh God, Derrick's probably freaking out. What time is it?"

"It's a little past noon, and to say he's freaking is an understatement."

"Shit, so he knows I'm here?"

"Are you kidding? He's been here all night! He just left a few minutes ago to get some coffee. I don't think the man's slept in at least twenty-four hours, but he refuses to leave."

"But… what about Eliza? Last time I saw him, he'd been heading to pick her up because Layla just up and left her home by herself in the middle of the night."

"They hadn't even made it back to the house when he got the call you'd been hurt. They came straight here. I just sent her back to my house with Noah a little while ago. She was crashed out in the waiting room. She didn't want to leave, was too worried about you, but Derrick put his foot down and made her go since she was all but dead on her feet."

My head flopped back on the thin, flimsy pillow as I thought about what that poor little girl had endured over the course of just a few hours. I lay there silently for several seconds before the sound of the door opening quietly had me shifting my eyes. Derrick stood with a coffee in his hand as he gently eased the door closed so there wasn't more than a tiny *snick*. Once it was closed, he turned for the bed, only to stop in his tracks at the sight of me watching him.

"You're awake."

I felt the tears begin to form at just the sight of him, and I wasn't sure why. Maybe it was the pain, maybe it was the meds pumping through my system, but something told me it was just *him*, having him close, having him *care* that made me overly emotional. The moment he saw the tears break loose, he rushed to the bed, nearly spilling his coffee on the way before Harlow snatched the cup from his hand and sat it down.

"Baby, what's wrong? Are you hurting? Let me get a nurse."

"No!" I shouted through the pain, grabbing onto his arm with my good hand and holding tight. "No, no nurse. I'm fine. I just…"

He sat alongside me in the bed and pulled me in his arms the best he could to prevent any pain, keeping me safe and secure as I cried into his shirt. He didn't say a word for as long as it took for me to get it all out, just trailed a hand up and down my back in slow, languid patterns.

"Christ, sunshine. I was so fucking scared," he whispered in my ear. "I thought I'd lost you. Never want to go through that again, baby. I'm pretty sure you just shaved a decade off my life."

I sniffled and nuzzled my face closer to his chest, needing his calming presence to ease me. "Derrick?"

"What is it?" he asked quietly, leaning in to brush the tears from my cheeks as those hazel eyes I loved so much stared back at me, full of concern mixed with just a hint of relief.

"I love you," I whispered. "I just love you, and I hate that I put you through this stress. You *and* Eliza. You've already had to deal with so much, now this—"

"Shh." He put a finger over my lips to silence me. "Stop that."

"B-but—"

"No." That one word alone left no room for argument. "I won't listen to you spout anymore bullshit, you hear me? None of this is on you. *None of it*. If anything, it's all my fault. If I hadn't pushed you into a relationship, you never would have been in that psychotic bitch's scope. It's on me. I'm the one that brought her into your life, and look what she did. She fucked with your bakery—"

I gasped. "So it *was* her. When I saw the damage, I guessed it might have been, but I wasn't sure."

"It was. We got the footage from your security cameras. And if that wasn't bad enough, now you're laid up in a hospital bed because of her."

"Wait. What?"

Derrick's eyebrows formed a deep V in confusion as he looked from me to Harlow. "She doesn't know?"

"Know what?" I asked.

"Well, we hadn't really gotten around to that part of the conversation before you walked in."

"What conversation?" I asked, starting to get frustrated at being ignored.

"Shit," Derrick hissed.

"Will someone please tell me what the hell is going on? I'm getting pissed and the only reason I'm not yelling right now is because it *really freaking hurts*. So somebody start talking."

Derrick looked back at me, remorse clouding his eyes. "Baby, Layla's the one that hit you."

My eyes went wide. "Holy shit," I whispered, then yelled, *"Holy shit!"* followed by, "Ow. Ow, ow, ow, ow. Shit that hurts." I hissed in a breath between my teeth and I hugged my battered ribs.

Derrick was over me in a flash, hovering over me, his expression revealing just how much he hated to see me in pain. "Baby, try to relax. What can I do?"

"I'm okay, I'm okay," I panted, trying slow breaths through the pain. Once I had it under control I looked back up at him. "That crazy bitch tried to kill me?"

"Well, according to her story, the hit was just an accident. She smashed the hell out of your place, then freaked when she saw you come in. She took off, but seeing she was drunk as fuck, she lost control of the car, hit you, then smashed into a light pole. She's looking at felony vandalism and aggravated DUI, and that's only her criminal charges. That doesn't even count what I'm gonna do to her in family court."

"Holy shit," I repeated again. "You're going to rake her ass over the coals."

"Abso-fucking-lutely. I've already talked to Walter. He's pushing an emergency custody hearing through. I'm stripping the bitch of every parental right she has. Then you're going to press charges. With no job, no sugar daddy, and no more child support to cushion her fall, she can't afford to dig herself out of this hole. She's royally fucked."

I asked the one question that had been weighing on my mind during his whole rant. "How's Eliza?"

He let out a whoosh of air and scrubbed his hands over his face. "Scared. Worried about you. I don't think she'd going to feel any better until she can lay eyes on you herself and see you're okay."

"She doesn't…" I trailed off and studied his face. "She doesn't know about Layla, does she?"

"No."

"Okay, good. I don't want her to. She's dealt with enough. All she needs to know is a drunk driver hit me. I don't want her carrying any more on her shoulders than she already does."

Placing his hand at the back of my head, he gently pushed so my cheek was resting against his chest. "Whatever you want, sunshine."

"Thank you."

"I'll just leave you two alone," Harlow spoke up. I felt like a crappy friend, because, until that moment, I'd totally forgotten she was still in the room with us.

"Okay, Low-Low. Thank you for being here."

She came around the side of the bed and kissed the tips of her fingers before placing them on my temple since my position against Derrick didn't allow for much else. "Always, babe. Just get better, okay?"

"I will."

"Good. I'll see you tomorrow." She rounded the bed and leaned in to press a kiss to Derrick's cheek, then slowly left the room.

Neither of us spoke. I simply lay against him, letting the rhythmic beat of his heart soothe me like my own personal lullaby. I don't know how long we stayed like that, and I'd nearly drifted back off to sleep when his voice rumbled through his chest.

"I love you, sunshine. With everything I am."

"I love you too, Derrick. Always will."

And with that, I fell asleep in the sanctuary of my man's arms. Despite the tumultuousness of the past several hours, I drifted with a smile on my face. Not even the aches and pains could keep me down as long as I had him.

27

CHLOE

I LOVED MY parents, I really did.

But I'd discovered a long time ago that I could only really handle them in small doses. It was around the time I entered into adulthood, when they tried to keep my nightly curfew intact.

I wasn't even living with them at the time!

Our relationship flourished when they moved to Arizona to get away from the cold a few years ago. Absence really did make the heart grow fonder... for about a week. Then I was ready to stuff them in their carry-ons and ship them back to Scottsdale.

They'd only been in Pembrooke for a day and I was already fantasizing about duct taping my mother to a chair with her mouth gagged so she couldn't talk.

Currently, she was doing her best to fluff the damned hospital pillow behind my head, trying to do the impossible and make it more than paper thin. She'd been at it for ten minutes.

"Mom."

"I think I got it." She fluffed again, only to have it fall flat once more. "Oh damn. Hold on."

"Mom."

"Just once second." *Fluff, fluff, fluff.*

"Mom."

"You'd think they'd give you something more comfortable. I mean, you're already in pain after all." My head continued to bounce like a bobble head while she attempted to beat the pillow into submission.

"Mom, really. I'm fine."

"I'll just get a nurse and see about getting a better quality pillow."

"Seriously. You don't need to bother them with that."

She kept fluffing away and I finally snapped. "Mom!"

"Jesus, Mary, and Joseph, Maureen. Will you leave the damn girl alone already?" My dad grumbled from his place in one of the stiff hospital recliners. He didn't even bother taking his eyes off the crossword puzzle in his hand to see that he'd said the completely wrong thing.

"Well excuse me for caring about my daughter's comfort, Bill," my mother harrumphed, slapping her hands on her hips and shooting daggers at him even though he wasn't paying attention. "I guess I should just let her suffer, huh? Tell her to rub some dirt on it?"

I giggled. I couldn't help it. This was one particular

argument they'd been having since I was five years old and it only got funnier as the years passed.

"One time!" Dad barked, slapping his crossword against his leg. "I said that one damn time, and you *still* won't let me forget it!"

"She had a broken arm, Bill!"

"How the hell was I supposed to know that? I'm not a doctor for Christ's sake."

"So you just *assumed* it was normal for a child's arm to bend that way?"

"Well it wasn't like she cried!" He took his eyes off my mom long enough to shoot me a wink. "My little girl's always been one tough cookie."

"A tough cookie with a broken arm that was left untended for *three days* until I got home from my girls' trip and finally took her to the ER!"

My father ended the conversation the way he always had. "Well she didn't die, did she? So I'd say I did a pretty damn good job, if I do say so myself."

A knock sounded on my hospital room door, bringing my laughter to an abrupt halt. "Guys," I said to my parents. "You know I love you and your own personal brand of crazy, but that's Derrick and he has his little girl with him, so can you *please* just be normal for like, ten minutes? I'm begging you."

My folks had already left Pembrooke by the time Derrick moved to town so, other than the brief exchange they'd had the night before when they got in, they'd never really met him. Once my mother announced she wasn't leaving my bedside until I was finally released, I'd insisted Derrick go home. He fought me on it, and I could see the respect shining in my dad's eyes as he watched the exchange between us, but I eventually won when I told him he needed to get Eliza home so she could unpack and get settled.

He finally relented, giving me a long, lingering kiss before pulling back and saying, "I love you, sunshine," loud enough for both parents to hear before finally disappearing out the door.

I'd spent the thirty minutes after filling Mom and Dad in on everything about Derrick and how our relationship came to be, then another ten minutes in hell — also known as my mother's delayed discussion about the birds and the bees and how important it was to make sure the condom hadn't reached its expiration date.

After that, I wished that the car had hit me hard enough to at least put me in a coma for a few days.

My father snorted. "*Pfft*. We're always nice."

"I didn't say *nice*. I said *normal*. I need you to act normal, Dad."

He lifted his crossword back to his eyes. "No can do, sugar plum. I am who I am. If your young man can't handle that then he's not good enough for you."

"He has a point," my mom decreed.

The knock sounded again and I cursed under my breath before calling, "Come in."

Derrick's head peeked around the door and he offered

me a smile that warmed me from the inside out. "Hey sunshine, got someone who's been dying to see you."

I grinned big and bright. "I've been dying to see her too." I was pretty sure my mom sighed.

He pushed the door all the way open and led Eliza into the room. The moment her eyes landed on me they went painfully wide and the smile slipped from her face, replaced with a quivering lip.

"Chloe," she whispered, voice so full of sorrow, eyes growing red and wet. It killed me not to be able to jump from the bed and go to her.

"Oh, no. Sweetie, please don't cry," I spoke up, wanting nothing more than to make her feel better. "I'm okay, I promise. It's just some bruises, baby. Come here." I opened my arms, desperate for a hug, but she shook her head, causing some of the tears to break loose as she took a hesitant step back.

"Baby girl?" Derrick asked, concern lacing his tone as he looked down at her.

"Please, sweetheart," I spoke through the lump forming in my throat.

"I don't—" she croaked, "I don't want to hurt you."

From the corner of my eye I saw my mother bat away a tear from her cheek. I was just about to speak up when my father suddenly rose from his chair and moved in Derrick and Eliza's direction, squatting down so he was eye to eye with the frightened little girl.

"Hey there, honey bunch. I'm Bill, Chloe's Daddy. It's nice to meet you." He stuck his hand out and held it there as Eliza tentatively reached forward and placed her tiny palm in his. "You must be Eliza."

She nodded. .

"I've heard a lot about you, Eliza," he continued. "And it's a pleasure to meet you. Now, I know it's a little upsetting to see her like this, but I promise you, my girl's tough as nails. Why, she even walked around with a broken arm for three days without so much as crying!"

Mom snorted.

Derrick's eyes bounced from my father to me in confusion.

Eliza gasped. "Really?"

"Yep," Dad exclaimed proudly, like I'd managed to win the Super Bowl or something. "Little arm was bent in an *S* and everything. Not one single tear."

Eliza's mouth hung open for a few seconds before she asked, "Why didn't you take her to the hospital?"

Mom snorted again.

"That's neither here nor there," Dad answered, standing to his full height and waving the question off. "Point is, she's strong, and a hug isn't going to do anything but make her feel better. And I bet *your* hug will be ten times more powerful."

Eliza's little shoulders lifted as though Dad's words gave her a new strength, and she released Derrick's hand and headed for me.

She leaned into my embrace, wrapping her arms around my neck as I held on tight with everything I had. I closed my eyes and pulled in a deep breath. Dad was right, just one hug from Eliza and I already felt a million times better.

"How are you feeling?" she whispered against my hair, her hold squeezing just a little more.

"So much better now, honey." I felt her sigh heavily. The tension seemed to melt from her body as she pressed closer to me, the fear of hurting me seemingly disappearing. I opened my eyes and smiled, my gaze landing on Derrick as he shook my father's hand, mouthing *"thank you."* Dad smiled in return and patted Derrick's shoulder with his free hand. "Any time, son."

At the sound of her sniffle, my gaze shifted to my mom to find her wiping away more tears as she stared down at me and Eliza, a knowing smile painted across her lips.

Eliza finally pulled back enough to look up at me, and I couldn't help but reach out and tuck a strand of dark hair behind her ear.

"I was worried," she told me.

"I know, honey. But I'm going to be just fine. Bones heal and bruises fade."

At that, she smiled genuinely and said something I hadn't been expecting. "Daddy said you're moving in with us!"

"Uh..." I turned my head to look at Derrick. "What?"

"Brilliant idea!" Dad clapped his hands and my mouth dropped open in shock.

"Bu-but."

"Oh, that's wonderful," Mom said dreamily, clasping her hands in front of her chest. *Damn it.*

"Uh, honey," I turned back to Derrick and glared. "Don't you think it's a little soon? I mean, we've only been dating for a few weeks! And things have been a little crazy during that time. It's not like it was a simple courtship or something."

He grinned that panty-melting grin and moved to the other side of the bed, pulling up a chair. "Do you love me?"

"Of course I do!"

"Good. And I love you, so it's settled."

"How is that settled?!" I squeaked, sending a twinge of pain through my ribs.

"Because you love my girl, you love me, and we're going to get married one day."

"Woohoo!" Eliza yelped, throwing a fist in the air. "I get to be a junior bridesmaid!"

"Oh, sweetheart," Mom practically swooned. "We've got to start planning immediately! With your coloring, I'm thinking ivory."

I shook my head, feeling a headache coming on. "Wait... just, hold on a second! I can't think!"

"No sense dawdling when you've found the one, sugar plum," Dad said, shrugging his beefy shoulder. "And your young man's a cop. It'll help your old man sleep better at night knowing you'll have someone who can protect you."

My eyes practically bulged out of my head at his declaration. My mom and dad were no help *at all*. "Don't you think this is something we should discuss in private?" I hissed at Derrick between clenched teeth.

"No can do, sunshine." He stood from his chair and

walked to my father, clapping him on my back. "Bill and I have to head over to your place and start packing up. The movers are coming early tomorrow morning."

"You already planned this?! When? *How?*"

"When your young man's got his mind settled on something, he doesn't sit on his ass, baby girl. He's a man of action. I can relate."

"Oh please," Mom rolled her eyes. "When's the last time you took action on anything, Bill?"

I knew that look in my father's eyes. It was a look that promised that anything out of his mouth was determined to make my ears bleed.

"Didn't hear you complaining when I *took action* last night in the hotel—"

"No!" I shouted, clapping my hands over my ears. "Just... *no*! Fine! I'll move in with Derrick, okay? Just, please, for the love of God, *Stop. Talking.*"

My mom chimed in, "It's perfectly healthy for two people our age—"

"Hit me with another car," I told Derrick. "I'm begging you. Put me out of my misery."

He walked back over to the bed and leaned down, planting a kiss right on my lips. "Sorry, baby. Already have plans for this afternoon."

"You suck," I grumbled.

"Bye, Chloe." Eliza grinned as she followed Derrick and my father to the door. "Dad said I could help Ms. Harlow pack all your girly stuff."

"She's in on it too?!"

"Uh huh."

I let out a defeated sigh, slumping against the bed and closing my eyes, knowing there was no point in arguing, that I didn't even *want* to argue. If I were being honest with myself, I really loved the idea of moving in with Derrick and Eliza. Like, *a lot*.

"Oh, and Chloe?" I lifted my eyelids and looked at Eliza.

"Yeah, honey?"

She fidgeted with her hands in front of her waist as she shifted from foot to foot. "You know those empty places you told me about? The ones that special people in your life come in and fill?"

"Yeah," I said softly, feeling the tears begin to well in my eyes.

"Well, I just wanted to let you know, you fill some of those places for me."

Damn being stuck in this stupid freaking hospital bed! I needed another hug!

"You fill those places for me, too, sweetheart," I sniffled as a tear broke free.

Eliza ran back to me and threw her arms around my neck as gently as possible, whispering, "I love you," into my hair.

My arms tightened. "I love you, too."

She pulled back, graced me with a beautiful smile then took off with my dad and hers.

And I was left feeling like that last empty space inside me had been filled so full it was overflowing.

28

DERRICK

*I*T WAS DONE.

It had taken a lot longer than I'd hoped, a few months where I was sure I'd gotten more gray hair every fucking morning, but it was finally done. And I could breathe easier knowing my little girl would never have to deal with the stresses her mother placed on her shoulders ever again.

She was mine, free and clear. All parental rights had been stripped from Layla when she was convicted on all the charges brought against her that night she nearly took Chloe from me. The judge didn't even bat an eye at declaring her unfit, telling her to her face how ashamed she should be, how she was one of the most selfish people he'd ever encountered, and how he hoped she somehow managed to pull her head out of her ass during her two to five years in prison.

I wasn't going to hold my breath.

I never tried to put Chloe in the role as a replacement mother, but there was no denying that she gave my little girl everything she needed. There were times when Eliza still missed Layla, or maybe the *thought* of what she could have with Layla. But every time she got sad Chloe was there, her sunshine shining down on the both of us, making everything all right.

Life was good. Chloe's bakery was still thriving. She'd even had to bring on more help to cater to the crushing demand of customers who'd been craving her pastries and coffee for the weeks she'd been closed for repairs. Gone were the before-dawn wakeups. She'd managed to loosen the reins and let her staff have more control, and as I'd predicted, they all proved that she'd made the right choice, bringing them on at Sinful Sweets. She'd struggled with the decision to step back, but knowing Eliza needed her time made the decision easier for her to make.

We still fought at times. She was a stubborn, hard-headed woman after all, but it was never over anything major. And the making up was so good there were times we picked fights for no other reason than to make up after.

She fit in my life so seamlessly, that as the days passed, I questioned how the hell I'd ever managed to live without her.

Staring down at the notarized documents in my hands, custody documents declaring Eliza could never be taken from me or used as a pawn to hold over my head again, I knew the second-to-last puzzle piece of my life had fallen into place. There was only one thing left to do.

"Come on!" I shouted, opening a desk drawer and tossing the documents inside. "We're going to be late!"

I was officially outnumbered in my own home. It had taken some adjusting, but over the past three months, I somehow managed to come to grips with the fact that my life had become overrun with all things female. Another thing I was learning to deal with? The fact that I'd never be on time for anything for the rest of my life.

"Coming, coming!" Chloe hurried down the hall and into the living room, her sandals in her hand. Christ, she hadn't even gotten her shoes on yet?

"You're lucky you're cute," I told her, leaning down to press a kiss to her lips before she bent to slide her feet through the complicated straps.

"And you're lucky I put up with your overbearing, pain-in-the-ass self."

"I consider myself lucky every single day." I grinned at her then looked back at the mouth of the hallway. "Eliza! Take the lead out!"

"Will you stop bellowing?" Chloe stood, shoes now on her feet where they belonged, and smacked me in the stomach. "She's almost finished."

Eliza came waltzing down the hall, and something sparkly caught my attention.

"What the hell is that?" I barked, pointing at my daughter's face.

"What?" she asked innocently

"*That!*" I moved closer and squinted. "Are you wearing *makeup*? Oh hell no!"

"Relax," Chloe rolled her eyes at me. "It's just a little lip gloss."

"She's nine years old!"

"I turned ten last week!" Eliza argued, propping her hands on her hips as she glared.

"Whatever, you're still too young for makeup. Go wipe it off," I demanded, only to have Chloe grab my arm and pull me toward the kitchen.

"Eliza, will you go wait in the car? We'll be out in just a sec."

My daughter all but skipped out of the house as I snapped, "But she hasn't wiped it off!"

Chloe's eyes got fierce as she jabbed her finger into my chest. "And she's not going to. It's lip gloss, Derrick, it's not like she's ready for a drag show or something. A little lip gloss isn't a big deal."

I threw my hands in the air in frustration. "Why the hell does she even need it?"

"Because. Ethan's going to be there today with Harlow, Noah, and the baby, and you already know she's got an insane crush on him. She wants to look pretty. She asked me to teach her how to put on makeup and I managed to haggle her down to just the gloss. *You're welcome.*"

"You know," my eye narrowed into dangerous slits, "this is all *his* fault. My baby girl never worried about shit like makeup until *him.*"

"Oh, for the love of God," Chloe groaned to the ceiling, not that there was anyone up there that would help her with an irrational, overprotective father. "You love Ethan!"

"Lov*ed*. Past tense. The moment I saw Eliza making googly eyes at him that went right down the drain."

"You're being ridiculous."

"Don't care." I crossed my arms over my chest and there was a slight possibility my bottom lip actually poked out.

She sighed heavily. "Look, Ethan's a great kid. He knows it's just a harmless crush and he doesn't do anything to egg her on. You need to relax, okay? Let's just go to the carnival, eat our weight in funnel cake, ride some rides, and come home." She came closer, placing her hands on my chest and standing on her tiptoes, speaking in a low, seductive voice, "If you behave all day today, I'll let you do that thing with the handcuffs tonight."

Yes, I was man enough to admit that I had to stop and weigh the pros and cons. "Really?"

"I promise."

And she had me. "Fine," I sighed. My woman played me like a sucker. Damned thing was, I didn't care. I loved it. "You're lucky I love you."

"So lucky." She kissed me with a smile on her lips. "And I love you too."

Chloe

I WAS FINALLY DOING IT.

I was finally on the Ferris wheel with the man of my dreams. The love of my life.

I smiled to myself as I looked out at the sun glistening off the lake before me as I sat, snuggled close to Derrick. The Ferris wheel made a slow, lazy loop around, and each time, the view from the top took my breath away.

"It's so beautiful," I breathed as the ride came to a stop with our bucket at the top to let more people on.

"Most beautiful thing I've ever seen," he answered, and when I turned to look at him, his gaze was directly on me. He leaned in and kissed me, and I got lost in how amazing it felt. Not just the kiss, but my life in general. I had my dream job, I lived in my dream town, and now I had my dream family. Derrick and Eliza were the last pieces of my puzzle. My life was complete.

Once the kiss ended, I rested my head on Derrick's shoulder with a contented sigh. The minutes ticked by and I finally sat up straight in order to look over the edge of our bucket. "I wonder what's taking so long."

"Oh, I paid the guy to wait for my signal before he let us down."

My head shot in his direction. "What? Why'd you do that?"

He smiled and kissed my lips again. "Because I have something I need to ask you, and having you trapped at the top of the Ferris wheel is kind of the perfect way to guarantee I get the answer I want, don't you think?"

Giddy anticipation built in my belly like a million butterflies taking flight, and I couldn't stop the crazy smile from spreading across my face. "Oh yeah, and what do you have to ask me?"

He reached down and pulled something from his pants pocket, keeping his fingers closed tightly around it. "Oh, I think you know."

I nodded. "I think so too, but why don't you ask anyway?"

"Chloe Delaney?" he started. I held my breath and waited eagerly. "Will you..." God! The suspense was killing me, "please stop leaving your damned shoes all over the house! For the love of God, woman! I nearly broke my neck last night! I swear, I have no idea what the hell women need with so many shoes. I'm thinking about getting a dog just so he can chew them all to hell."

"Derrick!" I shouted, smacking him in the chest.

"Okay, okay," he chuckled, opening his palm and revealing a beautiful ring. "Will you marry me?" he asked softly.

Tears immediately started falling as I nodded my head. "Yes," I sniffled, snatching the ring out of his hand and sliding it on my finger. "Yes!" I threw my arms around his neck and kissed him like my life depended on it.

"I love you," I said against his lips.

"I love you too, sunshine. More than anything."

"You were just kidding about letting a dog destroy my shoes, right?"

He laughed and pulled me against him tighter. "Maybe just a little bit." Once we pulled apart, he leaned over the edge of the bucket and shouted, "She said yes!" at the top of his lungs. Our loved ones below — along with some of the other people on the ride — hooted and hollered from below.

"And you said you'd never get married again." I couldn't help but tease as the ride started back up and we began our decent.

"Well, I never expected a curvy little bakery owner to waltz into my life and throw everything off course all because I called her by the wrong name. It took me a while, but I finally realized."

"Realized what?" I asked, staring up into those hazel eyes I'd been in love with since I first saw them.

"That I'd been waiting my whole life for you."

Yeah, I was most *definitely* getting my fairytale ending.

EPILOGUE

ELIZA

I FELT LIKE I'd been living in a fairytale all day long. Everything about my Dad and Chloe's wedding was so beautiful. I looked around the room, nothing but white Christmas lights twinkling all over as people danced and talked and laughed. It made me wonder what *my* wedding would look like. I would want it *just* like Chloe and Dad's.

I stood off to the side of the dance floor, watching my Dad and Chloe kiss as they swayed to the music. I was *SO* glad he picked her to marry. Chloe was the *best*. She even picked out the prettiest dress for me to wear in the wedding! I felt like a princess as I looked down at my feet, covered by the long skirt. I swished it back and forth, watching the material move around my legs like a wave. I felt like a grownup in that dress

My hair was pretty and done up just like Ms. Harlow's, and I even got to wear a little bit of makeup! I'd hoped it would make Ethan notice me, but when I finally got the guts to go over and talk to him a few minutes ago, he didn't even say anything.

I sighed as I remembered how handsome Ethan looked in his tux. He really was the cutest guy I'd ever seen, and I hated that I was so much younger than him. I heard Dad and Chloe arguing about it one night — they always liked to argue so they could make up after, going in their room to kiss and stuff. Dad said Ethan was way too old for me. That he'd gone through most of the cheerleaders in his school already.

I remembered my face getting hot as I listened in on them. I wasn't really sure what Dad was talking about, but I knew if Ethan liked high school cheerleaders, then there was no way he would like me.

"Hey there, kiddo." My eyes shot up off the floor. The sound of his voice made my stomach flip over and over.

"Uh... hey."

"What are you doing over here looking so sad?"

"I look sad?" I hadn't realized I looked sad. I guess thinking about Ethan had kind of bummed me out, but I hadn't realized people would notice. Especially him. "I'm not sad. I was just... thinking."

"What were you thinking about so hard?" He shoved his hands in the pockets of his tuxedo pants and smiled at me. It was the best smile I'd ever seen.

"N-nothing," I stuttered. Gosh! I hated when I did that around him. He probably thought I was stupid or something.

"Well, if you're not thinking about anything, and you're not sad, then why don't we dance?"

My mouth dropped open and I felt like my eyes were going to pop right out of my head. "You want to dance? With *me*?"

"Sure," he laughed. I loved his laugh. It made my belly feel funny, like there were butterflies in it or something. "We're basically family, right?"

My shoulders slumped at his question. I was in love with Ethan Prewitt and he only thought of me as part of his family. He'd never see me as anything more than a sister no matter what I did. "Oh, yeah… sure. Family."

One of his eyebrows hooked up in that really cool way. "Do you know how to dance?"

"I guess," I shrugged, feeling like such a dork for crushing on the coolest guy *ever*. "I mean, I know a little bit."

"Well then let's go." He reached for my hand and I felt goosebumps break out across my skin as he pulled me onto the dance floor.

"Your girlfriend won't mind that you're dancing with me?" My eyes darted all around the room as he put one hand on my waist. My body tingled from him holding me and I thought I could die happy, all because the coolest guy in *high school* was dancing with *me*. His hand was on *my waist* and he was staring Right. At. Me.

"Nah," he shrugged. "We broke up. She was kind of a pain in the ass." I giggled and felt my cheeks turn red. "You know, your dad's staring at me like he wants to shoot me." I jerked my head around to see Dad glaring right at me and Ethan. Chloe looked like she was trying not to laugh.

I turned back around, embarrassed. "He's just protective."

Ethan laughed again and I wanted so badly to lean in closer and press my ear to his chest so I could hear what his laughter sounded like close up. Lilly was going to *die* when I called her and told her that I talked to and danced with Ethan! She knew how much I liked him.

"Well, you can't really blame him, right? I mean, if I had a daughter that looked like you, I'd probably chain her down in the basement."

My forehead wrinkled as I looked up at him. "Huh?"

"I just mean, you're really pretty. I'd lose my mind if I had a daughter that looked like you," he shrugged like what he said wasn't the best thing I'd ever heard in my entire life.

I was pretty sure my heart stopped beating for several seconds. "You... you think I'm pretty?"

He shrugged again, "Well, yeah kiddo. You're really pretty. And when you get older, I bet you'll be gorgeous."

He thought I was pretty. And he thought I'd be gorgeous when I grew up! I only ever heard of people on TV being called gorgeous, or Chloe when my dad had really screwed up.

In that very moment I made a decision, a decision I'd hold on to for years and years. I was going to have my fairytale wedding one day, and I was going to marry the love of my life, just like Chloe and Dad.

Standing on the crowded dance floor at the most beautiful wedding I'd ever been to, I made a promise to myself.

One day I was going to marry Ethan Prewitt.

He just didn't know it yet.

The End
keep reading for a peek at COMING FULL CIRCLE, *book 2 in the Pembrooke series*

ENJOY AN EXCERPT FROM COMING FULL CIRCLE

Prologue

Eliza

I FELL IN love with Ethan Prewitt when I was nine years old.

It wasn't *real* love or anything. I was only nine—almost

ten—after all, but back then it was the most intense, consuming emotion I'd ever experienced in my young life. From nine to twelve I was a blushing, giggling, stuttering mess whenever he was around, and seeing as my Dad and his wife Chloe were best friends with Ethan's sister and brother-in-law, he was around *a lot*.

Ethan was gorgeous and popular and way too old for me — which only added to the thrill of it. But as time passed and we really got to know each other, that young, childish love evolved. I started to grow up, mature, and that immature infatuation turned into a friendship the likes of which I cherished above all else.

My relationship with Ethan was the most important thing in my life. It was him I went to when I needed advice, his opinion I held in the highest regard, his shoulder I leaned on whenever I needed someone to share my burdens with. As the years passed, that respect only grew.

He turned into the best friend I could have ever had. We told each other everything, confiding things we wouldn't dare tell anyone else. We shared our ambitions and dreams. We knew each other better than anyone else. I needed him. I grew to depend on him.

And looking back, I realized that was my biggest mistake.

Because needing someone didn't necessarily mean they needed you back. It was a lesson I'd learned even before Ethan came into my life. You could give a person all the love you were capable of carrying, but that didn't mean you'd get the same in return.

My mother hadn't taught me much in my life, but that particular lesson was the one that stuck the most, sad as it was.

There were people in your life who were supposed to care, supposed to do their best to protect you from all the bad. My father was one of those people, his wife Chloe another. It hurt to know my own mother, my flesh and blood, wasn't one of those people, and for that very reason, I kept my circle small. Only those who I'd go to the ends of the earth for and who I trusted to do the same for me were allowed in. I appreciated quality over quantity, and while keeping people out sometimes led to being lonely, I'd convinced myself that it was enough. I had everyone I'd ever need. I had Dad and Chloe, Noah and Harlow, my other friend Lilly.

And I had Ethan. Or so I thought.

I only had him for six years before I lost him.

Then I spent the next six regretting the fact that I ever let Ethan Prewitt in.

Chapter 1

Ethan

IT WAS YET another sleepless night where I spent hours staring up at the slow spinning ceiling fan above my bed. I tried counting the rotations hoping the monotony would clear my head enough to let drowsiness take over, but no such luck. I hadn't slept for shit since I took that hit on the field. The hit that fucked my knee to hell and took me out of the game for the rest of the season. I'd lived and breathed football for as long as I could remember, and now that it had been taken from me, I was left with nothing to do but think.

Not a good thing, especially since sitting idle was something I'd been avoiding like the plague for the past six years.

The warm, naked body next to me in the bed shifted and ripped me from my thoughts. How sad was it that I'd been so lost in my own head that I'd forgotten the woman sleeping next to me?

"Mmm," she hummed pleasurably. "Good morning, handsome."

My head rolled on the pillow to face the blonde currently pressing her fake tits against my arm. Amber. One of the few women in my phone who got repeat calls... not that those calls were all that often. But seeing as I was holed up in my apartment with a goddamned torn ACL and unable to hit up the clubs and bars with my teammates to pick up a random hookup for the night, my choices were limited.

Unfortunately, that also meant I'd been left with no choice but to invite her to my place if I wanted to get laid — something I made a conscious effort *never* to do until now.

"Morning," I muttered, sounding sullen despite having marathon sex last night with a woman more than happy to do all the work.

"You don't sound too happy," she purred, running her bright red nails across my chest. "How about I do something to put you in a better mood?"

My hands went to her hips and grabbed hold, stopping her just before she managed to throw her leg over my hip and straddle my waist. "Sorry, babe. PT will be here any minute, so I'm gonna have to take a rain check."

When her bottom lip jutted out in a pout, it took everything I had not to roll my eyes. But since I'd used her for sex and had no intentions whatsoever of calling her again after the night before, I figured the least I could do was be polite to the woman while I attempted to shuffle her out of my apartment.

"Gotta take a leak, then you should probably get going. No need for you to stay and be bored out of your mind while he's working my knee." I shifted her body away from mine and sat up, easing my left leg off the mattress so I could attempt to stand.

I hobbled awkwardly over to my crutches, the long brace on my leg making it more difficult as Amber spoke. "I really don't mind. Maybe I could help you out while you're recovering? Like cleaning and cooking until you can get around a little better?"

Oh Jesus. The hope shining her in eyes — eyes that had mascara streaked underneath, not a very good look — had me twitching to run, and if it wasn't for my blown-out knee, I had no doubt I'd already be locking myself in the bathroom. However, I wasn't that lucky; I was stuck in place while she crawled from the bed, revealing every inch of her body to me as she closed the distance between us.

Her nails traced along the waistband of my boxer briefs as she whispered, "Maybe I'll clean naked. It could be fun." Her lips tilted up in a seductive smile that held little effect since half her makeup had streaked into places it didn't belong, making her look more like a drunk clown than a seductress. My dick didn't so much as twitch.

Fuck me. That was one of the reasons I never had them over to my place, and I never stayed the night at theirs. Things never looked the same in the light of day as they did the night before.

"Maybe some other time, baby." I tried to smile, hoping it didn't look as forced as it felt. "Besides, you wouldn't want to put my cleaning lady Rosita out of work, now would you?" I gave her a little wink and let go of one of my crutches long enough to smack her on the ass.

As I pivoted toward the bathroom, the sound of my front door opening and closing sounded, followed by a loud voice. "Wake your lazy ass up, Prewitt. Time to get this shit started."

That time my grin wasn't fake at all. I probably shouldn't have looked so damned giddy, but I couldn't help it. Typically I hated PT, but just then I could have kissed Duke for saving me from having to physically remove Amber from my apartment.

"Looks like it's time to go, sweetness. I'll give you a call sometime."

With a forlorn expression, she turned and started

picking up her clothes, and I took that as my opportunity to take a piss. When I emerged from the bathroom, she was already dressed, but instead of being gone, she was standing next to my bedside table, the picture frame I'd kept there in every single apartment I'd lived in the past six years in her hands.

She looked up with a smile on her face. "Is this you when you were in college? You look so young!"

"Put that down," I grunted as I made my way in her direction. Before she could follow my command, I reached her and snatched the frame from her fingers, placing it back down exactly as it had been. No one touched it but me. Even Rosita knew just to dust around it.

"Sorry," she snapped in a snotty tone as I scooted the picture a centimeter over, tilting it so it could be seen perfectly from my side of the bed. "Is that your sister or cousin or something?"

I looked back down at the photo in question, taking in Eliza's bright, shining smile. My sister Harlow had taken it. She had a gift for photography and snapped the picture just as Eliza's head was tipped back in laughter at something I'd just said to her. My arm was thrown over her shoulder and I was grinning down at her with a pleased-as-shit look on my face that I'd been able to make her laugh. We'd been in my old backyard, it was the same house Harlow and her husband Noah still lived in. It was their daughter Lucy's fifth birthday party, and I'd driven back from college in Laramie to celebrate. It was the first time I'd seen Eliza in weeks. Having a full class load and football practice all the damn time, it had been hard for us to catch up. But when I got home that weekend, we'd picked up right where we left off.

It might have been weird to some, a twenty-one year guy so excited to see a fifteen year old girl, but it wasn't like that. She was my best friend. The best friend I'd *ever* had. I never felt the age gap when we were together. Maybe it was because she'd already experienced shit at a young age that no kid should have to go through, but she was mature... and so damn smart. And because of the shit her mom had put her through, she could understand feeling like an outsider. That was probably what bonded us the most.

Then I'd fucked it all up. Because about a year after that picture was taken, my feelings started to change. Feelings that fucked with my head in a major way and scared the hell out of me. Feelings I'd convinced myself were all kinds of wrong. Feelings I never, *ever* planned to act on.

So I left. I had no choice.

And the worst thing about it was, in the six years I'd been gone, my feelings hadn't lessened in the slightest.

"She's my best friend," I answered.

"Isn't she a little..." Amber's words trailed off, drawing my gaze away from the picture and back to her, "*young* to be your best friend?"

"We practically grew up together," I ground out, feeling an overwhelming sense of protectiveness where my relationship with Eliza Anderson was concerned, even if it wasn't the complete truth. It was the same feeling I felt for years any time someone questioned our friendship, or said anything negative about her in general. Because of my stupidity, we hadn't spoken in six years, but to this day, that desire to defend her, to defend what we had, hadn't lessened in the slightest.

Even if I didn't have her anymore.

"I need to get a quick shower," I grumbled as I used my crutches to help me pivot around, giving Amber my back. "I'm sure you can see your way out."

"So..." she called out hesitantly, but I didn't stop moving. "You'll call me?"

Not a fucking chance in Hell. "Sure. I'll be pretty busy with rehab and stuff, but I'll give you a call if I have time." With that, I shut the bathroom door on her. I trusted Duke to keep her from stealing any of my shit, and after the hard hit that thinking about Eliza caused, I was done.

As I stood under the hot shower spray, I went over the hundred ways I spent the past six years being the world's biggest asshole. It started with hurting the one person I was the closest with and ended with me waiting so long to apologize and make things right, that it was already too late. Looking back, I could have done things differently. But you know what they say about hindsight.

It's a motherfucker.

MY CELLPHONE RANG just as I popped a couple ibuprofen and downed then with the cold beer in my hand. Duke had left an hour ago, but because he was a sadist, my knee was throbbing like hell, which did nothing to help improve my earlier mood.

I reached into the pocket of my sweats and pulled the phone out, not bothering to look at the display as I answered with a curt, "What?"

"Holy shit!" a familiar voice cried from the other end. "He actually answered the phone! Noah! Quick! Look out the window and tell me if the world's on fire. This has to be the sign of the apocalypse."

"You're fucking hysterical, Low-Low," I deadpanned. "To what do I owe the pleasure?"

"What? Can't a sister call her baby brother and give him shit for being an asshole who never comes to see her or her family and barely has the time to talk on the phone anymore?"

My head dropped down as I rested a hand on the dark granite of the kitchen island and leaned forward. With a sigh, I told her, "I'm really not in the mood for this right now, Harlow."

"I don't give two shits what you're in the mood for Ethan. Last I heard from you, you were about to have surgery to repair the tear to your ACL. That was *eight days ago*! I had to hear from your *agent* that you were doing well and at home recuperating. You haven't answered a single call, you won't return any of my messages, and Noah said you've been ignoring him too. What the hell, man?"

"Harlow—"

Doing what she always did and ignoring the warning in

my tone, she pushed forward. "Lucy's been worried about you, and Evan's been beside himself since he saw you take that hit. Do you have any idea how hard it is to try and console a six-year-old when he thinks his favorite uncle just got his guts stomped on the field?"

"I'm his only uncle," I replied, but she wasn't finished.

"I'll tell you. It's really *freaking* hard, Ethan. You're his idol for Christ's sake. Lucy and Evan *adore* you. But you can't even bother with more than one or two goddamned phone calls to let us know you're okay and still alive?!"

By the end of her rant Harlow's voice got so high pitched, I started to worry for the dogs in their neighborhood. But she made her point.

"I'm sorry," I muttered through the line.

"Sorry, what was that? Couldn't hear you since you were mumbling. Try repeating it, and this time try and talk like a grownup."

Just like Harlow to give me shit, even when I was trying to apologize. She had never been one to just accept an apology. Oh no, she made you bust your ass to earn her forgiveness. No one knew that better than me and her husband Noah. She'd practically made the man jump through flaming hoops to win her back after breaking her heart when they were teenagers.

"I said, '*I'm sorry*,'" I repeated, making sure to enunciate. "You're right. I've been a prick."

She was quiet for a few seconds before stating, "Yes. You have."

"I'm really sorry, Low-Low," I said softly, using the

nickname I'd given her when I was little, hoping it would help to butter her up. "I'll make it up to you guys. I promise."

"Good. Because I've already told the kids Uncle Ethan's coming for an extended visit starting next week."

"You *what?!*"

"And don't worry. I've already cleared it with your agent and, lucky you, Fletch is a licensed physical therapist! What a coincidence, huh?"

It was bullshit was what it was. I wouldn't have been surprised if Harlow had this whole thing planned out, *including* having Noah's assistant coach Fletcher getting certified as a PT. "You're kidding, right? I can't just pick up and leave. I've got shit to do here, Harlow."

"Like what? You're out for the rest of the season and on limited activity until your knee's healed up, so don't give me that. It's been way too long since you've been back home—"

"That's not my home anymore, that's *your* home. Denver's my home."

"Call it whatever you want, but pack your shit. Duke said you can't fly just yet, so Noah and I are driving up to get you next Saturday. We'll crash at your place for the night and head back early Sunday morning."

"You talked to *Duke* too?" I asked incredulously.

"What can I say? Everyone around you, *except you*, thinks your family is freaking awesome. Now pack. I'm done playing this game with you. It's time I had my little brother back."

She hung up before I could say anything.

"Shit," I breathed as I dropped my phone on the counter, suddenly feeling more exhausted than I had before the phone call.

There was no way I was going to be able to talk myself out of this one. I was going back to Pembrooke.

Whether I liked it or not.

CLICK HERE TO KEEP READING

MORE PEMBROOKE TITLES

She's a romantic at heart.

Chloe Delaney had three very specific wishes, growing up. She wished to stay settled in the small mountain town of Pembrooke, where she grew up, to one day be her own boss, and to fall in love with a man who would be willing to go to the ends of the earth for her. With her roots firmly planted in Pembrooke's soil and her bakery, Sinful Sweets, thriving, two of her wishes have already come true. When a handsome single father moves to town, she's certain she's found the man to fill the role of wish number three. The only problem is, you can't force a frog to turn into a prince.

He isn't the Prince Charming type.

When Derrick Anderson moved from Jackson Hole to the small town of Pembrooke, he did it determined to wipe the slate clean. After eight years spent trapped in a miserable marriage, he's made a vow to never take the plunge again. He wants to be untethered, not tangled up in the strings that come with a committed relationship. He has his daughter, his career, and an ex-wife hell bent on making his life unbearable. His plate is already full. The only problem is, he didn't have a plan in place to protect his heart from her.

Neither of them were prepared for the course their lives would take. But once a rollercoaster begins to move, you can't just climb off, now can you?

The only thing they can do is strap in, hold on tight, and enjoy the ride.

She knew what it was like to feel unwanted.

At an early age Eliza Anderson learned a very hard lesson. Sometimes the people who are supposed to love you the most are the ones that cause you the most pain. She learned to guard herself, hesitating to let anyone close for fear of feeling that rejection all over again. Then Ethan came into her life, and what had started as a simple childhood crush morphed into a friendship she eventually came to cherish above all else. He was her safe place. Her rock. A shoulder she could lean on. Until he ripped it all away.

He knew what it was like to feel like an outsider.

Ethan Prewitt grew up learning that you couldn't always trust the people you loved the most to be there. That sense of security he craved had always alluded him, leaving him to feel like an interloper in his own home. He dreamed of escaping the small town of Pembrooke and building a life where he didn't have to depend on anyone but himself. What he never expected was for his friendship with Eliza to grow into something that meant everything to him.

Mistakes were made. Hearts were broken. But now Ethan's home and he's determined to make it right. It was time for their relationship to come full circle.

Because what they had was once in a lifetime.

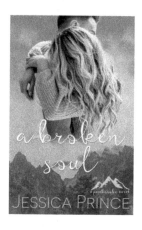

He's terrified of loving her.

Quinn Mallick already had his happily-ever-after, and in the blink of an eye it was ripped away from him. Now he's content to walk through the rest of his life carrying the weight of that guilt on his shoulders. He's convinced he doesn't deserve a second chance. But when the town's beautiful dance teacher turns her sights on him he finds himself questioning everything.

She's terrified of losing him.

Lilly Mathewson's once quiet, predictable life has been

turned on its head. Feeling alone and adrift, she finds her comfort in the most unexpected of places. Falling for the town widower was never part of the plan, but there is just something about the temperamental man she can't seem to let go of.

What started as two grieving people leaning on each other has quickly turned into something neither of them expected. Lilly is ready to take the next step, but how do you move forward when the man you love refuses to let go of the past?

Especially when the only hope they have of healing their broken souls is if they do it together.

ABOUT THE AUTHOR

Born and raised around Houston, Jessica is a self proclaimed caffeine addict, connoisseur of inexpensive wine, and the worst driver in the state of Texas. In addition to being all of these things, she's first and foremost a wife and mom.

Growing up, she shared her mom and grandmother's love of reading. But where they leaned toward murder mysteries, Jessica was obsessed with all things romance.

When she's not nose deep in her next manuscript, you can usually find her with her kindle in hand.

Connect with Jessica now
Website: www.authorjessicaprince.com
Jessica's Princesses Reader Group

Newsletter

Instagram

Facebook

Twitter

authorjessicaprince@gmail.com